NO LAUGHING MATTER

Lennox Brothers Romantic Comedy

TALIA HUNTER

Chapter One

Carlotta

I wasn't having the *worst* week of my life.

But only because I ate an awful lot of crap sandwiches when I was a kid. Metaphorically speaking.

There were some foul-tasting, unpleasantly chewy chunks in the sandwich life had served me this week, no denying it. But given a little time—and maybe a few dozen martinis—I could fix it. At least, that's what I was telling myself as I hauled my suitcase up the run-down wooden front steps of my mother's house.

Home.

For the first time in ten years, I was home to stay.

And I was *really* trying not to hate it.

But the wooden boards under my sneakers felt dangerously soft, as though they'd been so worn down by life they were thinking of giving up completely. A jasmine vine had spread so far across the wall, it was smothering the windows on one side of the house. The sickly stench of its flowers mingled with the smell of dog poop that wafted from under the porch.

And worst of all, I had no idea who my mother would pretend to be.

Neverland and the Emerald City were more real to Mom than California. She was the reason I'd been teased at school because I'd had no idea dragons or witches were make-believe. I'd assumed everyone had conversations with trees, and left bowls of milk out for fairies.

Thanks to the school bullies, I'd realized Mom wasn't just separated from reality, she'd filed for permanent divorce.

Lifting my hand to knock, I squared my shoulders and lifted my chin. No matter what fantasy world Mom was living in, at least now I knew what was real. Besides, maybe she'd become more grounded since the last time I saw her. Perhaps she'd answer the door in a pair of sweatpants and ask how I was. She might even want to hear about my life and offer some kind of sensible advice to help me fix my career implosion.

Okay, not that last bit. I wasn't completely deluded.

The door swung open. My mother was wearing an enormous layered dress, complete with petticoats—one of her Shakespearean costumes. She was holding a tumbler half-full of a clear liquid that was probably Gin.

"Carlotta!" She threw her free hand in the air like she was on a stage. "You've reached safe haven. Come in quickly, before our enemies see you."

Nope. Nothing had changed. As silly as it was to think it might, my stomach still tightened with disappointment.

What, you were expecting a hug? I silently asked my clenched stomach. Because doesn't everyone talk to their body parts?

"Hi, Mom," I said. "Thanks for taking me in. It won't

2

be for long. I'll head back to LA as soon as I get my career sorted out."

But my mother had already swept away into the living room with her full skirts swishing around her. And if I followed, I'd be returning to her world where fantasy twisted its way into reality until it became all but impossible to unravel them.

Maybe it wasn't too late to get back in my car and drive right back to LA?

If only I hadn't already sub-let my apartment.

With a resigned sigh, I hauled my suitcase into the small living room that now held even more books than I remembered. Enormous floor-to-ceiling bookcases were packed so full that books were overflowing onto the coffee table, dining table, and floor. The room even smelled like books, a musty, old paper smell.

"Let me guess." I motioned to Mom's dress. "You're teaching Shakespeare to your class?" Somehow she still held down a job as an English teacher at San Dante High School. I could only imagine how bewildering her parent-teacher meetings must be.

"Two households, both alike in dignity, in fair Verona." She set her glass on the coffee table with a dramatic flourish.

"Romeo and Juliet?"

She bobbed a curtsey. "I'm the nurse." As she straightened, Mom tugged a piece of candy from her sleeve, unwrapped it, and stashed it in her cheek. She sucked on hard candies like a chain smoker puffed on cigarettes.

"Where's Xul the Destroyer?" I asked, looking around. "Is he okay?" It was weird that Mom's elderly Basset Hound hadn't greeted me at the door.

"If you're referring to my faithful canine companion, his name's now Lennox."

"Excuse me?" I frowned. "Did you say you've decided to call him Lennox? As in Edward Lennox?"

Edward Lennox was Mom's neighbor and sworn mortal enemy. I would have thought I was past being surprised by anything she did, but surely she wouldn't have renamed her beloved old dog—quite possibly the only thing she'd ever truly loved—after the person she hated most?

"That's right. Lennox is in the garden." She led me to the back window, and I saw Xul digging in the rows of vegetables Mom liked to grow so she could pretend she was living in The Little House On The Prairie.

"But Edward Lennox still lives next door, doesn't he?" My uncomprehending gaze went to Edward's house, which was visible through the back window. "Why on earth would you rename Xul?"

"Allow me to demonstrate." Mom pushed the back door open and stalked onto the porch, standing at the top of the steps that led down to the garden. "Lennox, you shameless mongrel," she bellowed at the top of her lungs. "Desist your foul explorations! Extract your filthy snout from the dirt!"

Xul ignored her, intent on living up to his real name. Over the years, Xul the Destroyer had been responsible for a lot of dug-up vegetables. He had a thing for carrots.

Next door, a face appeared in the window, peering out with a scowl. No doubt Ed Lennox had heard Mom's shout. The woman who'd sublet my apartment in LA had probably heard it.

"Do you really have to do that?" I asked.

"Indeed I do." She looked gleeful. "It vexes Edward Lennox sorely. I only wish I'd thought of it a few years ago, when his hearing was better." She raised her voice again, bellowing even louder. "Lennox, you filthy cur! You despicable mongrel!"

The dog in question didn't seem to notice that he was being yelled at. I couldn't blame him. He'd been Xul for all of his twelve years, and probably assumed Mom was yelling at somebody else.

Still, I went past Mom and down the back steps to get him. Just because I'd lost my capacity to feel any embarrassment didn't mean I wanted my mother to keep yelling at poor Xul.

I was at the bottom of the steps, near the fence, when the back door of the Lennox house opened. A man jogged down Edward's back steps, moving more quickly than I would have imagined sixty-something-year-old Edward Lennox would be able to go. He stopped at the gate that separated the two properties and stared at me, as though surprised to see me.

It wasn't Ed Lennox.

This man was huge, with wide shoulders and bulging biceps. He was my age, and I recognized him instantly, though he had a scar on his neck that hadn't been there last time I'd seen him.

"Mason Lennox?" I was so shocked, I said his name like a question, as though I expected him to answer.

More shocking was the fact he *did* answer. "Hello, Carlotta. It's been a long time."

"Wow. You actually spoke to me."

As well as the scar running down the side of his neck that disappeared under his T-shirt, there was another scar on his forearm. A long line of light, ridged skin cutting up lengthways. Could he be Jason Momoa's sparring partner? A bare-knuckle boxer? Or a stunt double for the Incredible Hulk?

"What are you doing in San Dante?" he asked.

"What are *you* doing here?" I wasn't about to explain my career disaster, and how I'd come home to give myself time to get back on track. Not when looking at him made me feel so unbalanced.

Mason was my *first*. Well, to be clear, though he claimed a lot of firsts from me, the one thing he didn't take was my virginity.

But at thirteen years old, he was my first crush.

At fifteen, my first kiss.

He was the first boy to touch my boobs.

And most importantly, the first to break my heart.

But there was nothing boyish about Mason now. He was a man mountain, made up of muscle, hard edges, and a dusting of stubble, wrapped in a thick layer of sex appeal that was only enhanced by his scars, and the whole powerful-and-dangerous look that was definitely working for him.

He wore a faded gray T-shirt that had to have steel reinforcing for the seams to still be holding together, and he wasn't so much wearing his jeans as allowing them to hug him. Tightly.

Unfortunately, in spite of the way he'd treated me, he hadn't developed any deformities. Instead, just looking at him made my legs weaken.

Don't be ridiculous, I told them sternly. *He's not that good looking.*

My legs didn't bother to reply. They knew I was lying.

Mason Lennox had grown into the manliest hunk of manhood I'd ever seen. So the universe must have decided my crap sandwich wasn't already chewy enough.

"I'm here visiting my family." Mason leaned against the fence that separated the two back yards and I was momentarily afraid he'd take the entire thing down.

"Me too," I said. "I'm staying with Mom."

"You're not moving back to town?"

"No way." The idea forced a shocked laugh out of me. "I'll probably just stay for a week. Maybe two. Three at the most." Coming here had bought me a little breathing time with my bills. Time I'd use to figure out if there was a chance I could get my sponsorships back.

Mom hollered from the back step. "Lennox, you foul wretch, stop licking your penis!"

I didn't get embarrassed. Ever. A childhood with my mother had inoculated me against shame. Constant exposure to it had acted like the world's strongest vaccine, which meant I could laugh in the face of humiliation. In fact, I'd made a career out of encouraging young women to be happy in their own skin. My humor was shameless, and though it meant exaggerating my own flaws and exposing the most personal parts of my life, my cheeks no longer remembered how to blush.

So when Mason's brow furrowed, why did they feel a little warm?

Mason looked toward my mother, his expression a picture of puzzled confusion. Unfortunately, that only encouraged her.

"You malodorous animal!" she bellowed even louder. "Lennox! Remove your tongue from your genitals this instant!"

Mason's eyes were a very light, cold gray with just a hint of blue, like an ice storm in Antarctica. And as he turned his polar gaze back onto me, I felt it again. An utterly foreign sensation of discomfort: warm cheeks and a prickle across the back of my neck.

Whatever it was, I didn't like it.

"Mom's renamed her dog," I explained. "She isn't yelling at you, she's yelling at the dog." I dropped my gaze to Xul, who was licking his balls with vigorous enthusiasm. "And she's hardly being fair," I added. "If humans could do that, none of us would ever stop."

Mason let out a surprised laugh, and I bent to pick up Xul, interrupting his testicle appreciation session. As I hoisted him in my arms, he swiped his tongue across my cheek and over my mouth.

Mason's eyes widened with horror.

I choked, trying to wipe off testicle-flavored saliva with one arm while keeping hold of the wriggling, affectionate mutt with the other.

Mason wrestled with the gate for a moment, then came through to our side, tugging something out of his pocket with one hand. A white handkerchief, like a peace offering. "It's clean," he said.

I dumped Xul on the ground to take the handkerchief, using it to wipe my face. Dragging it across my lips, I made the mistake of inhaling deeply. It smelled of male cologne, an oaky male scent that made me think of handsome shirtless woodcutters chopping giant trees as tiny beads of sweat ran over their burly chests and rippling stomachs. I'd clearly been on a sexual starvation diet, because the scent sent tingles to my womanly parts and made my thighs tremble.

It also must have addled my brain, because I blurted, "You smell nice." Then I remembered how hurt I'd been when he'd stopped talking to me. "I mean, you smell slightly better than dog testicles."

He snorted another laugh, then shook his head. "I'd forgotten how funny you can be."

"How would you even know? This is the first time you've spoken to me in fourteen years. And by the way, you still owe me an explanation for the way you treated me back then."

"An explanation?" His brow furrowed. "But you know why everything happened the way it did."

"Are you crazy? How could I possibly know, when you refused to tell me?"

His puzzled frown deepened and he opened his mouth to say something, then closed it again. Shaking his head, he glanced back at the house where I could see his father scowling at us from the window. "I'd better go back in before Dad's head explodes." He held out a hand, wordlessly asking for his handkerchief back.

Though my still quivering thighs suggested I shove the fragrant handkerchief in my pocket so I could enjoy sniffing it later, I ordered them to pipe down and handed it over.

"Well?" I asked. "An explanation?"

Instead of answering, Mason turned to the gate that separated our two properties. As he opened it, Xul gave an excited bark and bounded through, pushing past his legs.

"Xul!" I called, but the dog ignored me. He ran to Mason's father's back stairs, lifted his leg and shot a stream of pee all over the bottom step.

"I'll get him," I told Mason, my voice almost drowned out by my mother's triumphant whooping.

I hurried through the gate, past Mason, to the foot of the stairs. As Xul bounded out of my grasp, the door at the top of the steps crashed open, and I caught a single glimpse of a red-faced, furious Ed Lennox, his outrageously hairy eyebrows crashing together like two skinny Pomeranians in a fight to the death.

I just had time to notice he was upending a large jug. Then an icy blast of water hit my face.

Gasping, I staggered backward. I wiped my eyes, breathless with shock. Cold water ran down my neck, dripping onto my T-shirt.

"Wha——?" I spluttered.

"Get your filthy dog off my property!"

"Dad! What did you do?" Mason was by my side in a moment, and this close I realized how wide his chest and arms really were, like he'd swallowed a barrel and it had gotten stuck halfway down.

"You're wet," he said to me, as though I might not realize my *Zombies Hate Fast Food* T-shirt was plastered to me and there was a cold breeze blowing. He put his hands on me, wrapping his big fingers around my upper arms. His touch was hot and he was towering over me. Then his scent hit my lungs, and it was even more delicious than on his handkerchief.

I could count the times I'd previously been lost for words on the fingers of no hands, and an observation like, 'You're wet,' deserved a quick comeback. But incredibly, I couldn't think of a single smart-assed retort. All I could do was stare up at Mason's handsome face and nod.

His irises were so much like shadowed glaciers, it should have been impossible for them to transmit a feeling of heat. But he was staring at my wet T-shirt as though I had D-cups. And when his gaze lifted to tangle with mine, it was hot enough to dry my shirt in a matter of seconds.

"You cowardly fiend," yelled Mom. "You despicable wretch! How dare you attack my daughter?"

Ed Lennox harrumphed. "If your dog pees on my property again, I'll have it taken away and locked up."

It was such a ridiculous threat, my voice—and my sarcasm—came flooding back with a vengeance. I stepped back, breaking contact with Mason. "Remind me, what's the phone number for the Doggy Detention Squad?" I called up to Edward. "Or were you going to call the Society for Stopping Soggy Stairs?"

Edward gripped his jug with one hand and pointed

with the other. "Get out of my yard, devil spawn! Back to your side of the gate."

"You lump of smelly ass dandruff!" shouted Mom. "You vile bumbaclot!" She sounded like she was enjoying herself.

"You can't go around throwing water on people, Dad." Mason's tone was sharp. "Apologize to Carlotta."

"Apologize for what? I had to wash dog pee off my step and she happened to be in the way."

I gave a loud, derisive snort.

"Trixie Watson is a menace!" Edward raised his voice. "The woman is certifiable, and I won't have her pets or relatives on my property."

Mom raised her voice even louder. "Edward Lennox has the brain of a beetle and a face like a basilisk's butthole."

"Mom!" I yelled. "Would you please stop making things worse?"

Mason folded his arms, glaring up at his father, and I was distracted by the impressive flexing of his biceps. "Dad, are you going to tell Carlotta you're sorry?" His tone was so hard, he could have used it to crack macadamia nuts, which are by far the most difficult nuts to crack. Come to think of it, his angular jaw could probably be used the same way. He could rent himself out to the Nut Hut for parties.

"Sorry?" His father snapped. "I'm not sorry. And if that dog doesn't get off my property, I'll…" He broke off as Xul lifted his leg and sprayed another stream of liquid onto his steps.

Mom hooted. I could hear boards creaking as though she were doing some kind of victory dance, but I didn't want to turn around and look. I was suddenly finding it hard enough to keep a straight face.

"Sorry about Xul, Mr. Lennox," I said. "He's old, and you know how the elderly have to pee every five minutes."

The old man made a choking sound. "Get that mutt under control, or I'll go inside and fetch my gun."

A muscle twitched in Mason's jaw. "You don't own a gun."

"Then I'm going inside to order one!" The door slammed behind Edward so violently, I winced.

"Who's a very good boy, Xul?" Mom cooed. "Who's my big, bad destroyer? Come to Mommy, Xuley Wuley. Come here, good boy."

When the dog ran to the gate, Mason opened it for him to get back through to our side. Tail wagging, he ran straight back to Mom. I moved to follow, and another crash came from inside, as though Edward had slammed an interior door.

Mom cackled again. "Did you see how angry he was? Now's the perfect time to crank call him." She hurried inside, Xul at her heels.

Sighing, Mason dragged his hand through his hair, giving it a tousled look that made me wonder if that's what he looked like when he woke up.

The mental picture was sudden, and all too vivid. Mason in bed, his hair messy. He was so big, his body would take up a lot of room. And when he sat up, the sheets would slip down his wide, muscled chest to reveal abs that rippled like roofing iron.

I swallowed, trying to lock down my rebellious imagination.

Then Mason gave me a heart-stopping smile. "Welcome back to San Dante, Carlotta. Are you having fun yet?"

A comedic retort might distract from the fact he was making my legs weak again, but I couldn't think of a single funny thing to say. That meant I'd been lost for words twice. For someone whose career depended on humor, it was a worrying sign.

Somehow, Mason Lennox was extinguishing my wit. He was crushing it out of existence with his macadamia-cracking jaw, his polar-storm eyes, and his butt-hugging jeans.

Just one more reason to be mad with him.

"This isn't my idea of fun." I folded my arms. "And your father isn't the only one who owes me an apology."

Chapter Two

Mason

I hated keeping secrets from Carlotta.

For the last six years I'd been pretending to be someone I wasn't, so lying was second nature. But I knew Carlotta's history, how she'd been mocked at school for believing her mother's wild stories. She'd deserved the truth then, and even more so now.

But I couldn't be honest with her, not even about things that had happened years ago. Those weren't my secrets to tell.

"I apologize," I said instead.

"What about an explanation?"

"I can only give you an apology."

She narrowed her eyes, her arms still folded, and I felt like I was sixteen again. I couldn't pick what exactly it was about her that had changed since then, but she was even more beautiful than I remembered. I liked the fine laughter lines around her eyes and the character the years had added.

"I'm surprised your mom and my dad haven't burned down each other's houses yet," I said to distract her.

The two small, wooden houses sat side-by-side. They'd once been almost identical, but not anymore. Dad's place was well cared for and freshly painted. Carlotta's mother's house had peeling paint and an overgrown vine that was threatening to swallow it. Some of the boards I could pick out as rotten, even from a distance.

"The two of them seem to be edging into Defcon One," agreed Carlotta.

"Nuclear war?"

"I probably shouldn't tell you this, but Mom's enriching uranium in her basement."

She sounded so serious I couldn't help but chuckle. But then, she'd always had a talent for making me laugh.

"I'd better go and make sure my father isn't really trying to buy weapons on the Internet." I moved toward Dad's front step. "It was nice seeing you again."

The breeze lifted the ends of her hair, blowing a few strands across her face. She brushed it back, her brow furrowed.

"Wish I could say the same. Not that it hasn't been super great reliving the fact you left town without a word and ignored me when you got back, but there are other things I enjoy more. Like root canals and anal fissures."

Ouch.

"Do you get a lot of anal fissures?" I asked, trying to soften her frown.

She drew her back up, lifting her chin. "You've forfeited your right to enquire about any of my body parts."

As soon as she said the words 'body parts', it became physically impossible for me to stop my gaze from flicking down to her wet T-shirt. And a sudden jolt of memory came over me with such force, for a moment I was sixteen again.

Carlotta and I had watched a re-screening of The Matrix. We'd both seen the movie at least three times on its first release, and the cinema was all but empty. From our seats in the back row, we shared a bucket of popcorn and murmured a commentary to each other, our feet propped up on the seats in front.

I'd kissed her a few times already, but I was keyed up as I waited for the perfect moment to do it again. Though I'd tried to sound normal, our next kiss was all I could think about and the anticipation of it had made me nervous.

Near the end of the movie, as Trinity kissed Neo, bringing him back to life, I'd turned in my seat and made an awkward lunge. Our shoulders had collided and our noses had banged together, and for a moment it was so embarrassingly awful I'd waited for her to laugh.

Then her lips had opened under mine, tasting of popcorn and salt, and the muffled, eager sound she'd made had extinguished all thought.

It wasn't even a conscious movement that had brought my hand up to forbidden territory. I'd only intended to put my hand on her waist when it accidentally brushed the underside of her breast. But she made the same sound again before taking my hand to place it where she wanted it. With my heart beating in my throat, I cradled her breast. That curve had felt both perfect and vital, as though I'd just discovered the meaning of life. The way her body had melted into me, pushing into my hand, had been a religious experience.

I'd felt like I was on the precipice of something big. Something irreversible.

I'd thought I was falling in love.

It was a memory that had stuck with me, still so visceral

that I could close my eyes and breathe in the buttery smell of popcorn.

"Mason?"

I blinked, coming back to reality. "Did you say something?"

"The only thing I want to say to you is goodbye."

Her dismissive tone told me how much everything had changed. Now she'd rather have a painful medical condition than talk to me. And if she still didn't know what had driven me away back then, I couldn't blame her for hating me.

I watched her walk away before going up the back steps into Dad's house. He was beetroot red, pacing up and down beside the window he'd been peering through. "Why can't you arrest Trixie Watson?" he demanded.

"Because she's done nothing wrong."

He made a spluttering sound. "Done nothing *wrong*? She's been annoying me for years, and now she's sending her rude daughter and that flea-bitten animal to torment me." He looked ready to explode, so I put on a soothing tone.

"It's time to end the war, Dad. Make peace with the Watsons."

"Trixie's a public disgrace. I demand you lock her up and throw away the key."

I stopped in front of him so he couldn't keep pacing. "Do you know how childish you sound? How long has this feud been going on? A dozen years? More?"

"That shrew has been——"

"Stop! No more complaints about Trixie. And enough talk about arresting her. You can't say things like that, even in private." I glowered at him. "I work as a bodyguard, remember?"

"You could have the local cops arrest her."

"Dad—"

He huffed. "Forget I asked. Next time, I'll call the police myself."

I shook my head, striding into his kitchen. "What did you eat last night?"

"Something green. And that means it was healthy."

I opened Dad's freezer to check the supply of nutritious meals I'd filled it with. They were all still there, untouched. And when I peered into his trash bin, it was filled with empty packets of junk food.

"Ice cream?" I asked, spotting the empty container. "That green stuff you ate, did it have a sweet peppermint flavor?"

"So what? It's still green."

I rubbed my forehead, wishing there were a way to get through to him. "The doctor said you couldn't have—"

"I like ice cream." He folded his arms, his lips in a stubborn line. "I've been eating it all my life and I'm still here, aren't I?"

"Not for much longer if you keep ignoring your doctor's orders. Vegetables aren't poison. If you try some, you might even like them."

"I eat fruit."

"Jelly donuts don't count."

"They're raspberry. That's fruit!"

"It's not enough to just take your medicine, Dad. Lifestyle changes are important too."

"You're one to talk, the number of times you've almost died."

"Not on purpose." I realized I was rubbing the scar on my arm and dropped my hand. "Maybe Kade will make you some healthy meals you'll actually eat."

Dad's overgrown eyebrows shot up, his expression lightening. "What? Is Kade coming home?"

I nodded. "He gets here on Tuesday. Taking a short break from filming." I still couldn't get over the fact my brother had become a celebrity. His TV cooking show, *Kade Cooks*, was a runaway success.

Dad rubbed his hands together. "I'll ask him to cook ribs. He does them better than anyone."

"We'll have a family dinner when he gets here," I promised.

My brothers were non-identical twins, and the three of us were close, though we didn't live in the same city. Asher lived here in San Dante, while Kade was usually in LA. As for me, I'd been in Houston, although that could change now the drug dealers I'd been working for were behind bars. I'd been undercover for six years, acting as a bodyguard for some of the biggest scumbags in the Medea drug cartel. But a few weeks ago my DEA taskforce had swooped in and mopped most of them up.

Six years of stress, danger, injuries, and secrets had finally paid off. I'd thought I'd be overjoyed, but instead I was restless. So when my brother Asher had called with information connecting his neighbor to the cartel, I'd come running.

My work was everything. Other people could take vacations; I'd rather keep taking out bad guys.

"Great idea." Dad sounded gleeful. "Ribs for the whole family."

"Kade makes a nice broccoli side dish."

"That's disgusting. Wash your mouth out. With bacon." Dad stomped back into the living room and lowered himself into the recliner next to his bookcase full of conspiracy theory books. Aliens in government, their plan to cull the human race, and the Illuminati's diabolical plans. In his own way Dad was just as fond of fanciful stories as Trixie Lennox.

"If you're looking for something useful to do, you could go next door and help Carlotta's mother with some house repairs," I suggested. "Her porch looks like it's about to fall down."

"You think so?" He rubbed his chin, his gaze going up to the ceiling.

I narrowed my eyes. "What are you plotting?"

"Just wondering if I could help her porch fall down by tying a towrope around the foundations and—"

"I asked you to fix her house, not destroy it. A peace offering." Then I shook my head at myself, because I was wasting my breath. "Anyway, I need to get back to work." I went to the door.

"I hope you're not planning to see that Watson girl again? She's almost as bad as her mother."

"Not unless she starts enjoying anal fissures."

"What?"

"Nothing. I'm leaving now, so try to stay out of trouble, okay?"

Dad grunted and I gave him a nod, pretending he'd agreed. Better for my peace of mind that way.

Chapter Three

Carlotta

The next morning, to my horror, I discovered Mom didn't drink coffee and had none in the house. I decided to walk Xul to Natalie's café, which was on Calle Colina, about five minutes inland from the beach. Nat's parents had owned the café for the entire time I'd been alive. I used to go there after school to drink milkshakes so thick they could barely be sucked up a straw.

Outside the café, I paused a moment, looking through the glass, searching for Natalie. She was wiping tables, her long dark hair pulled up in a ponytail. She wore black-rimmed glasses that made her eyes look enormous, and she had an amazing figure I used to envy, before I grew to like my own bottom-heavy shape.

She'd been running the café since her father lost the use of his legs, but it still bore his name. *Mack's Place* was printed across the front of her T-shirt.

Looping Xul's leash around one of the outdoor chairs, I told him to stay before pushing open the door.

Nat's face lit up when she saw me. "Carlotta! I was wondering when you'd get here." She threw down her cloth and rushed to hug me.

"It's great to see you, too." Grinning, I hugged her back. "I've missed you." I pulled away so I could see her face, and gave her a sympathetic look. "I'm sorry I couldn't make it to your Mom's funeral."

"I know. It's okay."

"How's your father?"

She'd told me how hard he'd taken his enforced retirement from the café.

"Dad's worse than ever. You want a coffee?"

"I'd kill for one. Seriously, I'd be willing to commit murder and do jail time."

She laughed. "Sit down and I'll get us both one."

Even though it was early January and there was a cold breeze, I took an outdoor seat so Xul the Destroyer could sprawl under my chair. Natalie brought our coffees out, then put down a bowl of water for Xul before she settled onto the seat opposite me.

"How long will you stay in San Dante?" she asked.

Before answering, I took a sip of the elixir of life, taking my time to properly savor and worship the hot, delicious liquid, giving it the respect it deserved. Nat made great coffee.

"I'm not sure," I said, after swallowing reverently. "My Instagram account was hacked and my sponsors have deserted me."

"I saw." She scrunched her nose. "I follow you, remember?"

Of course she'd seen it. I'd been locked out of my account for a few days, and it had been beyond ugly.

"When anyone Googled me, they used to get perfectly good naked photos. Now they get carnage."

Nat leaned closer, dropping her voice. "Naked photos from your stroll through the park? Did you really do that, or was it faked for the camera?"

"I really did it. And it was fun. You should try it sometime."

She laughed, letting out one of her sudden guffaws that always made me smile. "I promise that will never happen."

"It was World Naked Day. That's a real thing, you know. I didn't make it up." I had to add that, because it was totally the kind of international holiday I *would* invent.

"I can't believe you didn't get arrested."

"There were only a few joggers around. But I did happen to stroll close to a couple of guys doing yoga on the grass. They were looking up at me, and that's my best angle." I winked. "Their downward facing dogs may have gained an upward facing tilt."

"You didn't so much as blush?"

"Nope. It felt good. I had the grass between my toes and the wind in my hair." I nodded to my lap. "All of my hair."

"That's what I was wondering." She dropped her voice even lower, though there was nobody else sitting at the café's outdoor tables. Or the indoor ones, for that matter. "What level of grooming did you choose for your naked stroll? Full bush, landing strip, total nude?"

"Semi-full bush, but with tidy pruning. Short back and sides, so to speak."

The photos had been taken from behind, showing nothing more explicit than my ample bare bottom, love handles, and what little side boob I had to offer. But exposing a hairless vajayjay to the park's early morning exercisers would have been a step too far. Even for me.

"Wise choice." Nat nodded her approval. "Tasteful coverage."

"I had a ton of positive feedback from young women who thought I was brave to show my cellulite. And my caption about the brand of moisturizer I was using to prevent my naked thighs from chafing paid my rent for a month."

Nat's coffee cup froze halfway to her lips, her eyes widening. "Really? They gave you that much money?"

I sighed wistfully. "Can you believe it? Encouraging body positivity, *and* getting paid for it? Best job in the world. At least, it was."

"I wouldn't care if they gave me a million dollars, I still wouldn't shed my clothes in public."

Teasingly, I pulled my T-shirt up, flashing my waist. "I'd strip right now for a second cup of coffee."

"I should take you up on that. Might bring in a few customers." She gazed through the front window into her empty café and sighed. "Couldn't hurt, anyway."

"Business has been slow?"

"I don't want to complain when things are worse for you. You've had some seriously nasty comments since those duck pictures. Are you worried?"

I shrugged and drank more of her delicious, life-restoring coffee, acting casual so she wouldn't suspect how terrified I was that I might have managed to throw away my career for good.

"I'm doing my best to win some goodwill back," I said. "I've explained I was hacked. Hopefully my followers will start to believe me."

"What about the death threats?"

"I reported the worst ones to the police. I just wish I could convince people that I'd never hurt any animal, let alone a duck."

"Of course you wouldn't."

"My hacker has to be obsessed with ducks. But the original pictures I took were supposed to be light-hearted. And I wouldn't even have thought of taking them, except the big warning sign at the park was so..." I trailed off, searching for the right word.

"Blunt?" she suggested. "Extreme?"

"Exactly." I sat back, nodding. "See, you get it."

I'd had the bright idea to pose for pictures in a park down the road from my house, in front of a large sign that warned visitors not to feed the ducks.

In big letters across the top it read, *Bread Can Kill*.

"The gun made out of bread looked funny." Nat lifted both hands to mimic the way I'd posed in front of the sign with the gun, blowing away imaginary smoke from its muzzle like a secret agent in a movie.

"You'd think a bread gun would be harder to make. But damp bread is easy to shape." I sighed. "If only it hadn't dropped crumbs while I was posing with it."

"You gathered a big crowd of ducks. All those cute little ducklings."

"The ducklings only made the later photos seem worse." I'd worn a skin-tight black body suit like a comic book villain, and hammed it up with my bread gun while the ducks crowded around.

"What was that caption?" She grinned. "Time to quack down some carbs, mother duckers." She drawled it just like I'd imagined when I wrote it. At the time, I'd thought it was hilarious. Now it just made me cringe.

"It was supposed to be a tongue-in-cheek send up of low-carb diets. The whole point was to link to nutritional information, and the only reason to add funny photos was so more people would click through."

My mystery hacker had decided to punish me for

supposedly threatening ducks by hijacking my platform to raise awareness of duck cruelty. They'd taken over my account and altered the pictures so it looked like I was pointing the bread gun at ducks that had actually been slaughtered. And the dead ducks the hacker had added to the photos were a critically endangered breed.

"I know you were hacked." Nat reached over to pat my shoulder. "Even if nobody else believes you."

"Thanks, Nat." I took a deep breath, willing myself to let the stress go. "Anyway, let's change the subject. Tell me why the café's so quiet?"

She grimaced. "Let's not talk about that either. Mack's Place is *my* dead duck."

"Before we drop the subject, is there anything I can do to help? Nudity included."

"Thanks, but I'm pinning my hopes on somebody buying the café and taking it off my hands."

"I'm sure the right buyer will come along." I tried to sound confident. "In the meantime, how's your writing going? Have you finished your novel? Can I read it?"

A car had pulled up outside and was discharging a load of elderly ladies. They were chattering nonstop, all dressed in matching pink shirts with *ViaGranny* embroidered on their front pockets.

I blinked at them.

Ten years since I'd left town and the ViaGranny Gang were still hanging out together, and by the looks of things, as rowdy as ever. Their name was a combination of Viagra and Granny, and I'd heard they offered stamina-enhancing pills to any potential—probably elderly—male lover who might catch their eye.

The grannies were too busy chattering to notice me, and I wasn't sure they would have recognized me anyway. But when Nat saw they were bustling into the café, she jumped up. "I'll be back in a minute," she promised, heading inside after them.

While I waited for her to serve the ViaGranny Gang with coffee and cakes, I pulled out my phone, searching for the photo I'd taken this morning. Xul had decided to sleep with me, and I'd woken up with his butt in my face. I'd reached for my phone without disturbing him, and snapped a picture while giving the camera a groggy smile over his hind legs. My bed hair was crazy, I had sleep in my eyes, and some dried drool in the corner of my mouth. But that was all part of my ongoing campaign against unrealistic retouched photos damaging the confidence of real-life women.

I typed in a caption. *Woke up at Mom's house, praying her dog doesn't fart. #RealisBeautiful #LottaLaughs #SanDante*

With one eye screwed shut and the other only half open, I took a deep breath and posted the picture, putting my phone down afterward before I accidentally read any nasty comments.

I believed in what I was doing, so I'd keep going without sponsorship. But it would be a lot harder if I couldn't fix this. Before the duck pictures, I'd partnered with some amazing companies promoting body confidence. Now they'd canceled their contracts and distanced themselves from me. They didn't even want me linking to their websites.

"Sorry." Nat sat back down next to me. "We may not get to talk much because my chef hasn't turned up. *Again*." She looked around, checking the grannies had settled into their chairs.

"You want me to help out in the café?"

Her eyes widened and she shook her head so firmly I worried she'd get whiplash. "I follow you online, remember. I've seen photographic evidence of your kitchen disasters."

I wrinkled my nose at her. "You can't cook either."

"Which is why I hire a chef, so I can stick to making coffee."

"Wait," I said, remembering something. "Didn't Kade Lennox used to work here?" Then I blinked, the full memory coming back. "Oh, wait, that's right. Didn't you *date* him?"

I'd been in LA, busy with acting classes, when Nat had messaged me to say she'd hooked up with Mason's brother.

She nodded. "We went out for a little while. Is it weird you dated his brother?"

It was totally weird, but I shook my head because that's what friends do. "Not weird at all. What's strange is that I only got back to town yesterday, and I've already run into Mason." I grimaced. "He irks me." That was an understatement, but the most annoying thing was how Mason had taken up residence in my head.

"Really?" She raised her eyebrows. "You must be the only woman in existence who's ever had a negative reaction to one of the Lennox brothers."

"It's his eyes. They're like ice one minute and on fire the next."

"He looks at you and his eyes light up?" She leaned forward. "You think he's still got a thing for you?"

I snorted. "Who cares? He's a bumbaclot."

"What's a bumbaclot?"

"No idea. But Mom shouted it at Mason's father, so it must be insulting."

A businessman strode into the café and Nat jumped out of her chair. "I'd better go and serve him."

"And I'd better take Xul home."

"I'll see you later." Nat snapped her fingers, her face

brightening. "Hey, I've been invited to a party tonight. Want to come with?"

"What kind of party?"

"At one of the oceanfront houses. Probably be swarming with pretentious twatwaffles. Lots of opportunity to trip over your own feet and make a fool of yourself."

I grinned. "Sounds like a plan. I'm in."

Chapter Four

Mason

I was sitting by the window in one of the large spare bedrooms in my brother's oceanfront home. Looking through my camera's viewfinder, I focused its long zoom lens to snap photos of the guests mingling around his neighbor's swimming pool.

The house next door was brightly lit, but I was sitting in the dark with just a small, dim lamp by my side. My eyes had adjusted well enough to the gloom that I could make notes in my notebook.

Asher's cat was asleep on the bed I'd pushed to the far side of the room. Nemesis was a sleek black cat with startling yellow eyes and a disconcerting level of intelligence. Much like Asher himself, though my brother's eyes were dark gray.

I was alone in Asher's house.

Or rather, I was supposed to be alone. But straining my ears, I caught the soft, barely-there creak of floorboards.

Somebody was creeping in quietly, trying not to be

heard. In fact, their footfalls were so quiet and careful, they must have taken off their shoes.

They were trying to sneak up on me.

"Hi Asher," I said without turning around.

The soft sound stopped.

"I was trying to surprise you," my brother complained good-naturedly. "You must have ears like a bat."

I lowered the camera. Asher had the darkest hair and eyes of anyone in my family, and he usually dressed to match. Tonight he was wearing a dark gray suit with no tie, and blended into the shadows as well as any cat burglar.

"It's my job to sniff out miscreants who are up to no good," I told him.

"I've never been called a miscreant before. I like the way it sounds." Asher crossed soundlessly to the bed and unbuttoned his jacket before sinking down next to Nemesis. He leaned back with a sigh, stroking the cat, who looked up and yawned before settling back to sleep.

I frowned. Though my brother's tone was light, the heaviness of his sigh told a different story.

"What's wrong?" I asked.

"Long day, that's all. I'm going to sit here and enjoy the darkness for a moment, then I'll grab us a couple of beers."

"No beer for me. I'm working."

"The local guys have gone for the night?"

When Asher had called me with suspicions about his neighbor, I'd notified local law enforcement, and asked them to set up a surveillance operation. With a small player like Santino, I'd usually just leave the bust to the locals, but with Asher right next door I'd stepped in to make sure it went down without a hitch.

The local team were pleased when I volunteered to work with them, seeing as I'd spent the last six years inside

31

the Medea drug cartel and knew how it operated. And when I'd discovered Santino was connected to a cartel member I had a personal beef with, I was glad I'd gotten involved.

"I volunteered for the late shift and sent the rest of the team to get some sleep," I told Asher. "Seeing as I'm the one who can identify any cartel members if they show up to Santino's party."

Asher glanced through the window at his neighbor's house. The crowd was clearly visible around the swimming pool, and a loud bass beat punctuated the sound of talking and laughing.

"Anything interesting happening?" he asked.

"Four-Finger-Frankie is one of the guests."

"Let me see." Asher took the binoculars and peered through them.

"He's wearing a blue shirt, talking to Santino."

Though we'd last seen Frankie over a dozen years ago, neither of us would be likely to forget the face of the sleazebag who'd sold drugs to our mother. He was too small a fish in the Medea cartel to have been caught when we took down the sharks, but I couldn't wait for him to join them behind bars. The idea of getting some form of justice for what Mom and my brothers had suffered was what had motivated me to become a DEA agent in the first place, and the reason I'd agreed to go undercover.

"When do you get to make arrests?" asked Asher.

"First we need to find out how Santino's bringing in shipments, and who he distributes to. We want to catch him in the act."

Turning back to the window, I snapped off some photos of Frankie and Santino talking to each other.

Four-Finger-Frankie was in his late fifties, bald as a baseball, but with a thick gray beard. He was a violent, low-ranked hood with delusions of grandeur. Rumor was he'd lost the pinkie finger on his left hand when he'd pissed off the wrong gangster. But if that were really the price he'd paid for being an asshole, it was a miracle he still had the rest of his digits.

Santino was a whole different category of bad guy. In his early thirties, about my age, he'd apparently paid cash for the house next to Asher's. It had been built a few decades ago, around the same time as Asher's, so it was a little dated. But beachfront properties in any condition didn't come cheap.

Santino looked more like an up-and-coming entrepreneur than a drug dealer. He wore an expensive-looking suit and chunky gold rings, and had a short, dark beard. He owned a local importing business that made only a fraction of the money he liked to flash around, but compared to Frankie he was smooth and discreet.

Four-Finger-Frankie was a thug, while Slick Santino pulled the strings.

I took more photos of Frankie as he headed to the area behind the pool where a bar had been set up, complete with bartenders to serve the guests champagne and fancy cocktails. The house was crowded, with rich, well-groomed men and women packed around the pool area, talking, laughing, and drinking Santino's booze. I recognized a few actors, one or two politicians, and a couple of trust fund wasters with a reputation for trashing expensive cars and hotel rooms. The party would most likely go all night.

"I'm getting a beer." Asher said. "Okay if I turn the light on in the kitchen?"

"Just shut the door first."

As Asher walked away, I zoomed in on the crowd, noting two newcomers to the party. When they came into focus, my stomach took a dive.

"Shit," I muttered.

"What is it?" Asher paused at the door.

I didn't answer because I was too busy swapping the camera for the binoculars, jamming them to my eyes to make sure I wasn't seeing things.

Dimly I heard Asher walking back toward me, but most of my attention was focused through the binoculars. More specifically, I was focused on a woman in a silver dress, with shoulder-length hair.

Her back was to me, but I didn't need to see her face to recognize Carlotta. She had a distinctive figure, with her top half small and athletic, and her hips rounded and full. Her body looked sensational in a silver dress, and my binoculars focused themselves on her ass as though they had a mind of their own. I drank in the sight of her hips swaying as she moved.

But what the hell was Carlotta Watson doing rubbing shoulders with drug dealers?

Another woman was with Carlotta, and I recognized her too. Natalie had been Carlotta's best friend in high school, and was currently running Mack's Place, the café her family had owned for years.

Carlotta turned toward me so I could see her face, and my breath caught. Dressed up for a party, she was so beautiful, I couldn't do anything but stare.

Lipstick made her lips look even fuller and plumper than usual. Even more kissable. Her hair framed her face in a silky waterfall, and her dress shimmered like liquid. Her eyes sparkled when she laughed, and all the lights around the swimming pool seemed to brighten.

A man approached Carlotta, and my heart sank when I realized it was Santino.

"What are you looking at?" Asher sounded close

enough that he must be beside my chair. "Stop gaping and use your words."

"It's Carlotta Watson and Natalie Williamson."

Asher let out a low whistle. "What are they doing there?"

"My question exactly." I kept my gaze on Carlotta, scrutinizing her expression as she spoke to Santino.

There was always an underlying softness to her face, as though a smile were her default expression and every other emotion needed more effort. But right now, her smile looked forced. Was she giving Santino the kind of polite greeting you'd give to a stranger? Or maybe that was wishful thinking, and I was just seeing what I hoped was true.

"I didn't even know Carlotta was back in town," said Asher.

"She just arrived."

"You think she's one of Santino's dealers?"

I jerked the binoculars down to scowl at my brother. "Are you crazy?"

"Not according to my shrink. When did you last see Carlotta?"

"Yesterday, when I went to check on Dad."

"And before then?"

"Not since high school."

"So you don't know for sure she isn't involved with the cartel?"

He was right. I clenched my jaw, lifting the binoculars back to my eyes.

Asher let out a sigh. "I'd better go over there."

"What?"

"I'm inviting myself to Santino's party so I can ask Natalie to leave." Asher stayed as calm and matter-of-fact as always, even when my voice rose.

"You can't. What if Frankie recognizes you?"

"Last time he saw me, I was fifteen. Besides, I doubt he even remembers Mom, let alone her kids."

"I can't risk it."

Asher shrugged, already heading to the door. "You know how Kade feels about Natalie. If he discovered she'd walked into a den of criminals, he'd expect me to get her out."

Asher was right. Our brother Kade had fallen for Natalie years ago. They'd dated for a while, and though I had no idea why they'd split up, I was pretty sure Kade's feelings for her hadn't changed.

If Kade were here, he'd insist we rescue Natalie from the party. And as Kade's twin brother, Asher clearly felt it was his job to step in.

"Don't you dare blow my operation," I growled at Asher's back.

My brother let out a loud breath that was his version of an eye roll. "Give me some credit."

"Get Carlotta out too."

"What if she's involved with the drug ring?"

"Just get her out of there, okay?"

I couldn't make out much more than Asher's shape as he stopped out of range of the dim lamp, in the shadows by the door. But I could see the tilt of his head and could imagine his thoughtful expression.

"You're letting your personal feelings sway you," he said. "I thought it was important to bring the entire cartel down?"

I glowered at him. He knew I'd give my life to put every one of those assholes behind bars. Hell, I almost had. But my gut was telling me to protect Carlotta.

"Are you going to stand around talking all night?" I asked.

Instead of answering, he bent to put on the shoes he'd left by the door, then buttoned his jacket.

"Don't loiter over there," I told him. "Stay under the radar, and avoid both Frankie and Santino."

"I've got this."

As soon as he left, I jammed my binoculars back to my eyes, waiting for him to appear next door. I was already regretting letting him go. No matter how smart and capable my brother was, I shouldn't be letting him saunter into the middle of my operation. Not when there was so much at stake.

But it was too late to stop him now.

Chapter Five

Carlotta

Winter in San Dante wasn't exactly freezing, but it was cold enough that I was regretting I hadn't worn a coat.

Instead, I had on a slinky silver dress and high heels. Another mistake. My feet were already sore, and in future I'd have to remember that high heels were for events with chairs, not parties so crowded there was barely room to stand next to the pool.

This was a ritzy house. Though the architecture was a little dated, it would be worth a fortune because it was practically on the beach. But at night, standing on its brightly-lit deck, the no-doubt impressive view of the ocean looked more like an expanse of black nothingness. Over the obnoxious loud music, I couldn't even hear the surf.

"Fun party," said Nat to the man she'd introduced as Santino, a regular customer at her café.

"It's more fun now that you're here." Santino gave Nat

a smile. He'd made a beeline to us as soon as we'd arrived, and the way he was looking at Nat, it was obvious why he'd invited her to his party. Not surprising seeing as Nat was a knockout, especially in the little black dress she was wearing. Her long dark hair was loose and she was wearing her glasses, as usual. They were thick enough to make her eyes look enormous behind them.

Santino had sharp features, and a short beard. He was wearing a nice suit and several gold rings, which I couldn't help but notice because he was smoothing the front of his suit as though worried it might wrinkle. Not bad looking, but I could tell Nat wasn't interested. Her smile was polite rather than flirty, and her gaze kept drifting away from him.

"Let's go to the bar and grab a drink," Nat suggested.

The three of us threaded our way through the crowd, cutting close to the swimming pool on our way to the bar. We hadn't quite reached it when Santino stopped. "This is Frankie," he said, introducing us to a tall, bald man with a gray beard, who was about Mom's age. He was thickset, with old, faded tattoos on his forearms, and small, mean eyes.

"It's nice to meet you," said Frankie, looking me up and down before giving me a toothy smile that made me instantly uncomfortable. "You look lovely," he said. "Carlotta, is it? I like your dress."

"Thanks." He was standing too close, but the swimming pool was right behind me, and this area was so crowded it was hard to move away.

"What do you do, Carlotta?" he asked.

"We're looking for the bar." I misunderstood on purpose, because I really wanted a drink, and if we moved toward the bar I might be able to escape him.

"Carlotta's an influencer," said Nat.

"Not anymore," I muttered. "My sponsors have stopped replying to my emails."

"Does that mean you're looking for work?" asked Santino, smoothing his suit jacket again.

"I'm actually looking for a martini. Though I do have bills that need to be paid, so a job would be good too."

Santino dug in the pocket of his suit and handed me a business card that smelled of his cologne. "It's your lucky day. I'm hiring."

His job title was printed under his name. "Importer and Distributor," I read. "What do you import and distribute?"

"Gifts and novelty items. Pretty things." He flashed his handsome smile at Nat. "Not as pretty as you are, Natalie." She rolled her eyes, but Santino's gaze was back on me. "I need someone to do odd jobs."

"Well, if you're looking for odd, I couldn't be any odder."

"Does that mean you're interested?"

"That depends. Is the work illegal, immoral, x-rated, abusive, exploitive, or uncomfortable?"

"Nothing like that." He held up both hands, chuckling. "Just office work and a little driving."

"I waitressed while I was at acting school, but I've never done office work."

"You'll like it. Give me your number." Santino handed over his cellphone, and I punched in my number before slipping the business card he handed me into the small bag I had slung over my shoulder.

"I'll get us a drink," said Nat.

Frankie leaned in. He was a big guy, and he was standing so close I couldn't get around him. "I'm a social media expert," he announced. "I can solve the problem with your sponsors."

"Really?" I hesitated. Nat was already moving away, and I wanted to go with her. "Shall we talk about it at the bar?"

Frankie didn't move. "I own a PR company. I know how things work."

Nat turned back. "Are you coming, Lottie?"

I argued with myself for a moment. Frankie looked more like a man who robbed convenience stores than a social media expert, but maybe he really did have some wisdom to share. In spite of the sleazy look he'd given me, he had to realize he was way too old for me and maybe he wasn't aware he was crowding me.

"I'll help you get the drinks." Santino joined Nat. "We'll bring them back."

Nat raised her eyebrows at me, and I nodded my agreement.

"So," I said to Frankie when Nat and Santino had moved away. "What do you think I should do?"

"Forget about work. You should let me look after you." He gave me a suggestive leer.

I groaned, regretting my decision not to make a break for it when I had the chance. "Seriously?"

"Of course I'm serious. You're beautiful, and I'm rich and powerful. I'm a very successful man."

"How nice for you. It must be such a comfort in your advanced years."

He leaned closer, not taking the hint. "Women like spending time with me." When I took a startled step backward, right to the edge of the swimming pool, he closed the gap, lowering his voice as though he were sharing a secret. "My friends get the best of everything."

"My friend quota is full, but I'll be sure and let you know if a place opens up."

"Baby, I'm talking about being *special* friends. Ask me

nicely, and I can make all your problems go away." He ran his index finger down my arm and I saw his little finger was missing.

I gave a disbelieving laugh. He was so over the top, he had to be messing with me. Maybe he'd made a bet with someone that he could get a woman to knee him in the balls in her first fifteen minutes at the party.

"Are you being ironic?" I asked. "Perhaps you're performing a one-man play about how the MeToo movement has enabled women to speak out more freely when faced with inappropriate behavior?"

"Be sweet to me, baby, and I'll be sweet to you." He brought his face uncomfortably close to mine, and I noticed his pupils were dilated. In fact, they were huge. And he was sniffing. I'd assumed his sinuses were reacting to the cool evening, but what if there was another explanation?

Though I didn't do drugs, I knew what it meant when someone was talking too fast and sniffing, with eyes like the dark side of the moon.

"Hey Frankie," I said sweetly. "Would you please get out of my way before I slip off one of my shoes and stab my heel through your eye socket?"

He chortled. "You're beautiful, baby, but you're wound too tight. I have something that'll loosen you up. Something to make you feel great."

"I don't do drugs." I tried to figure out how to get past him when the guys on either side of him were built like three-hundred-pound NFL players, and crammed together with their backs to me, forming a wall I couldn't push through.

"Come on, baby. Let me take you to heaven."

"I'll stick to planet Earth. Or Mars, if colonization ever becomes a viable option. But as the saying goes, heaven can wait." I shoved against the nearest linebacker, but he was too busy talking to the guy beside him to notice. It felt like trying to perform demolition work without a bulldozer.

"Then have dinner with me," said Frankie. "Have you ever been to Pierre's? Best restaurant in New Orleans, and most people can't get a table."

"No thanks." I peered through the linebackers. Where was Nat?

"I'll fly us there in my plane, and we'll have the best oysters you've ever tasted."

"I'm allergic."

"To oysters?"

"To men with planes." I fumbled inside my bag, trying to tug out my phone. Maybe I could message Nat to hurry up and rescue me?

Before I could pull it free, a male voice came from behind Frankie's back.

"Excuse me."

Frankie turned to look at the man who'd interrupted him, finally giving me a little room. For the first time since he'd cornered me, I felt like I could breathe.

The newcomer was gorgeous. But then, all three of the Lennox brothers were like catnip for the eyes. Asher was two years younger than Mason, and a little shorter and leaner, though he was still well muscled. Asher's hair and eyes were darker than Mason's, and he had a graceful way of moving.

The smile I gave him probably showed how relieved I was to see a friendly face. "Hey, Asher. It's been a while."

"Sorry to interrupt, Carlotta, but would you mind coming with me?"

"Happy to." I tried to dodge around Frankie, but he moved to block me.

"She's not going anywhere." Frankie narrowed his eyes at Asher. "This is a private party. Were you invited?"

"I have something to discuss with Carlotta."

"She's staying right here." Frankie stabbed a finger into Asher's chest. "And you need to leave before I have you thrown out."

Outrage made my voice shrill. "I'll go with him if I want to."

"You're not going anywhere with him, baby. You're with me."

My mouth dropped open. I was so stunned, words failed me.

"There's no need to get aggressive." Asher's tone was calm, and he seemed as unruffled as ever.

"I'm never aggressive, jackass." Frankie poked Asher in the chest again. "Now fuck off before I shove your teeth down your throat."

Okay, that was it. Now he'd officially made me angry.

"I'm not *with* you, Frankie, and I will never eat any kind of food with you." I planted my fists on my hips. "I won't set foot in your car, your plane, your house, or your garden shed. The answer to any question you ask me will always be no. Nein. Neit. Non. Nope." I wracked my brain, trying to remember how to say no in more languages. "Nouch," I said finally. As far as I knew it wasn't a word, not in any language. But would a drug-addled creep know that? I didn't think so.

"You heard her. Now step back and let her get past." Asher sounded bored, and I wondered if his apparent level of calm was a mask he could put on. Maybe the more tense he got, the more serene he was able to sound, like how I sometimes found myself wearing a strained smile when my feelings were hurt.

"Get out of here, jackass." As Frankie swung around to

snarl at Asher, his elbow landed in my ribs hard enough to make me stagger backward.

One moment, there was concrete under my heel. The next moment there was only air, and I was falling backward into nothing.

Then I hit the water.

The freezing shock of it squeezed the air from my lungs. It closed over my head, and I dragged in a breath that turned out to be liquid.

Instinct made me kick to the surface, and I was already coughing when I surfaced. The water I'd swallowed burned back up my throat, and the strength of my big hacking coughs almost sunk me again.

My lungs hurt and my eyes were burning, my vision blurry. My wet hair was plastered over my face, and I pushed it out of the way, blinking.

Asher crouched on the edge of the swimming pool, reaching to haul me out of the water. He heaved me up, and I stood dripping on solid ground. Nat finally appeared, carrying two drinks and wearing a shocked expression.

A few moments ago, the party had been loud. Now there was dead silence. Even the loud music had stopped. I could feel everyone staring, but nobody was laughing.

Yet.

Lifting both arms theatrically, I paused with them angled up, and then took a low bow.

My dress had turned transparent. It stuck to my body like wet gossamer paper, and as I lowered my head, I saw the clear outline of my underwear.

I mentally fist pumped.

In a stroke of completely unplanned good luck, I'd worn my novelty Star Trek panties that had Spock's face on the front, and *To Boldly Go Where No Man Has Gone Before* printed across the back.

Staying down in a low bow, I swiveled around so everyone could see my butt, which was rounder than most. I held still for a moment, then wiggled my hips. If *that* didn't make them laugh, nothing would.

Somebody whooped as a ripple of laughter ran through the partygoers. When I straightened, people started clapping. I grinned, and indulged myself by taking another bow.

The laughter, wolf whistles, and applause slowly petered out. People turned away to resume their conversations. Except for the drug-addled creep standing next to Asher.

Frankie was staring at my body, his gaze devouring my wet dress. His eyes held a ravenous gleam, as though he was a stoner at two in the morning, and I was the last burger at the drive-through. I wasn't self-conscious about my body, but Frankie's creepy gaze would make a nun crave a baggier habit.

Glancing back down, I saw my panties had become almost as transparent as my dress. Maybe Frankie was checking out how Spock would look with a beard.

"You okay, Lottie?" Nat was looking around for somewhere to put the drinks.

Instead of answering, I shivered. Now the cold sea breeze was hitting me, instantly dropping my body temperature.

Asher stripped off his jacket and wrapped it around me. I didn't object, though it was an expensive looking jacket, and the pool's chlorine would probably ruin it.

Which reminded me. My high heels were at the bottom of the pool with my shoulder bag and… dammit, my cell phone. I'd have to leave this party barefoot and phoneless.

"I'll take you home." Nat shoved the drinks she was

carrying at the nearest bystander. "Here, you can have these."

"I live next door," said Asher. "You can dry off there."

Frankie tried to elbow Asher aside. "She can dry off here." But Asher had his feet planted, and Frankie seemed to be having trouble getting past him.

"I'm g-going with A-Asher." I was suddenly so cold, my teeth were starting to chatter. Catching a glimpse of a relatively clear path to the house, I grabbed my chance to dash toward the door.

My dress already felt clammy, and being wet had turned it scratchy. On the plus side, the crowd was miraculously parting for me, probably because I was soaking wet and nobody wanted me to drip on their nice clothes.

I had to go through Santino's house to get to the street, and I made it inside and all the way through the living room and hallway to the front door. Nat and Asher were behind me, presumably stopping Frankie from following. But when I flung the door open, a man was standing right outside, blocking my exit.

"M-Mason?" I yelped.

Chapter Six

Carlotta

I was so surprised to see Mason, I stumbled over the front doorstep. And because I was cold and my bare feet were so numb they were starting to lose feeling, my stumble turned into a fall, and suddenly the ground was accelerating toward my face.

Mason grabbed me before I hit, setting me back upright on unsteady feet.

"Are you okay?"

"Y-y-yes." My teeth were clattering together like castanets. "C-c-cold," I added, by way of explanation.

Mason slid his arm around me, though my wet hair and clothes were going to soak his T-shirt. He seemed to be generating heat, like a giant walking furnace, and I felt instantly warmer.

"I'm o-okay," I said. "You d-don't n-need to—"

"Come next door." He didn't loosen his arm, but hustled me down the path toward Santino's front gate.

"You live next door?" asked Nat from behind us.

"I'm staying with Asher."

The path was cobbled with decorative stones, and my numb bare feet stumbled again, despite Mason's grip.

"Quicker if I carry you." Mason bent to put his arm under my knees.

"W-what? No, you c-can't—" I let out a squeak as he swept me into his arms.

Though I grabbed around his neck, I wasn't in danger of being dropped. Not when he was cradling me with his enormous muscles barely flexing. But for several long strides, all I could do was hang on. All words had deserted me. The strangeness was overwhelming.

Mason Lennox was carrying me to his house?

No, this had to be some kind of hallucination. I couldn't really be pressed against Mason's wide chest, getting his T-shirt wet and dripping pool water onto his jeans.

Mason turned up the driveway of the house next door. Asher caught up, then strode ahead to open the door. Once inside the house, I expected Mason to put me down. Instead he maneuvered me through the hallway and into a bedroom.

Mason's bedroom.

The bed was made, but it had clearly been slept in, and the closet door was ajar, giving me a glimpse of some clothes on hangers. Beside the bed were a couple of crime novels and an old fashioned alarm clock. A doorway at the far end led into a private bathroom.

Being in his bedroom felt intimate and surreal, especially as I was plastered against his wet chest with his scent filling my lungs. His face was close enough to mine that I could study the square cut of his jaw, his rough shadow of stubble, and how the hard lines of his face contrasted with the soft curve of his lips. His eyelashes were surprisingly long and dark, considering his eyes were so light. And the scar on his neck must have been a deep wound, because I could see lots of little lines crossing it where the stitches had been. The scar disappeared beneath his T-shirt, running beneath his collarbone. How low did it go?

"We have to stop meeting this way," I said in an unsteady voice. "People will talk." I could only hope Mason couldn't feel the way my heart was beating too hard, as though being in his arms had pushed it into turbo mode.

"Your teeth have stopped chattering."

"I feel drier. Which is more than I can say for your shirt." I let my gaze run down to the wet fabric slicked against tempting slabs of muscle, and it was all I could do not to press my nose to his neck and breathe in his fresh oak scent.

He grunted, setting me on my feet. When he stepped away, his heat went too, and I pulled Asher's jacket tighter around me.

"The bathroom's through there." His voice was gruff. "Clean towels are on the shelf. While you have a hot shower, I'll find you some dry clothes."

I looked around, but Asher and Nat hadn't followed us into the bedroom. "Um. What just happened? I mean, how did you turn up again out of nowhere? And why bring me here when you don't even like me?"

"Who says I don't like you?"

"What's going on, Mason? You ignored me for years, then you literally sweep me off my feet and carry me into your bedroom? Why would you do that?"

"You were cold, wet, and barefoot. What was I supposed to do?"

"Oh sure, you make it sound logical." I blew out a frustrated huff of air. "But why do you suddenly care?"

He gave a one-shouldered shrug, turning for the door. "You needed help."

"So you had to pick me up and carry me away?"

He glanced back. "Asher says I have a compulsion. I can't resist a damsel in distress." He surprised me with a quirk of his lips, and whatever I was about to say died on its way up my throat. His smile was lopsided, boyish, and totally endearing. If his scent had made me think of shirtless woodcutters, his smile was an unexpected tumble of puppies.

"Well, this damsel had the situation covered," I managed to mutter. "For future reference, I'm perfectly capable of carrying myself."

"Got it." He shot me a wink as he left.

Rooted to the spot, I watched him go. Then I swallowed hard, shaking my head at myself. I wasn't about to let myself fantasize about Mason Lennox, of all people.

Been there, done that.

Shutting myself in the bathroom, I stripped and got into a piping hot shower. And as the water chased the cold from my bones, I gave myself a pep talk.

There was no point in trying to figure out Mason's mysterious behavior. After growing up with Mom, I couldn't handle anyone who wasn't straight with me. Besides, he'd already proven he was a villain, not a knight.

After my shower, I peeked out of the bathroom. Some neatly folded clothes had appeared on Mason's bed. Giant-sized sweatpants and a hoodie that hung to my knees.

I could hear Nat, Mason, and Asher talking in the next room. Mason's voice was a low rumble, and he must have said something funny, because Natalie laughed.

While I was trying to make out what they were saying, I put on the clothes, rolling up the arms and legs. My underwear was too wet to put back on, and I had to keep hitching up the sweatpants or they'd end up around my ankles, but at least I was warm. And the clothes smelled faintly of Mason's delicious cologne. Shirtless woodcutters again. Why his scent made my thoughts drift down that path, I had no idea.

Whatever.

I was about to go and find the others, when the door opened and Nat came in.

"I'm sorry I left you with Frankie." She looked around curiously. "I didn't know he was such a jerk."

"That's okay. I get to wear these fashionable clothes, so it all turned out for the best." I hitched up the sweatpants and did a little jig, making fun of the way I was swimming in Mason's Hulk-sized clothes.

She lifted her eyebrows. "What was the deal with Mason carrying you?"

"He seems to think he's a superhero. Clearly he's delusional."

She sat on the bed, bouncing a little as though to test its springs. "All three brothers are super hot."

I gave a reluctant nod, because I couldn't argue. "I did get to cop a feel of Mason's rock-hard pecs, so it wasn't all bad."

Her grin was mischievous. "How hard, exactly?"

I mimed running both hands over a large, perfectly-formed male chest. "He can probably open beer bottles with his nipples."

She let out a wistful sigh. "I've missed you, Lottie. I'm so glad you're back."

"I missed you too. It's a shame I can't stay long. I've sublet my apartment while I sort out my income problems, but it's only short term."

Her smile turned a little sad. "Well, it's nice to hang out again, even if it's only for a week or two."

I sat next to her on the bed, wishing we lived in the same city. I'd made friends in LA, but nobody knew me like Nat did. "I'm sorry I haven't called you more often."

"We've both been busy. Besides, it doesn't matter. When we see each other it's like no time has passed."

"That's true. Hey, is there something going on between you and Santino? He seemed like he was into you."

"Santino?" She wrinkled her nose, pushing up her glasses. "He comes into the café sometimes, and he's a good tipper. I went the party to be polite, because I try to be nice to my regulars. There aren't that many of them."

"He offered me a job. You think he's legit?"

"Apart from his terrible taste in friends, he seems okay." She hooked her head toward the kitchen. "Want to go have a drink with the hot Lennox brothers? Or would you rather take off?"

"Do you mind if we go? I'll call us an Uber." I looked around for my cellphone before I caught myself. "Dammit, I forgot my phone's at the bottom of Santino's swimming pool."

"I'll call the Uber." Nat concentrated on her phone for a minute. "They're busy tonight. Closest one is fifteen minutes away." She lifted her head and sniffed. "Do you smell something delicious?"

"Shirtless woodcutters. You smell it too?"

She shot me a puzzled look. "What? I'm talking about chocolate."

Now that she mentioned it, I could smell chocolate. "Come on," I said. "Let's investigate."

We found our way back to the kitchen, and discovered Asher sitting on a stool at the kitchen island, while Mason stood at the stove, pouring bubbling brown liquid from a saucepan into a mug. Both had changed their clothes. Mason had on a fresh gray T-shirt, and Asher was wearing dark blue jeans and a dark charcoal shirt. A black cat was lying on the couch, studying us with bright yellow eyes. I moved closer to pet her and she lifted her head regally, allowing me to scratch under her chin.

"That's Nemesis," said Mason. "I made you hot chocolate to warm up your insides."

"We also have wine and beer," said Asher.

"Wine please." Nat took the stool next to him.

While Asher poured her a glass of wine, I accepted the mug of hot chocolate Mason offered and took a sip. It was as delicious as it smelled.

"There's one thing that's bugging me, Mason." I slid onto the stool next to Nat, cupping the mug with both hands. "Why is it that every time I see you, I get wet?"

Nat coughed a laugh that sprayed droplets of wine over the counter. "Sorry." She clamped her hand over her mouth. "Gross."

Mason rolled his lips between his teeth, clearly trying not to laugh. Only Asher looked impassive.

"I mean, my clothes get wet." I rolled my eyes, pretending I hadn't made the joke intentionally. Inside I was sighing with relief. At last, I'd managed to crack a joke in front of Mason. Sure it was a lame sexual innuendo, but last time I'd been unable to even manage that much.

"Have you warmed up now?" asked Mason.

I nodded. "Thanks for the shower and clothes." I looked at Asher. "And thank you for rescuing me from the swimming pool. I hung your jacket in the bathroom, but it probably needs emergency dry cleaning."

"You're welcome."

"What did you want to talk to me about at the party?"

"Nothing important."

"What do you mean? You were so insistent, it had to be something urgent."

Asher met my gaze. "I was going to warn you not to fall in the pool."

I narrowed my eyes at him, and Nat snickered. Then her phone dinged and she glanced at the screen. "Our Uber's almost here."

"Cancel it," said Mason. "I'll drive you home."

I shook my head. "Thanks for the offer, but you can climb down from your white stallion now. I'm not a damsel who needs rescuing, remember?" I turned to Nat and dropped my voice to a loud mock-whisper. "I thought he might have figured that out when he saw the Vulcan on my panties."

"Spock's only half Vulcan," said Nat with a shrug.

Mason looked from her to me as though trying to pick which of us was the craziest one. "I don't have a horse, but a perfectly good car. No saddle required."

Nat took another gulp of her wine, and set the glass down when her phone dinged again. "As much as I'd love to take a ride with you guys, our Uber's right outside."

Chapter Seven

Mason

Carlotta climbed into the Uber's back seat and lowered the window. "Thanks for the dry clothes, Mason. I'll return them."

"Just don't tell your mother who the clothes belong to," Nat warned Carlotta. "Or she'll build a bonfire and burn them."

The sound of drunken laughter drifted from Santino's house, and every light was blazing. In my six years as a cartel bodyguard I hadn't run into Santino or Frankie, so if they saw me on the street they wouldn't know me. Still, I didn't want to loiter in front of Santino's house for a moment longer than necessary.

"Next time, keep away from people who push you into swimming pools," I said to Carlotta, trying to subtly warn her away from Santino and Frankie.

She nodded. "Especially obnoxious drug fiends." The driver started the car, and Carlotta pressed the button to slide the window back up.

"Drug fiends?" I asked sharply.

She nodded. "Frankie's a—" The car started to pull away and her window slid shut.

I stared after the car for a moment, then turned to Asher. "Did you hear that?"

He nodded. "You think she's involved?"

"Of course not. Come on, let's get back inside."

He gave me a sideways glance, but followed me up the path. "I realize you have a pathological need to protect everyone you're close to, but you need to be objective," he said.

I kicked a stone out of my way with more force than necessary. "Which is why I'll run a background check on Carlotta anyway, even though she's not likely to be in the system, or have a record."

As soon as we were inside, I went back to the still-dark spare bedroom so I could watch the partygoers crowded into Santino's house. Asher followed me as far as the door.

"Why did you turn up at Santino's place?" Asher leaned against the door frame. "That wasn't part of the plan."

"Nobody saw me."

"Frankie might have followed us out."

"You're the one who spoke to him after I told you to keep clear. He didn't recognize you, did he?"

Asher shook his head. "I told you he wouldn't."

Truth was, neither of us should have gone near the house. But when I'd seen Carlotta fall in the pool, I'd rushed out without caring.

Which was so incredibly stupid, I should slap myself.

As a bodyguard I'd won the trust of key members of the cartel. Although those members were now in jail, my cover and reputation were intact. After helping the local team arrest Frankie and Santino, I could head back to

Houston and get to work taking down more cartel members. But if Frankie or Santino learned I'd been involved, word would get around.

Six long years of living and breathing my work meant I couldn't afford to take any risks.

"It's easy to see why you like Carlotta," said Asher, reading my mind. "But you need to be careful."

My father and brothers knew I was a special agent with the DEA. They also knew I'd been working undercover, though I hadn't given them any details and I'd sworn them to secrecy. I was pretty sure they'd figured out my job was dangerous. Hell, they'd seen my scars.

"I'll have to put Carlotta and Natalie on the list of party-goers. The surveillance team will look into them to make sure they have no links to the cartel." I clenched my jaw, hating the idea of anyone prying into Carlotta's private life. "I know they aren't involved. There's no way. But if I leave them off the list and they're somehow connected, it could come back to bite me."

"You could eliminate them as suspects yourself."

"You just told me to be careful."

Asher shrugged. "Then let the local team look into them. I'm going to finish my beer."

Once he'd disappeared into the kitchen, I turned my attention back to the party, taking photos and making notes. It wasn't until several hours later that the last of the guests left the house next door, and I had time to log into my laptop and request records on Carlotta from the police database. The request would take a while to process, so in the meantime, I Googled her.

Hundreds—no, thousands—of results popped up. Apparently, Carlotta was Internet famous. Some duck pictures were the top results, then… naked photos?

My mouth went dry.

I clicked through to Instagram, and saw Carlotta walking naked in what looked like a public park. It had to be early morning, because the golden light made her skin glow. A series of photos had been taken from behind, showcasing her body to perfection. I clicked on the first, and it filled my screen. Carlotta was twisting to smile over her shoulder at the camera. Her hair was swinging and the light caught it like a halo. The motion showed off the pert outline of her breast, and the breathtaking beauty of her ass.

She was a work of art. A masterpiece.

I was so captivated by her naked form that it was a long time before I even noticed the other people in the picture.

A couple of joggers were gaping at her, their eyes wide and their mouths open. They were frozen mid-run, their expressions so shocked that I snorted a laugh before clicking to the next photograph.

The second picture had caught one of the joggers stumbling over his own feet. The other was too busy staring at Carlotta to notice his friend was about to plow into him.

In the third picture, the joggers were both sprawled on the ground, their necks craned to follow Carlotta as she strode, seemingly unaware of them, out of the shot.

I chuckled. It was a clever sequence, beautifully timed. And there was no way the shock on the joggers' faces wasn't real.

Carlotta's user name was LottaLaughs, and her follower count was... Whoa. Almost a million followers? Was that even possible?

I went back to Google and randomly clicked on some of her other photos and videos. There were hundreds of them, showcasing all kinds of wacky stunts and candid shots. She had photos of herself in a changing room trying on padded bras, photos mid-faceplant, photos of epic cooking fails.

Clicking on the picture with the most views, I rocked back in my chair.

Dead ducks?

The picture wasn't from Carlotta's feed, but had been tagged with her name. The caption was: *LottaLaughs can't delete this!!!*

The picture was gruesome because someone had added realistic blood and gore to the foreground. Carlotta was in the background, grinning as she pointed a gun made from...was that bread? But there was no way the Carlotta I knew had shot anything.

In the last six years, I'd seen plenty of blood and a whole lot of ugliness. I'd worked for criminals who'd slaughter people without a thought, let alone care about a few dead birds.

Carlotta was the opposite. When we were teenagers, she'd named all the spiders outside her window. And it hadn't been just because of her mother's stories about spiders being able to trap people's souls in their webs.

Carlotta wasn't a hunter. Hell, she wasn't even holding a real gun.

Then I glanced at the comments. My stomach tightened as I read the first one.

Ugly bicth a nasty human bean. Im goona mess her up I sware.

"Shit," I muttered. There were over five thousand comments on the picture, and the first one was mild compared to some. They clearly thought Carlotta was an animal abuser.

I heard a grinding sound and realized I was grinding my teeth. This was bad. Very bad.

An entire online mob was out to get her.

I checked the newest photo on Carlotta's Instagram feed and found a photo she'd taken of waking up with her mother's dog. Only she'd tagged the photo with the name of the town, and I closed my eyes and muttered several curses. San Dante was a small enough place that a crazy follower with a grudge would probably be able to find her.

I was still sitting in the dark, so the feel of something brushing against my leg made me jump a foot into the air.

Asher's black cat had crept up so silently, I hadn't heard her. Nemesis was little more than a shadow, but I could just make out she was carrying something in her mouth before she dropped it at my feet.

"What's that?" I said out loud. When I picked it up, it turned out to be a piece of cloth.

I got up, stretching my stiff legs, and turned the light on in the hallway to examine what Nemesis had brought in.

A pair of plain, white cotton panties.

Not Star Trek panties.

I'd only caught a glimpse of Spock's face, but the memory of Carlotta standing in her wet, transparent dress was permanently engraved into my brain.

Where could Nemesis have found these ones? Natalie was the only other woman who'd been in the house today, and she'd stayed fully dressed.

Nemesis stared at me with unblinking yellow eyes, giving nothing away.

"Where did you get these?" I asked her anyway.

The cat arched her back, stretching her front legs.

"From Santino's party next door? Are you bringing me clues to help bring him down?"

Nemesis yawned and turned her back on me, padding silently away and disappearing into the shadows. Asher had mentioned she liked sneaking into neighboring houses and bringing home trophies, but this was the first time I'd seen proof.

Sighing, I carried the panties into the kitchen. It was time to get some sleep, but I'd leave them on the counter and ask Asher about them in the morning.

"You're still up?" asked a voice from behind me.

I turned to see Asher rubbing sleep from his eyes. He wore black pajamas, and his hair was messy. His disheveled appearance made me smile. He didn't look like the owner of Lennox Construction, or like one of San Dante's biggest success stories, but like the kid he'd once been.

At an age when most young people were focusing their energy on dating, surfing, or studying, Asher had been working two jobs and saving every cent. He'd taken a big risk and borrowed more money than I could imagine to start building houses, and then apartments. Now he employed a large team of builders and his company, Lennox Construction, had just scored the contract to build San Dante's new library and post office.

And Asher had recently bought the house we were in, which had to be worth a couple of million. San Dante had once been a sleepy small town, full of artists and alternative lifestylers. But it was only a couple of hours from LA, and it was becoming a celebrity hot spot. Oceanfront houses were in hot demand.

"I'm heading to bed." I handed him the panties. "Your demented cat dropped these on my feet."

Asher didn't seem surprised, but I'd never met anyone as good at hiding their feelings as he was. Friends had complained they couldn't read him, but I could usually tell what he was thinking.

"Nemesis has been going through a sock phase lately," he said with a yawn. "She hasn't brought in panties for a while."

I frowned. "You can't let your cat steal from people's houses." I looked down at the cat in question, who'd reappeared and was threading her lanky body around Asher's ankles. "I should arrest her."

Asher ran a hand over the top of his head, smoothing his hair. "Nemesis gave you the panties. Maybe she's trying to tell you something."

"Like what?"

"Like you should keep your pants on. Stress is the nation's biggest killer." He stepped over the cat and padded into the hallway to open the linen closet, then bent to pull a box from the bottom shelf. It was stuffed with all kinds of stuff, including plenty of socks.

I gaped at the size of it. "You can't just shove this stuff in the closet, Ash. That's all stolen goods."

Asher gave me a level stare and I was sure he was thinking about all the food and money I stole when I was seventeen. Just because I'd had to feed my brothers hadn't made it okay. But doing the right thing now was the only way I knew how to atone for what I'd done back then.

"Relax, Dick Tracy," he said. "It isn't the crime of the century. Besides, what do you want me to do? Go door-to-door offering panties to strangers?"

"If your cat's so clever, get her to take all that stuff back."

Asher added the panties to the box. "I used to try to return things, but it took too long finding the owners. Now I just hang onto the stuff in case someone comes looking for something." He pushed the box back onto the shelf and closed the door. "Did you decide what to do about Carlotta and Natalie?"

"Yes."

"And?"

"I'll rule them out as suspects myself. I can draw them

into a conversation and find out why they were at the party without raising suspicion. Better than having the team dig through their pasts."

It was Carlotta's naked photos that had helped me decide. Of course they were already out there for everyone to see, so it made no sense for me to feel so protective, but I couldn't stand the thought of a whole team of cops standing around a screen gaping at her pictures.

"How will you start a conversation with Carlotta?" asked Asher. "I'm not sure you're her favorite person."

"I'll ask her out for coffee."

My brother blinked. "On a date?" In his understated Asher way, he managed to sound incredulous.

"Why not?" I asked, as though I really believed Carlotta wouldn't turn me down.

"You think Carlotta's okay with everything that happened between you two?"

"Actually, she has no idea what happened. Her mother never told her. She doesn't know why we went to Mexico, or why I wouldn't talk to her when we got back."

"No wonder she doesn't like you." Asher rasped a hand over the stubble on his jaw as he digested this information. "Are you going to tell her?"

"How can I? She used to complain she couldn't trust her mother, and she never knew what was real and what was a lie. If I tell her what happened, she may never speak to her mother again."

"Agreed." Asher gave a decisive nod. "You can't tell her. It has to be her mother who does it."

"If Trixie Watson hasn't shared the truth with her in the last fourteen years, she isn't likely to do it now." I rubbed my forehead where a dull ache had started. "I hate that I can't be honest with Carlotta. I feel as bad as her mother."

"Her mother's lying because she's ashamed. She had an affair. You're trying to save the world."

"Go ahead, make me sound like a moron."

"I'm your brother, that's my job." He turned on his heel and headed back to his bedroom, then stopped in the doorway and looked back. "So you're really going to ask Carlotta out?"

"That's my plan."

He cracked a rare smile. "Let me know what she says. I haven't had a good laugh in ages."

Chapter Eight

Carlotta

T he next day was Saturday, and I went out early to pick up a new phone and get my number transferred. I'd barely arrived home when my new phone rang. It was a number I didn't recognize, and for a moment, weirdly, I wondered if Mason could be calling me.

"Hello?" I flopped onto my bed, staring at the posters of famous actresses I'd plastered the walls with when I was sixteen. Back then, I'd thought one day I'd get to accept my own Academy Award. Turned out all those hours practicing my speech would have been better spent studying for good grades.

"This is Santino," said the man on the phone. "I'm calling about the job we discussed at my party last night."

"Oh." I sat up quickly. "Hi."

"Are you still interested in some part-time work?" His businesslike tone was reassuring. At least he wasn't hitting on me like his obnoxious friend Frankie.

"I'd like a job. But what exactly would I be doing?"

"My office manager broke her ankle and needs some help while her leg's in a cast. The pay's good and the hours are flexible."

"You said it was office work? Like answering phones and stuff?"

"No phones, but there will be some driving. You have your driver's license, right? Sometimes I need things collected and dropped off."

"I have a license. And a car."

He told me how much he'd pay, and I whistled. "Per hour?"

"When I need stuff picked up, I have to be able to count on you. Will you meet with my office manager on Monday? The address is on my business card."

I grimaced. "Which is at the bottom of your swimming pool."

"Oh. That's right." His business-like tone loosened up. "Hey, I'm sorry about Frankie. He's not usually such an asshole."

"Really? Because it seemed like he'd had a lot of practice. He was so good at it, he could turn pro."

Santino chuckled. "That's a good one. So I'll send you the address and tell Faith to expect you Monday morning?"

"Absolutely, boss."

And just like that, I had a regular job.

It was a relief, because I was running out of money. It was also depressing. I'd been over the moon when sponsors had started contacting me to tell me they liked my message of confidence. Discovering I could make money from my passion for positive social media was a revelation. And after the trainwreck of my failed acting career, the best day of my life had been quitting my waitressing job to do something I loved.

But now, that really could be over.

When I left my bedroom to find Mom, she was wearing pink stretchy pants and a bright top instead of a Victorian-era costume. She had on fluffy bunny slippers complete with cute bunny faces and sticking-up ears, and her mouth was red from the candy she'd been sucking. Her long silver hair was usually piled on her head in a Victorian up-do, but today she was wearing it loose, with sparkly bobby pins to hold it back.

In other words, she looked like a sixty-year-old toddler.

While Mom waved a colorful feather duster ineffectually around her vast collection of books, I rolled my sleeves up to get a start on some of the other chores that had to be done around the house. Mom was clearly not keeping up with the repairs the place needed, and I was feeling guilty because it had never occurred to me that I should come home occasionally to lend a hand.

Mind you, it obviously hadn't occurred to my brother Declan either. Not that it was the right time to suggest he come home to pitch in. Not after his wife had just left him and he was trying to put his life back together.

At least cleaning the black grime off the inside of Mom's kitchen windows was a good way to keep my mind busy. Scrubbing them kept me from obsessing over the hateful comments in my Instagram feed.

I was wiping the last window when I heard a knock on the front door. Xul barked from his dog bed in the living room, but didn't bother getting up.

"I'll answer it," said Mom.

As she opened the front door, I straightened to listen. A male voice said, "I'm here for Carlotta Watson."

My stomach turned over. It couldn't be the bumbaclot from last night, could it? Frankie the obnoxious drug fiend?

When I went to the door, I saw a tall, thin stranger shifting nervously from foot to foot. He had oily hair that was long enough to touch the collar of his long, dark overcoat, and—what was that faded black tattoo on his neck supposed to be? Wonky bunny ears? An inkblot? Maybe he'd turned himself into a walking Rorschach test and asked everyone he met what they saw in him.

"Hi," I said, as Mom walked back to the kitchen. "Can I help you?"

The man stared at me without speaking for a moment, his gaze intense. While he stared, I studied the black shape on his neck and finally realized it was a silhouette of a flying bird, half hidden under the collar of his overcoat.

"It's you," he said. "Lotta Laughs. I wasn't sure you'd be here, but here you are."

"Who are you?" A bad feeling was starting to churn in my stomach. He was still shifting from foot to foot. His eyes were buggy, as though they might fall right out of his face, and his hand was shoved deep into the pocket of his overcoat.

Uh oh.

I'd been so transfixed by his tattoo, I hadn't focused enough on his weird outfit. Hemp sandals. Bare legs. And a long woolen overcoat. It may be winter, but it was a sunny, mild morning in Southern California. Not really overcoat weather.

"I found you," he said. "So I can give you what you deserve."

I took a step backward. His was the kind of coat worn by flashers and perverts, and if he was naked underneath it, I couldn't imagine it would be pretty.

"This is for the ducks!" The man yanked his hand out of his pocket and hurled something at me.

The object he threw hit my face and exploded.

Wet. Slimy. Blinding.

My vision went red. I gasped and stumbled backward, trying to wipe slime out of my eyes.

"Duck deaths are no joke!" he yelled. Then, over my own shocked and gasping breaths, I heard the man running away, his sandals thudding down the steps.

Xul barked madly, his paws clacking as he trotted along the hall toward me. Mom's slippers slapped on the floor along with him.

"Carlotta? What happened?" Mom's voice rose. "Is that paint? Did that man throw paint at you?"

My eyelashes were gummed together and my eyes were starting to sting. "Lead me to the sink. Help me wash it off my face."

Instead, she pushed past me. Her bunny slippers slapped the ground harder as she rushed out the door. "Come back here!" she shrieked from the porch. "Face me, you sniveling, chicken-livered coward. You think you can throw paint in my house? Nobody does that and gets away with it. Nobody!"

"Mom," I called. "My eyes are burning."

"I'm a warrior! You hear me? I could break your neck with one finger. I could disembowel you with one of my toenail clippings!"

Giving up on Mom, I felt my way blindly down the hall, searching for the nearest source of water. I could imagine her chasing the duck lover down the street, her bunny slippers bobbing behind his flapping overcoat. It would make a funny picture, except she was so caught up in whatever vigilante fantasy she'd created in her head, she'd completely forgotten about me.

I should be used to that by now. So why did it still hurt more than the paint in my eyes?

I was almost at the kitchen when I heard the front door slam shut and she took my arm. "This way."

Surprised, I stumbled blind with her guiding me, until my hip hit the counter and I heard water gush from the faucet.

"Here. Let me sponge it." A cold, wet cloth ran down my face, wiping gently over my eyes.

I leaned over the sink, more worried about red paint staining Mom's floor and counter than about the cold water soaking my clothes. At least Mom was here helping me, rather than on the street trying to perform a citizen's arrest, or attempting a Karate chop she'd read about in a book.

"Let me put my head right under the faucet." I fumbled to feel where it was so I could cram my head into the right position. With the cold water running over my forehead and eyes, I took the cloth away from Mom and scrubbed hard at my skin, cleaning the paint away.

"He didn't blind you, did he?" I heard the rustle of a candy wrapper, then a sharp crack as she crunched on the candy like she did when she was angry, rather than sucking on it. "Do you know who that man was?"

"Someone with a serious devotion to ducks."

"I'm calling the police. We need squad cars, helicopters and SWAT teams." Another crunch of candy. "They can chase him down with dogs."

"Don't, Mom. He's long gone by now. I'll call the police after I've cleaned up the mess."

"Why did he attack you?"

"I told you how I was posting photos on the Internet to help women feel more confident? He's one of my followers." Turning off the faucet, I felt for a dry cloth.

Mom huffed with impatience. "Carlotta, that makes no sense."

I wiped my face and blinked at her, intensely relieved to be able to see again. Xul was sitting in the corner, watching us with his head tilted as though trying to figure out what on earth we were doing.

"My Internet account was hacked. Someone added some gruesome pictures to make people think I butchered rare, protected ducks." I used the rag to scrub my hair. "That man probably saw the pictures and got angry."

Her brow furrowed. "I like my ducks roasted, with plum sauce on the side."

"Please don't say that to anyone who comes to the door."

"If that man comes back, I'll roast him, then carve him."

"I'm surprised you're taking this so well," I said honestly. "You're not going to rend your clothes or gnash your teeth?"

Mom was shorter than me, but she tilted her head back so she could glare down her nose. "I may be dramatic on occasion, but today you have me beaten." She gestured at my clothes, and I had to admit she had a point. I wasn't just soaked and bedraggled, I looked like I'd dismembered an entire cheerleading squad with a chainsaw.

I bent with a clean rag to clean up the red liquid that had dripped from me, following the trail all the way to the front door. Luckily, the paint washed up easily and hadn't stained the floor. In the hallway I found the remains of the water balloon that had smacked me right between the eyes.

Once I'd finished cleaning, I went back into the kitchen to drop the scrap of rubber into the trash. Mom was wiping the last splashes of water off the counter.

"There are a lot of crazy people in the world," she said

without a trace of irony, the ears on her bunny slippers flopping as she turned to face me. "If I dig a moat out front and fill it with a carnivorous fish species, do you think sharks or piranhas would be—?"

A loud rapping on the front door cut her off.

We stared at each other with wide eyes. Xul barked at the door. My heart hammered. Every muscle was tight.

The rapping sounded again, harder this time. More insistent.

Xul growled, a low, menacing sound that was completely unlike him. It raised the hairs on the back of my neck.

I swallowed hard, gathering my courage. "I'll get it."

"Don't move." Mom threw down her cleaning cloth and drew herself erect, tossing back her hair and pushing her sparkly bobby pins more firmly in place. "You stay right there, Carlotta. I'm going to answer the door, and if it's that detestable duck delinquent, I'll tell him to get plucked!"

She stomped down the hallway and tore open the door, Xul at her heels. From the kitchen I couldn't see who might be standing outside. But I could hear Mom clearly.

"You!" she exclaimed. "What are you doing here?"

I frowned. It didn't sound like what she might say to the man who'd thrown paint at me. Xul let out a small bark, but it was one of his happy barks, not threatening.

"Begone foul demon," boomed my mother. "Scuttle back to the darkness from whence you came."

Chapter Nine

Mason

In my six years as a bodyguard for the cartel, I'd been stabbed three times and shot twice. I'd earned the trust of the scumbags I'd worked for by taking hits that had been meant for them. I'd never flinched from danger.

But when the waist-tall, pink-clad, bunny-slipper-wearing English teacher in front of me started shouting like Gandalf facing down the Balrog, the strength of her rage made me take a step back.

Which was a mistake, because the porch's rotten boards let out a loud groan and sagged under my weight. Things would go from bad to worse if I crashed right through them.

"Good morning, Mrs. Watson," I said, trying to position myself across some of the less rotten boards. "I'm here to see Carlotta."

Trixie had something hard in her mouth, and it made

an angry sound against her teeth when she pushed it into her cheek.

"No member of the Lennox family is welcome on my property," she snapped. "Leave now, or I'll set my dog on you."

Xul stepped onto the porch next to me, adding extra weight the boards didn't need. When I looked down at him, he wagged his tail and stretched up to lick my hand.

Carlotta appeared behind her mother, and I raised my eyebrows, taking her in. Her hair was wet and tangled, some of it plastered to her scalp and some sticking up. Her clothes were soaked too, stained with red liquid. And was that a splatter of red on the wall behind her?

"Hey," I said. "You're wet again. Is that your thing?"

She didn't laugh, and her mother's mouth pursed like a cat's butthole.

"I came to make sure you were okay after last night's accident," I added, trying not to let my gaze drop to her body where her wet clothes were plastered against her. "Could we talk in private?"

"Accident? What accident?" Her mother narrowed her eyes, blocking the door. "Carlotta, this house has only two rules. The first rule is No Lennoxes."

"Mom, may I speak to Mason privately please?" Carlotta tried to get past her mother, but instead of allowing her through, Trixie Watson started to shut the door.

"What's the second rule?" I put up a hand to stop the door from closing.

"The second rule is No Lennoxes!"

"Mom, don't be rude." Carlotta ducked under her mother's arm. "Please give us a minute."

"I would have called but I didn't have your number," I said. "So I thought I'd drop by."

"Carlotta doesn't want to see you," Trixie declared from behind her daughter.

"Mom, would you please go inside and let me talk to Mason in private?"

"But Carlotta, the Lennox family are pure evil. His father—"

"Mom!" She swung on her mother. "Please, just give us a minute."

Trixie's eyes widened and she sucked in an outraged breath, drawing up ramrod straight. She was vibrating with indignation, her bunny ears trembling. Her gaze dropped to Xul, who was now leaning the weight of his body against my leg as though he was determined to get the creaking boards to break.

"Well," Trixie huffed. "If you're going to consort with demons, don't blame me if you start growing horns." She spun on her heel and strode off down the hallway.

Carlotta stepped onto the porch and closed the front door. Xul and I moved back to make room for her, and a different set of porch boards groaned under my feet like they were in terrible pain.

"If you came to collect your clothes, they're in the washing machine," Carlotta said. "I can drop them by later."

"Actually, I came to ask you out for coffee."

Her eyes widened and her mouth dropped open. She couldn't have looked more stunned if I'd stripped naked while singing show tunes.

"Coffee?" she repeated.

"Do you drink coffee?"

"When? Now?"

"Does now work for you?"

Carlotta glanced down at her wet, red clothes.

"Because you took one look at me and thought I was dressed to go out?"

"You look great." I wasn't exaggerating. Even red and wet, she was beautiful. "But go ahead and change if you like. I'll wait." I folded my arms and leaned against the porch railing as though I wasn't afraid it would disintegrate under my weight.

Her brow furrowed. "Why would I go for coffee with you?" There was no anger in her eyes, only confusion.

Standing in the sunshine, Carlotta looked so much like the teenager I'd fallen in love with, I felt a sharp twinge of nostalgia. She belonged to the years before I'd learned how ugly the world could be.

"We used to like spending time together," I said.

"Before you decided to ignore me."

"I've apologized."

"But you haven't explained."

I motioned to her red shirt. "Tell me, who did you kill?"

She folded her arms. "A man who refused to explain."

I offered her a smile. Maybe I couldn't be honest with her, but at least there was something I could do for her. "How about a deal. If you agree to have coffee with me, I'll arrange to have your porch fixed."

She blinked, her gaze going down to the battered old boards sagging under me. "Fixed?"

"Before the wood gives way under your feet. Or my feet, which is a lot more likely." The boards groaned again as I spoke, and to my ears it sounded like a final warning before catastrophic failure.

"But why would you fix Mom's porch?" She pushed wet hair back from her face and I watched the tendrils drag across the smooth curve of her cheek.

"Do we have a deal?" I asked.

"First I need answers. Why do you want to take me for coffee? Why would you fix Mom's porch? And—"

"Would you prefer hot chocolate?"

"And," she repeated firmly. "Do you really think Mom would let a Lennox do anything for her?"

"Your mother doesn't have to know. Asher has lots of builders working for him, and I'm sure he'd loan me a couple of guys for an hour or two. They could replace the rotten boards while your Mom's at school teaching. It wouldn't take long."

She folded her arms, tilting her chin up. "And what happens when Mom comes home?"

"She won't fall through the porch and break her neck."

The boards under my feet gave an ominous crack and Xul let out a small whine.

"You're serious about this?" she asked.

"I'm risking my life just standing here."

"All I have to do is go for coffee with you?"

"Decide quickly. Any moment could be my last."

She studied me wordlessly for several seconds, and I held my breath, hoping I'd convinced her.

"Tomorrow morning," she said finally. "Ten o'clock. But we meet at Nat's café, so I don't have to deal with Mom."

"Deal." That was perfect. I'd get to talk to both Natalie and Carlotta, and it would be easy to bring up Santino's party.

"See you then."

"Wait." I put out my hand to stop her turning away, and her skin felt damp and cold. Like when I'd picked her up and carried her into Asher's house, I had an overwhelming urge to put my arms around her and warm her up. To keep her safe. But she glanced down at my hand with a small frown, as though my touch was unwelcome.

I dropped my hand. "Will you tell me why you're wet and stained red?"

"Because a stranger threw paint over me."

"What?"

She huffed out a breath. "I've been making my living on social media, only I upset someone by pointing a bread gun at some ducks, and they hacked my account to make the entire world hate me as much as they did. Then some guy must have found out where I was, and decided I needed red paint to really learn the error of my ways."

My pulse kicked up. If she was still wet, I must have just missed running into her attacker. "Have you reported it to the police?"

"Not yet."

"Come to safer ground and tell me exactly what happened. From the beginning."

She sighed, but followed me down the steps to the sidewalk. "A man knocked on the door and asked to talk to me. He had good aim. That's it. That's all I know."

"Did he arrive in a car?"

She frowned as though she was trying to remember, and I was struck by how clear her almond-colored eyes were. Most people would be hysterical after being attacked in their own home. But though Carlotta seemed a little shaken, she was obviously resilient.

"I don't remember," she said slowly.

"Picture it happening, like you're replaying a movie. The man's standing at the door. What's behind him? Is a car parked at the curb?"

"It happened too fast. He said he was doing it for the ducks, then he threw the paint. After that, I had my eyes closed."

"What did the man look like?"

She tilted her head, frowning. "Why do you sound like a cop?"

I was careful not to let my expression tighten. "I watched a documentary. The best way to remember the details is to relive the event in your head as soon as possible after it's happened."

"The man was wearing an overcoat, and I thought he was going to flash his junk at me." She wrinkled her nose. "Maybe that's just the way my mind works."

"What color was his hair?"

She closed her eyes. "He had long, light brown hair, and a tattoo of a bird on his neck. His nose was thin. His eyes were too close together and they bulged. His mouth was small and pinched, so he looked super serious, and a little self-righteous. Like the type of guy who if he were granted one wish would choose the punishment of evildoers instead of world peace."

Her eyes flicked open and I gave her an impressed nod. "Great description. I bet not many people could describe a stranger so well."

"Want to hear me describe you?"

"Not really."

"Smart choice."

"So you'll go to the police right away and tell them everything?"

"Now you sound less like a cop and more like somebody's mother. Not my mother, because she was insisting on a SWAT team and helicopters. But somebody's mother."

"Go to the station now. You can tell me how it went when I see you tomorrow morning at ten."

"I'll look forward to it." Her lips twitched. "Like after eating something bad, when your stomach is cramping and you just want the diarrhea already, to get it over and done with."

I couldn't hold in a laugh. "I'd better go before you run out of insults and have none left for tomorrow."

"Don't worry, I'll save you some."

Chapter Ten

Carlotta

"You're meeting Mason here?" Nat was reaching into the café's food cabinet to get a muffin, but she froze, her head twisted to look at me. Her eyebrows lifted in twin arches of surprise.

"He asked me out for coffee."

"And you agreed?" She grasped the muffin in her tongs and pulled it out.

"It's weird. But he was persuasive."

"There he is." She nodded toward the door.

I turned. Mason's large frame was taking up the entire doorway. With the size of his shoulders, he almost had to ease in sideways.

"Hi," he said with a playful smile that set off his square jaw to perfection.

I frowned back at him. Mason was way too gorgeous for comfort. His were the type of good looks I needed time —and plenty of coffee in my system—to brace for.

"Coffee's ready," said Nat. "Grab a table and I'll warm your muffins."

"I ordered for you," I told Mason.

He quirked an eyebrow. "Should I be worried?"

"We're all out of hemlock, Lottie." Nat slid our coffees across the counter. "Will arsenic do instead? Two hundred milligrams will kill him, or I could use a fraction of that if you just want him to have a very bad day."

"How do you even know that?" Mason asked.

Nat leaned on the counter. "I'm writing a novel about a café owner who kills the customers she doesn't like."

"It's how Nat makes it through each day." I gave my friend a sympathetic look, because she'd inherited a café she didn't want to run.

"Here." Nat picked up one of the coffees and handed it to Mason with an innocent smile. "If you notice a strange, bitter aftertaste, just add sugar."

"Let's sit over here." I carried my coffee to a table by the window. Since Mason had asked me out, I'd been thinking about all the things I wanted to know, and I didn't intend to waste any time.

"Thanks for showing up." He eased into a seat that looked too small for him. "I wasn't sure you would."

"I need to know why you left town, and I won't let up until you give me an answer."

"Why is it so important?"

"Because when I was fifteen, I was convinced there was something wrong with my boobs."

He almost choked on a sip of coffee. His gaze dropped to my chest before bouncing back to my eyes. "What?"

"You felt my boobs the day before you left. We were at the movies. It was *The Matrix*."

He swallowed, his Adam's apple bobbing. "I remember."

"So I figured once you realized my bra was padded, you must have decided you were done with me." I gave a one-shouldered shrug. "Fifteen-year-old girl logic."

His light eyes darkened. "Wait. You thought I left San Dante and went to live in Mexico because you were wearing a *bra*?"

"Not really. I mean, your mother took your brothers away too, so it'd be pretty extreme to assume you *all* left because of a sad lack of boobage. But the reason you didn't tell me you were going, or say goodbye?" I screwed up my face. "I'm not sure how I decided your silence was boob-related. But the teenaged brain is a self-conscious, paranoid mess, and thanks to Mom, I was no stranger to dodging around logic. So crazy or not, that's the conclusion I reached."

His shock was raw, etched into his expression. "I had no idea." He shook his head. "Your breasts are great. No, better than great. They're spectacular. If you ever started to doubt that, you shouldn't have."

He sounded so sincere, my thighs quivered. I ordered them not to be fooled, and gave him a skeptical look. "I appreciate you're trying to be nice, but you don't need to exaggerate. I know my own bra size. You were the first boy I let touch my boobs, and I didn't let anyone else get past first base for a long time afterward." I sipped my coffee, trying not to let his stricken expression get to me. "At least it ended well. I turned my body issues into a positive message, and it kicked off my entire social media career."

He leaned in, his expression so earnest it made my heart squeeze. "I'm not exaggerating about how spectacular your breasts are. They're incredible. I used to dream about them. And not just occasionally."

"You did?"

"Cross my heart."

I pursed my lips. "Well, I want to believe you, but you haven't proven yourself trustworthy."

"What can I do? Take a lie detector test to prove how much I like your breasts?"

"Do they rent those out? Where would we get one?" I realized I was teasing him, and wondered when I'd stopped being angry about what he'd done. But he was so contrite, how could I not soften?

"Carlotta, when you let me touch you, I thought..." He broke off.

"You thought what?"

A hint of his disarmingly playful smile tugged at his lips. "Let's just say, I'll never forget that momentous occasion. *The Matrix* has always been my all-time favorite movie."

My insides had gone gooey, and I couldn't help but smile back. "My fifteen-year-old self thanks you for saying that."

"My sixteen-year-old self wants to kiss you again."

Okay, who'd turned up the heat in the café? I put my coffee cup down and gave him a stern look. "Why didn't you tell me you were going away? I mean, you must have known your Mom was leaving your Dad and moving to Mexico."

"I didn't know until Mom took us."

"What?" I rocked back, surprised. "Why not?"

He shrugged. "Mom hadn't planned it in advance. She was as unpredictable as your mother, remember?"

"What did I miss?" Nat appeared over Mason's shoulder, and I blinked, realizing the rest of the world had dropped away while we were talking. Wrenching my attention from Mason was like breaking a spell.

Nat put our muffins down, then slid into the seat next to me.

"Thanks." I gave her a smile, pretending not to be disappointed about her bad timing in joining us. I had a feeling Mason wouldn't want to talk about our past with Nat listening.

"How'd you enjoy the party the other night?" Mason looked between Nat and me. "Before your unscheduled swim, I mean."

I rolled my eyes. "The guy who cornered me was the worst. An obnoxious tweak weasel."

"A tweak weasel?" He frowned. "What's that?"

"He was on drugs. As high as the Mars Rover, and I spotted about as many signs of intelligent life."

"Who was he?" Mason was toying with the handle of his coffee mug, and I couldn't stop staring at his hands. They were just as big as the rest of him, but he had surprisingly nice fingers. Like an oversized pianist. They seemed nimble, and I could imagine how good he'd be at caressing my…

"Um." I cut off my line of thought. "Just a jerk trolling for a hookup, I guess. I was unlucky enough to catch his eye."

Mason turned to Nat. "You'd never met him before either? Who invited you to the party?"

"One of my customers. I went along to be polite, and asked Lottie to come because she makes everything so much more fun." Nat cut a muffin into quarters, put a piece in her mouth, then spoke around it. "Hey Mason, how'd you get those scars?"

"I'm a bodyguard."

"You must be protecting mobsters to have so many scars," Nat said.

"Or you're guarding someone clumsy." I eyed the long scar on his muscled forearm. "A nerdy tech billionaire with his head so far in the clouds he keeps stumbling off cliffs, and you have to dive after him."

"You figured out my secret." Mason grimaced. "Nobody's supposed to know. Now Elon's going to be pissed."

I leaned in. Just because I was used to make-believe didn't mean I wanted anything less than the truth. "But seriously, what's the deal?"

Mason's long fingers stilled on the handle of his cup. "Sorry, I can't say. Client confidentiality."

"Are you working while you're in San Dante?" Nat asked.

"I'm on vacation."

"You live in Houston, right?"

"How did you know?" Mason frowned. "Did Kade say something?"

Nat flushed. She didn't get flustered easily, but now it was her turn to play with her coffee cup. "I haven't spoken to Kade in years."

A businessman strode past us into the café. He was snarling at someone on his phone while he charged up to the counter.

"Ugh," groaned Nat. "I know that guy and he's always in a hurry. I'd better get behind the counter before he starts complaining." She got up and hurried to take his order.

Mason looked around at all the empty tables. "The place should be busier than this, shouldn't it?"

"Apparently the café's been quiet lately. Nat wants to sell it." I lifted my cup slowly to my lips, thinking out loud. "If I can win my followers back on my side, there might be some way I could help her promote it."

"Win them back?" Mason shook his head. "After yesterday's assault, you need to stop posting online and close your account."

I almost choked on my coffee. "Are you crazy? I've been building followers for years. I'm not abandoning everything I've worked for."

"Carlotta…" He reached across as though to touch my hand and my stomach flipped over. Then he seemed to change his mind and drew his hand back. "Please be more careful. You need a proper security system, and to stop opening your door to strangers. Most importantly, don't upload any photographs that can identify where you live. If you've tagged any pictures with your location, you need to delete them right away."

His expression was so concerned, I felt a familiar—and unwelcome—tug on my heart.

One of the things I used to love about Mason was the way he'd seemed to care so intently about me. Growing up with Mom had been like playing a supporting role in a one-woman show about her. But Mason had always made me feel like I was the one in the limelight.

Before his mother took him to Mexico, I thought he was the most caring guy I'd ever met. Which was why it had hurt like hell when he'd turned back up in San Dante a couple of years later and pretended I didn't exist.

"I'll be more careful," I promised.

I'd be careful of *him*, as much as any rogue followers with a grudge. It would be all too easy to forget everything bad that had happened and fall for his charms all over again.

"How are you going to win your followers back?" he asked.

"They like funny stories, so I'm going to keep coming up with new ones until I find something that takes off."

"What kind of stories?"

I drank more coffee as I considered the question. "I

think women are overexposed to pictures of people looking perfect. So I do the opposite. Like when I go swimsuit shopping. Instead of boring selfies in a bikini, I might take a photo of a fitting room filled with a mountain of discarded suits. I'll wear one that's all wrong for me, and ask the shop attendant to pose with her face buried in her hands, like she's helped me try on so many, she's losing the will to live."

He put his coffee cup down. "Do you always play up your flaws and make yourself look bad?"

"That's pretty much my brand. It's how I do funny."

"You're funny when you don't sell yourself short."

"But that way I can help other women feel okay about being less than perfect, and I never get embarrassed so it's win-win."

"I bet I could embarrass you." When I gave him a skeptical look, he shrugged. "Not saying I'm going to. Just that I could."

"Go ahead and try. You'll fail."

"Challenge accepted." He nodded like we'd made some kind of formal agreement, and I wondered if I'd somehow, accidentally, just agreed to see him again.

"But anyway," he went on. "I have to admit something." He reached across the table and tucked a strand of hair behind my ear. "I can't see any flaws."

His fingers brushed my cheek before his hand dropped, and the gesture sent a hot flush of blood surging through me, flustering me.

I lifted my coffee cup to my mouth, and simultaneously made a rude sound. I'd intended it to be a gentle scoff of disagreement. Instead, it came out as a loud fart noise, and coffee sprayed from the cup.

Mason laughed, and I grinned with him, relieved that the moment of intimacy was over, because it definitely couldn't have been what it seemed. There was no way Mason Lennox was flirting with me.

Was there?

"See?" I grabbed a napkin to wipe coffee off my face. "I made a fool of myself, and I'm not embarrassed. It's my superpower."

He moved the muffin plates out of the way as I wiped splashes off the table. Our hands bumped together, and I felt an inexplicable thrill.

So. Weird.

My body seemed to think I was still fifteen years old. I'd regressed back to the days when holding his hand would get me excited.

"You have other superpowers as well," he said.

"Like my spectacular breasts?"

His smile bypassed my brain and went straight to my thighs, setting them quivering again without my permission.

"Among other things." His eyes weren't the color of Antarctica now. In fact, I used to have a well-worn pair of flannel pajamas that had faded to that soft, warm shade of blue.

I sat back in my chair, feeling suddenly dizzy.

On Wednesday, I'd hated Mason Lennox.

On Thursday, he'd surprised me just by speaking to me.

And today, somehow, we'd started talking like we used to when we were dating, swapping jokes and flirty remarks, while he went out of his way to make me feel good.

How had I gone from being angry with the guy who'd broken my heart, to falling for his compliments? No, not just falling for them. I was getting tingles in all kinds of places.

What in the sweet holy bejeebus was going on?

Chapter Eleven

Carlotta

Mason's pocket was buzzing.

He tugged his phone out and frowned at it. "I'm sorry, I have to go. It's a work thing."

I blinked. "But it's Sunday. And I thought you were on vacation?"

"I am. But this is something nobody else can handle."

"A bodyguard emergency? Does a body urgently need guarding?"

"Something like that." He paid for our coffees and muffins, and said a quick goodbye to Nat. "How'd you get here?" he asked me.

"I walked."

"My car's outside. I'll drop you off at home."

His car was a matt black sedan that turned out to be a rental. Mom's house was only a couple of minutes away from the café, but after I slid into the passenger seat, I turned hopefully to Mason.

"You still haven't told me why your mother took you to

Mexico, and why you wouldn't talk to me when you came back. Will you tell me now?"

His expression closed in like a storm cloud descending. "You really don't know?"

"How could I?"

He seemed to be concentrating very hard on the road in front of him. For some reason, he didn't want to tell me anything.

Why keep secrets? What did he have to hide?

"If you can't be honest with me, I don't want to talk to you at all," I said. "I can't deal with lies, secrets, or fantasies. Not from you. I've had more than enough from my mother."

He seemed startled at my rough tone. "You deserve to know everything. But I can't tell you."

"That's not good enough."

He took his eyes off the road to meet my gaze, and the intensity of his eyes made me swallow. "I'd be sharing other people's secrets, and that wouldn't be fair to them. But I'll make you a promise. As soon as I get their okay, I'll tell you everything."

As he turned back to the road, I let out a long breath, my anger softening. "That seems reasonable," I agreed.

Mason's secret probably had to do with his dead mother, and maybe he wanted to check with his brothers before sharing things she may not have wanted others to know. I couldn't imagine what might have stopped him speaking to me when he got back from Mexico, but I believed he'd tell me when he could.

"What did you do about the guy who threw red paint on you?" asked Mason. "Did you go to the police?"

"I went. They filed a report, but didn't seem very concerned."

"When Asher's guys fix your mother's porch, I'll check your locks and make sure the house is secure."

"You don't have to do that."

"I want to make sure you're safe." He said it with such sincerity that I studied his profile, wondering why he cared so much.

Hadn't he mentioned he couldn't resist a damsel in distress? I couldn't remember him wanting to rescue anyone at sixteen, so it must have been a compulsion he'd developed in the years since then.

One thing I did know was that his face was hard to look away from. As big and tough as he was, there was a sharp beauty in the angle of his cheekbones. The cold lightness of his eyes was just a thin layer of ice that could easily melt, and his hands, though large on the wheel, were deft and sure.

My gaze dropped to the scar on his neck.

"Is that why you became a bodyguard?" I asked. "To keep people safe?"

His expression seemed to tighten, though the change was so small I wasn't sure I hadn't imagined it. Then he nodded ahead. "We're here."

He stopped in front of Mom's house and strode around to my side of the car as though intending to open the door for me, but I was too quick for him and clambered out onto the sidewalk.

"When's a good time to arrange the repair work for the porch?" Mason stopped an arm's length from me.

"I picked up a part-time job, and I start in the morning. Let me see how that goes, because I'm not sure how many hours they want me to do."

"Congratulations. What kind of work?"

"In an office." I was fumbling with my phone, feeling weird and awkward. "Want to swap phone numbers so you can check in about the porch?" Why was I suddenly all thumbs?

He handed me his phone to enter my number, and as I handed it back, I glanced at the house. A curtain was twitching.

"Mom's watching," I said. "She's going to think there's a Romeo and Juliet vibe going on between us. Two feuding families. A forbidden love. Wouldn't that be ironic, considering how much she likes Shakespeare?" I laughed, amused by the thought. "Such a shame we're not really in love. Mom's even reading Romeo and Juliet with her class right now, and going to school dressed as Juliet's nurse."

"She still does that? I remember how much you hated it when we were kids."

"I hated all the teasing. But that was before I developed my superpower."

He followed my gaze to the twitching curtain, then gave me a sideways look. "You think I can't embarrass you?"

"I know you can't."

"Not even if we give your mother her Romeo and Juliet moment?"

"What do you mean?"

He couldn't possibly be suggesting what I thought he was.

But he stepped closer, and my heart sped up. The pale blue of his irises had darkened and heated, so they didn't remind me of flannel pajamas anymore. Not unless the pajamas were flammable.

He put his hand behind my shoulder, pulling me in. Then his hand slid from my shoulder to the back of my neck, behind my hair.

My heart was skipping as though it couldn't believe what was happening. There was a soundtrack playing in my head that consisted of just the words *Oh My God* being repeated over and over.

Mason's hand felt soft on the back of my neck. He bent his face to me, his gaze playing over my lips. My legs trembled.

"Fair Juliet, will you grant me a kiss?" His voice was a soft rumble.

I opened my mouth to speak, but no words came out. The movement of my lips made his gaze intensify, the fire in his eyes burning hotter.

His mouth was close enough to brush mine, so close that if I swayed forward a little, we'd kiss.

I wanted him to kiss me so much, I couldn't breathe.

But this was *Mason Lennox*, and I'd kissed him before.

Been there, had my heart ripped out.

Still, it wasn't like I'd ever let him hurt me again. Just like going along with Mom's fantasies, I could enjoy a kiss from the hottest guy I'd ever known without getting emotionally invested. I'd learned how to protect myself.

"Juliet?" His murmur tickled my lips, his warm breath carrying hints of coffee. His eyes softened, their heat becoming contained.

He was waiting for me to say yes or no.

Though his tone was carefully casual, I could sense the tightness in his muscles, his body coiled like a spring. His hand was still on the back of my neck, his fingers applying no pressure.

He wouldn't move unless I gave him an answer, and there was only one answer I could possibly give. Just one tiny word for me to say. Only my throat was frozen, my voice buried so deep I couldn't force even the smallest word out.

The first time we'd kissed, I'd been just fifteen years old. When he'd flicked his tongue over mine, I'd finally realized why so many songs and movies and books were dedicated to something so simple as two people pressing their mouths together.

He was the one who'd taught me to love kissing. More specifically, I'd learned to love kissing *him*. So it would have been physically impossible for me not to lean forward now and offer my lips to the God of Kisses Past.

As our mouths brushed together, he gave the softest, most intimate sigh I'd ever heard, like he was sighing just for me. His fingers tightened on the back of my neck and his tongue gently teased my lips, encouraging them to part.

His lips were sinfully soft, his mouth an invitation to pleasure. He slid his other hand around my waist to draw my body against his. Then he kissed me with an intensity that made me gasp into his mouth.

He kissed me like he *owned* me. Like he'd signed all the papers and had me delivered.

He kissed me with his mouth, his body, and his *soul*.

Heaven help me, but I loved the way that felt.

My body softened against his like ice cream on a hot day. He was rock hard. And not just his biceps, either. If I'd somehow missed the signs that I wasn't the only one being turned on by the best kiss in the entire history of kisses, I could feel the proof jutting into my stomach.

I could dimly hear a sound, but it didn't seem important. Not as vital as what Mason was doing to me, that was for certain. But the sound repeated itself again and again, slowly filtering through the gooey, lust-filled mush my brain had become.

"Carlotta *Watson*!"

This time I recognized the sound as my mother's furious shout. She must have called my name a few times, because when I finally managed to drag my mouth away from sweet Mason heaven, I realized Mom was standing on her porch with her face bright red, yelling so loudly the entire street must have been wondering what was going on.

As was I.

I was a grown woman of almost thirty, and my mother was shrieking like that time she caught me making a booger sandwich.

What? I was four. Okay, seven. Whatever.

"Wow," said Mason softly. He blinked at me, looking a little stunned.

I made some kind of grunting sound in response, aware that I probably looked completely shell shocked. My entire body was quivering like a plucked guitar string.

His lips hitched up. "You make an excellent Juliet, but I'd better go before your mother decides to reenact a Shakespearean tragedy and thrust a dagger through my heart."

I dredged up the scraps of my self-composure, wrapping it around me like a shredded cloak.

"Goodbye, Romeo. You should know that Mom's more likely to use poison, so be on guard for an apothecary bearing potions." Amazingly, my voice came out almost steady.

A loud bang came from Mom's house and I jumped. My first thought was that she'd used a pistol instead of poison, until I realized she'd stormed back inside and it was the violent slam of her front door.

Chapter Twelve

Mason

At the café I'd received a reminder that the surveillance team were holding a debriefing meeting. But after dropping off Carlotta, I couldn't pretend to feel bad about already being late for it. Grinning, I drummed on the steering wheel in time to the song I'd turned up to ear-bleeding levels on the stereo.

When I came back down to earth, I'd probably think of all the reasons our impulsive kiss had been a bad idea. But working undercover had meant living in a state of constant anxiety, and being able to let go enough to enjoy small victories helped keep me sane. So while the memory of kissing Carlotta was fresh, I intended to bask in it.

The surveillance team was gathered in a meeting room at the local station. There were five local detectives involved, including Luke, an old friend. I nodded to him as I joined them. The lead detective had some photos on the table in front of him, and gave me a quick recap of what I'd missed.

"I was just saying that Four-Finger-Frankie's been confirmed as Santino's supplier. And we're now certain Santino's transporting the drugs through his business." The detective tapped a large photograph of Santino's importing office. "He uses his legitimate business to hide his dirty deeds."

He added a photograph of a woman in her mid-to-late twenties with her short black hair gelled into spikes. "This is Faith Lea. She seems to be his main courier, but he has several other people working for him and we're still confirming their level of knowledge and involvement." The detective put down four photos of men, and one of another young woman. "He likes to recruit mostly clean-cut, middle class types with no priors. They probably don't know what they're getting into, at least at first. He either uses them without their knowledge, or brings them into his business with promises of easy money."

"Is that one being duped?" Luke pointed at the photo of Faith.

"This one? She's in it up to her eyebrow piercings."

The team talked strategy for another half hour, and the meeting had barely wrapped up when my phone rang. My chief in Houston was calling.

"How's California?" he asked when I answered. "You bored yet?"

I went into an empty interview room and shut the door for privacy. "We're getting close to making arrests in the surveillance operation," I told him.

Griffin grunted, and I could picture him on the other end of the phone, most likely in his office even though it was Sunday. He was in his fifties, grizzled and tough. Ambitious. He pushed all his agents hard. "I never wanted you to get involved in that op," he growled. "Santino and

Frankie are nobodies. Leave them to the locals, and get your ass back to Houston."

My throat tightened. I held the entire Medea Cartel responsible for Mom's death, but Frankie was the one I blamed most. "What's your hurry?" I kept my tone casual so Griffin wouldn't guess how invested I was in the operation. "Now the cartel's fragmented, it's all about mopping up the smaller players."

"Another cartel's already expanding into Medea territory. The fun thing about our job is there'll always be more bad guys, and I need you here to get friendly with them."

"But a new cartel won't know me like the Medea guys. I'd have to prove myself all over again."

"They know your reputation."

"I thought you wanted me to take a break for a few weeks?"

"Change of plan. Diamond's moving in."

I sat down heavily on one of the interview room's hard chairs. "Diamond? Into Medea territory?"

"That's what they're saying."

"Shit." If the Medea dealers had been animals, Diamond was the meanest, most ruthless predator of all. His reputation for cruelty and savagery made even the most hardened Medea death merchants flinch.

"Lennox, we need to take down Diamond. I know the asshole's dangerous. Even his most trusted lieutenants die young. But you're the only agent who has a chance of getting what we need."

"Another six years?" The thought made me feel like I'd swallowed a block of ice. "There's no way I'd live that long."

"Not six years. We have a single focus, just him and his inner circle. This time we won't spread such a wide net."

"How long?"

"A year. No longer. Not unless it gets messy."

"That's still a long time to be around Diamond."

"This is what we live for, Lennox."

"Or what I'll die for."

"At least you'll die pretty."

"Don't you get a fat salary, Griffin? Use it to buy yourself a pair of glasses."

He chuckled, and it was a rough sound, rusty with lack of use. "I miss your pretty face, so you'd better drop the surveillance and get back to Houston. We need you on the ground right away."

I dragged a hand through my hair, shaking my head even though he couldn't see me. "There's a good team here, and they'll have the arrest wrapped up in a few days. I'm sticking around to make sure my family don't get dragged into it. My brother lives next door to the target, remember?"

"Then I'll send another agent to replace you." Griffin sounded impatient. "You need to take a big step back from the investigation, you hear me? We can't risk anyone connected to the cartel asking questions about you." His tone softened. "I know going back in with Diamond is a lot to ask, Lennox. But I can count on you, can't I?"

"I'll think about it."

I hung up and sat still for another minute or two, wishing I hadn't picked up the damn call. I'd have to do what the chief asked. But the thought of spending a year with Diamond and his pack of thugs made me sick to my stomach. Medea had been bad enough. Diamond was a whole new level of viciousness.

There was no way I'd make it through untouched. It would change me, and not for the better.

Cursing, I went out of the interview room and found

Luke in the break room pouring coffee. He had his phone crammed between his shoulder and his ear, and I figured he was talking to his new girlfriend, Willow, because he was telling the person on the other end that he loved them, too. I waited until he'd hung up and picked up his coffee before I spoke.

"Hey Luke, I have to step back from the team."

He turned to face me so fast, he slopped coffee over his hand. Cursing, he shook it, then licked off the last of the liquid. "You're stepping back, Mason? Never thought I'd hear you say that."

"Never thought I'd be forced to say it, but they're sending another agent to replace me."

"We'll miss having you on the team."

"Me too. But I know I can trust you guys to take down Frankie and Santino."

"Don't worry, we'll put them away."

Once I was back at Asher's house, I settled on a stool at the kitchen island with my laptop. The information on Carlotta I'd requested from the police database was waiting for me.

As expected, Carlotta didn't have a record. But she'd filed more than one police report in the last few days. As well as having paint thrown at her, Carlotta Minerva Watson had been the recipient of several online death threats.

I blew out a breath, staring at the reports. The details were brief, and nothing had yet been done. The complaints were low priority and still hadn't been assigned to a duty officer.

The few details included that the threats had all come from one online account, and had been repeated and explicit. The account name was FowlFetish.

When I searched online for the account, I found myself

scrolling through a wall of outrage. FowlFetish was nasty to a lot of people, but he was particularly vitriolic about Carlotta. His profile picture was a duck with a gun and a bloody beak standing on top of a dead hunter.

His account was set for maximum security, which would make it difficult to trace. But I called a friend in the computer forensics department. Todd and I had worked together years ago, and he owed me one. His social skills were a blunt weapon, but in the digital world he had a genius-level IQ.

"It's Sunday," he said when I gave him the details of the account I wanted him to check out. "I don't work Sundays."

"Would you check it out for me when you *are* working?"

"What's the case number?"

"No case number."

Todd blew out his breath. "Mason—"

"I need a favor off the record. It's for an old friend in San Dante. Some asshole turned up to her house and assaulted her, and it could have been the person behind the FowlFetish account. He's been sending her death threats since her account was hacked."

"How'd he know where your friend lived?"

"She used a San Dante hashtag. It's not a big place, and she's staying at her mother's place. They have the same last name."

Todd groaned.

"Can you find out who FowlFetish is?" I asked.

"Maybe. I'll take a look when I get some time, but if this comes back on me—"

"It won't. I take full responsibility."

I gave him all the details I knew, and I'd just hung up when Asher came in carrying a food carton.

"You want donuts?" he asked.

The suggestion made my stomach growl. "Sure do. I'm starving." The muffin I'd had at Natalie's café wasn't nearly enough.

Asher frowned, examining my face. "Has something bad happened?"

"What are you talking about?"

His eyes were like bullets. "What's wrong? Something related to the surveillance? Santino's discovered he's being watched?"

"The surveillance is going fine. They're getting closer to an arrest."

Asher's frown deepened. "Come and eat on the back deck. We need to catch up." He took the box of donuts outside.

I hadn't even been thinking about Diamond when Asher came in, but his weird sixth sense had struck again. My worry over going back undercover was probably what he'd seen in my face.

When I went out to the back deck, Asher was sitting at the table, selecting a donut from the box. I took the chair next to him, confident Santino wouldn't be able to see us. Asher's house was built higher than Santino's and we were shielded behind a small privacy wall that still allowed us a great view both of Santino's place, and San Dante beach. For the hundredth time I wondered how my little brother had managed to borrow enough money to buy a beachfront house. But I knew from experience there was no point in asking questions. Asher was too tight-lipped. Besides, I just wanted to enjoy a view I wouldn't get to see again for at least a year.

Choosing one of the donuts from the box, I bit into it with relish.

"Did you question Carlotta about the party?" asked Asher.

I nodded, swallowing a mouthful of donut. "We had coffee at Nat's café. She and Natalie are both in the clear. Officially off the suspect list."

He raised his eyebrows. "She agreed to have coffee with you?"

"I had to promise I'd fix her mother's porch." I licked donut glaze off my lips. "Actually, I told her a couple of your builders would fix her mother's porch." I gave him a mock salute with my half-eaten donut. "And on behalf of the Drug Enforcement Administration, thank you for your generous assistance with my investigation."

"You're doing a favor for Trixie Watson? Does that mean you've forgiven her?"

"Whatever happened between Trixie and Dad was a long time ago. Ancient history. And it's time we all stopped holding a grudge." Saying the words aloud felt surprisingly freeing. All the years I'd been mad with Trixie, all I'd done was hurt Carlotta. Besides, in the face of my imminent return to Houston, staying angry about an affair that happened years ago seemed ridiculous.

"But after everything Mom said about Trixie—" Asher started.

"Mom had a lot of poison to spread. You trust her judgment?"

"Of course not."

"Then it's time to end the feud between our families. And what better way than fixing Trixie's death trap of a porch?"

Asher let out a small sigh. "I agree we should end the feud. But do you need to use my builders to do it? They're already behind schedule."

"You're not financially stretched are you? Are you

waiting for me to leave before you tear down this house, or sell it, or whatever? I'll only be here a few more days."

"You're going back to Houston?"

I nodded. "As soon as we arrest Frankie and Santino."

"I'm planning to tear down this house," Asher said, his gaze lingering on a shapely young woman doing yoga on the beach. "But not yet."

"Do you owe a lot of money for it?"

"The money I owe is just numbers on a piece of paper. It's not real until somebody wants me to give it back."

"Then let's hope they don't come asking for it."

He nodded, shooting me a look that was all too serious. "Let's hope."

I studied my brother while I finished my donut. Asher was the smartest person I knew, but nobody was infallible. Problem was, if he got himself into trouble over his financial deals, I had no idea how I'd help him.

"What's the next step in the investigation?" asked Asher.

"Somebody threw red paint over Carlotta. I have a friend helping me look into it."

He put down the donut he was eating, and wiped powered sugar off his fingers with a napkin. "I'm sorry that happened to her, but I was asking about the drug dealers next door. Arrests are likely in the next few days?"

"It seems that way."

"It seems that way?" Asher's eyes narrowed and he scrunched the napkin into a ball. "Has Carlotta reported her assault to the local police?"

"She did."

"Then you should let them deal with it so you can concentrate on doing your job."

"The surveillance operation isn't my job anymore. I've had to step back."

"So you've stopped caring about arresting Santino and Frankie?" He sounded annoyed, which wasn't like him.

"Are you okay?" I asked.

He let out a breath as he threw the balled up napkin onto the table. It wasn't until I saw his muscles loosen that I realized he must have been tense.

"Yes," he said. "Sorry. Bad day, that's all."

"Another bad day? Problems at the building site?"

"Nothing I can't handle."

"You want to talk about it?"

"Do you want to talk about Carlotta?"

"What about her?"

Asher leaned forward. "Why does your expression change every time you hear her name?"

"What? That's ridiculous." I tried to think about anything except kissing her, knowing Asher would see it all over my face.

"You two used to get on pretty well, as I recall. Seems you still do."

"Why wouldn't we? She's fun to be around. What's not to like?"

"So your casual questioning of her over coffee turned into a real date?"

I shrugged, unable to hold back a small smile. "Turns out we still have a connection." Then I thought of my call with Griffin and my smile disappeared. "But I'm leaving soon. Besides, she keeps asking about what happened when we left, and I can't keep refusing to tell her."

I bit into another donut, and red jelly oozed from the inside. It was the color of the shirt Mom had been wearing the day our lives changed forever.

That day I'd been a little late home from school. When I arrived, Mom was in the driveway, standing next to the car. She'd clearly been crying for a long time, because her eyes were bloodshot and narrow, as though her tears had shrunk them into slits.

As soon as I saw her, my heart sank. I dropped my school bag to look for Kade and Asher, who usually arrived home before me. I was relieved not to see them, though I wished Dad was around to help calm Mom down.

"Get in the car," Mom snapped at me, grabbing my arm and digging her fingers into my flesh.

"No." I tried to yank free from her grip. "I have to go. I'm meeting Carlotta."

"You're not meeting your slut girlfriend." Her voice rose to a scream. "Get in the car."

"Don't talk about Carlotta like that."

She brought her face close to mine. "Get in the car." Spittle hit my face. Her voice was a dangerous hiss, and she looked more furious than I'd ever seen her.

When she dragged me to the car, I realized with a shock that my brothers were already in the back seat. Asher's angular face was set with anxious dread. Kade was uselessly yanking the door handle, trying to escape, although Mom had locked them in.

Mom wrenched open the passenger door and tried to shove me into the car. When I resisted, she hurled herself into the driver's seat and the engine roared into life. I tried to open the locked back door, yelling at my brothers to get out. Asher lunged forward, scrambling through the gap in the seats to escape through the front passenger door, but the car lurched forward and threw him back against Kade.

Mom was going to kill them.

Cursing, I jumped into the passenger seat. I barely managed to shut the door before Mom took off, tires screeching.

She took the first corner too fast, and I grabbed the door handle, hanging on for dear life as I craned my neck around to check on my brothers. "Put your seat belt on," I ordered Kade, seeing that Asher was already fastening his. I was only two years older than the twins, but for once Kade listened to me and yanked it around him.

"Let us out, Mom," he begged. "Please."

"Mom, stop." I tried to sound calm. "You're too upset to drive right now. Take us home and let's talk about whatever's wrong."

"You want to know what that bastard's been doing?" Mom snarled, squealing around another corner. "He's been banging your girlfriend's mother."

It took me a moment to work out what she was saying, and when I did my heart compressed painfully small. "What?" I asked dumbly.

"Your father and the slut next door have been fucking behind my back. Ed couldn't keep his dick in his pants. And that bitch, Trixie Watson, couldn't wait to wrap her legs around him."

My stomach was in knots. I felt like I was going to be sick. But I looked back at my brothers, their pale faces rigid with shock, and forced myself to stay calm for their sake. "Don't talk about Dad like that."

"You knew what was going on!" She turned a furious glare on me, the car swerving as her attention left the road. "Your bitch girlfriend already told you. She and her mother have been scheming and laughing."

I swallowed down bile. Every conversation I'd ever had with Carlotta was running through my mind.

"All this time the Watsons acted innocent." Mom accelerated around another corner. "Smiling at me and carrying on with you, like they weren't stabbing me in the back. I should burn their house to the ground with them inside it."

"Let us out of the car," ordered Asher, his voice tight. "Do it now, before anyone gets hurt."

She let out a manic laugh, baying like a hyena before biting off the sound. "*Before* anyone gets hurt? It's too late for that."

"Where are we going?" I demanded.

"We're going to start a new life, away from the cheating asshole I was stupid enough to marry."

"But where?"

"Wherever the wind blows." Her mood suddenly changed, like it so often did, and a humorless smile crept over her face. But her smile was too wide and I could see too much white in her eyes. When she turned her smile on me, cold fear prickled over my skin. "It's going to be an amazing adventure. Just me and my darling boys on the road together, in search of a new home. You boys love your mother, don't you? The three of you are so much more loving than your father. You'll take care of me, better than he ever did."

Something wet was running down my wrist. The sensation brought me back into the present, and I realized a blob of jelly was sliding down my arm.

"Shit." I grabbed one of the paper napkins from the table to wipe the mess. Then I dropped the uneaten part of the donut onto another napkin. I'd lost my appetite.

"You okay?" asked Asher.

I looked out to the ocean to banish the ghosts of the past. "Yeah. Just… memories."

He nodded, his eyes softening as though he understood. "Talk to Trixie," he suggested. "Suggest it's time Carlotta knew the truth about what happened back then, and why Mom took us away."

"Getting Trixie to listen would be close to impossible."

"If you have feelings for Carlotta, it's worth trying."

I frowned at his suggestion. "I don't have those kind of feelings for her. It's not like that. Sure, I like spending time with her. But we're not dating."

"Hmm," he said in a non-committal tone.

I shot him an annoyed glare. "We're not. It can't happen, and it won't."

"Whatever you say."

"With my job, how could I have any kind of relationship? It's impossible."

"Am I arguing?"

"You sound like you're not, but that's exactly what you're doing." It was an Asher thing. He was a master at it.

"If I were arguing, I'd tell you a relationship might not be impossible," he pointed out.

"Asher."

"And I'd explain why."

"Asher!"

He lifted both hands. "Never mind. You're not dating Carlotta. There's nothing going on between you two. Not a single thing."

I shook my head. "Would you stop that?"

He widened his eyes, blinking slowly. "Stop what?"

Chapter Thirteen

Carlotta

Romeo and Juliet was no longer my mother's favorite Shakespearean play.

After my kiss with Mason, she spent the rest of the day stomping around while heaving dramatic sighs. Dinner was mostly silent, until she started muttering about betrayal and paraphrasing lines from Macbeth, urging me to wash away imaginary blood I'd presumably spilt when I'd stabbed her in the back.

"Out, damned spot! Out, I say!" She pointed at my hands. "Yet who would have thought your mother to have so much blood in her?"

Honestly, I was just relieved she wasn't lying on the floor covered in ketchup, pretending to be a corpse.

On Monday morning, I drove my crappy Toyota to the address Santino had given me, where I found a warehouse full of crates. Attached to it was a small, messy office. A young woman was sitting at the desk in the office, gossiping on the phone.

I'd worn a smart skirt and matching top, but the woman at the desk had spiky black hair, two eyebrow piercings and a nose ring, and she was wearing a black Metallica T-shirt and leather mini skirt. On one leg was a large cast covered with graffiti, mostly band names and curse words. A pair of crutches leaned against the desk.

When she saw me, she ended her phone call. "Hey, you must be my new assistant. I'm Faith."

"Carlotta," I said with a smile. "Nice to meet you."

"I'd get up, but I broke my ankle." Faith motioned to her cast. "In the mosh pit at a *Soul Slaughter* concert. Totally worth it. Stayed to the end anyway, moshing on one leg." She gave me the heavy metal sign with one hand, holding up her index finger and pinky to make horns.

"Cool?" It came out as a question by mistake. "Um. Cool. That's why you need an assistant?"

She nodded. "I can still answer the phone, but it's harder to get around the office and I can't do Santino's pickups. That's the main reason you're here."

"His pickups?"

"Sometimes Santino sends me to pick up stock. It's usually just a few boxes that'll fit into your trunk."

"What kind of stock?"

"All kinds of things. Like this, for example." She moved a stack of papers on the desk, uncovered a round black-and-white ceramic animal about the size of a fist, and held it up.

I blinked. "What is it?"

"A fat cat paperweight."

"It's not a raccoon?"

She dropped it back on the desk with a thump. "Blows my mind what people will buy." She made a kaboom sound with her mouth, with matching hand gestures like her head had just exploded.

"So you drive around and collect boxes?" I glanced into the warehouse full of crates.

"Most get delivered, but I like it when I get to pick a few up. Gets me out of the office." She screwed up her face. "Won't be able to do it again for a few weeks, though. This cast is too heavy on the accelerator. When I tried driving, I almost took out the side of the building. Tore off my wing mirror."

"Probably safer to wait then." I tried not to laugh because she looked so serious. "Anyway, I'm here to assist, and Santino said you'd talk me through it."

"You can start with the filing. That's my least favorite job."

I ran my gaze across the towering stacks of paper that covered the desk and floor. "Is it?" I asked weakly.

"Here are the filing cabinets." Grabbing her crutches, she limped to the tall metal drawers. "Everything gets filed by date. Purchase receipts go in this cabinet. Invoices get matched with delivery documents, then they go in that one." Her cellphone rang and she waved at me to get started before thumping awkwardly down on the chair to answer it. "Yeah?" she demanded. "Oh, hey. You heard about me and him? Nah, he's a swamp rat. I'll tell you what I told him." She leaned back, lifting her leg to settle her cast on the desk, ignoring the papers that crumpled beneath it. "I told him he was a swamp rat. And you know what else? He's a moron. I told him that, too. I said it to his face."

Her conversation sounded like it might take a while, so I opened the cabinets to check their contents, then started work on the nearest pile of paper.

While I matched the documents, I thought about Mason.

He'd already broken my heart, he was keeping secrets,

and I couldn't trust him. In other words, he was the last person in the world I should want to kiss.

But none of that had mattered while we were doing it.

Our crazy chemistry defied logic. I'd thrown caution to the wind, and once I started it had felt too good to stop. Even now, I couldn't stop smiling when I remembered kissing him. He was exactly wrong for me, and I craved more.

But maybe the fact he was so clearly everything I *didn't* want in my life was a good thing?

Because I already knew I couldn't trust Mason, I could handle him in the same way I coped with Mom. I'd built a protective wall against her fantasies, and knew to doubt every word she said. If I didn't lose sight of the fact that Mason was equally untrustworthy, I could enjoy spending time with him without getting attached.

I could kiss him again. I could flirt with him, and maybe he'd take those big, capable hands of his and run them over my body. With a little encouragement, he might caress my—

My cellphone rang.

I jumped in the air with a shriek loud enough that Faith broke off her conversation. Tugging my phone out of my pocket, I saw it was Santino.

"How are you doing?" he asked. "Faith keeping you busy?"

"I'm filing some paperwork." I glanced over at Faith, but she'd turned her attention back to talking about the swamp rat moron.

Santino chuckled. "That'll keep you occupied for a while, seeing as I can never get Faith to file anything. But I need you to pick up some cartons for me."

"Sure thing, boss."

He gave me the address and Faith paused her phone call long enough to give me a wave as I left.

My destination turned out to be a private house in a run down suburb. When I knocked on the door, an eye appeared on the other side of the peephole.

"Hey," I said. "I'm Carlotta. Santino sent me."

The door opened and a sour-faced, rough looking man in dirty jeans and a dirtier flannel shirt gave me a surly grunt. "Open your trunk."

I went to my car to do what he said. When I turned back, he was carrying four cartons out of his house all at once. They weren't big cartons, but they looked heavy, and he gave another grunt as he loaded them into my trunk.

"What's in the cartons?" I asked.

"Says it here." He tapped a sticker on the top of the closest one and I peered at the smudged printing.

"Duck W. L. Scent," I read the only thing the sticker said. Then I frowned. "What's that? Nothing to do with actual ducks, is it? I have bad history."

He scowled. "Just take the cartons, lady."

Rude.

"What about paperwork?" I asked, thinking about all the filing back at the office.

"No papers." He spat on the ground, narrowly missing my tire, before trudging back up to the driveway to his house.

"Wait." I slammed the trunk closed, and when he grudgingly turned back to face me, I gave him my widest smile. "It was a pleasure to meet you. I didn't catch your name, but I can't wait to get to know you better at our Friday night work drinks. Thanks for being so welcoming!" I dropped him a saucy wink before sliding into the car and driving away. Watching him in the rear vision mirror, I grinned at his confused face as he stared after me.

When I pulled up outside the warehouse, Faith hobbled out to show me where to stack the cartons. Then I followed her into the office.

"Santino said I should pay you in cash. Don't worry about the official tax stuff." She collapsed back into her chair, lifting her cast back onto the desk. "That okay with you?"

"He doesn't want me to fill in any forms?"

"We're informal around here." She waved a hand around the papers piled up like snowdrifts.

I wanted to protest that she could be crossing a line from informal to illegal. Then I thought about the thuggish-looking guy I'd picked up the cartons from, and paused to wonder why anyone would send an off-the-books employee to pick up stock at all, when a legitimate distribution business would surely have regular delivery drivers.

"Where's the restroom?" I asked Faith, pretending I hadn't seen it when I was unloading the cartons.

"Go through the warehouse. It's on the other side." She picked up her phone and was already complaining about her boyfriend to whoever was on the other end by the time I'd walked out.

I went straight to the cartons I'd unloaded and checked Faith was still on the phone and not looking my way before prying one open. Then I reached in to pull out one of the small boxes that were tightly packed inside.

"Water lily scented duck soap," I muttered, reading the cartoon lettering on the bright yellow box. "What the hell?"

Whatever water lily scent was supposed to smell like, the stench coming from the box was exactly like puke. But I opened the end of the small box and tipped its contents onto my palm. Wrinkling my nose at the bright green duck-shaped soap, I shook my head.

"See what you did to me, Mom?" I muttered aloud.

I couldn't believe I'd let Mom into my head. After growing up with her fantasies, now I was letting myself imagine all kinds of wild things. For a moment there, I'd wondered if Santino might be some kind of criminal mastermind, and this warehouse a front for nefarious activity. Maybe a smuggling ring. Counterfeit money or drugs. Organized crime. Mafia hits. Or the illegal duck penis trade.

But unlike Mom, I didn't live in fantasyland. I was firmly planted in the real world where I didn't meet crime lords at parties, and I was holding nothing more sinister than soap. Sure, it was green, puke-scented, duck-shaped novelty soap, which made it hideous and pointless. But it definitely wasn't illegal.

Of course Santino was legit. Imagining anything else had been a product of my Mom-enhanced, overblown imagination.

And the fact my hand now stunk of puke? Well, that just proved one thing beyond all doubt. Faith had been right.

People would buy anything.

Chapter Fourteen

Carlotta

That night, Mason didn't call.

I tried not to be disappointed. It wasn't like I was really expecting him to call so soon. And just because I couldn't stop thinking about kissing him, didn't mean he was having the same problem. Looking the way he did, there was no way he'd go through sexual dry patches like the one I'd been weathering. He probably kissed women all the time.

The next day, I worked in Santino's office again and got back to Mom's house that afternoon, just before she did. She was pulling in behind me as I was climbing up the steps to her front door.

That was when I smelled it.

"What the hell?" As I got to the top step, I gagged and pinched my nose.

In front of Mom's front door was a big pile of stinking manure, complete with flies buzzing lazily around it.

"What is that?" Mom hurried past me and leaned

around the mountain of poop to unlock the front door. "Xul? Are you there? Are you okay?"

Her dog came padding out, yawning. He sniffed the pile of crap and wagged his tail.

Mom turned to me, her eyes wide and dark in her pale face. She must have decided to bring her class's Romeo and Juliet lessons to an abrupt end, because she was wearing a severe, high-necked puritan's dress with a red letter 'A' sewn on the front, and her hair was covered with a gray bonnet. She'd clearly switched to teaching *The Scarlet Letter*.

"This is an outrage," she snapped. "The last straw!"

"Whoever dumped this must have known we were both out. They could have been watching the house." My stomach was churning, and not just because of the smell. The trench coat guy who'd thrown paint at me must have struck again. Did he hate me that much?

"He's not getting away with this." Mom growled. "I demand retribution!"

I stared down the street, looking for movement. "I can't see anyone, but that doesn't mean he's not still around. We should go in and call the police."

Mom disappeared into the house, and I hesitated a moment longer, doing another check up and down the street. When I turned to go in, Mom hurried back out holding a large egg carton. She strode down the steps with the egg carton in one hand and her skirts lifted with the other.

"Mom?" I called. "Where are you going?"

She didn't slow down. "You think I'd let Edward do this without striking back? That man has no idea who he's dealing with."

I blinked. "Ed Lennox? No, Mom, it wasn't—"

She was already out of earshot, charging down the

sidewalk toward her neighbor's front steps, Xul trotting at her heels.

I raised my voice, rushing after her. "Mom. Stop. I don't think it was Ed Lennox who did it."

"Behold the righteous rage of Athena, goddess of war!" She pulled an egg out of the carton.

"Wait, Mom. What are you doing?"

"Stand back, Carlotta. Revenge is my birthright!"

She hurled the egg. It hit its target with a loud crack, exploding over Ed Lennox's front door. Xul barked joyfully, capering around Mom's feet.

Ed's door flew open. He stared at the mess, his jaw slack and his hairy eyebrows jumping. "What are you doing?" he roared. "You devil woman!"

Mom laughed gleefully, grabbing another egg out of the carton.

"Don't," I yelled, running in front of her. "Stop!"

"Get back, Carlotta." She drew her arm back and Ed darted back into the house, slamming the door behind him.

"He didn't leave poop on your porch." I waved my arms frantically in front of her to stop her launching the egg she was holding.

"You're either with me or against me. Now get out of my way." Mom tried to push past me, but I wouldn't let her.

"Stop. You're egging the wrong guy. The porch pooper was probably the man from Saturday."

She frowned, lowering the egg. "The man from Saturday?"

"You've forgotten the duck lover who threw red paint on me?" My voice rose with indignation. "I was attacked, Mom. That's not something most mothers would forget. You could at least *pretend* to care."

"But don't you see? Edward *sent* that man. He's behind all this. It's part of his plan to drive me into an early grave."

"So he has minions now? Mom, come back to reality." I glanced back at the house. Ed was still inside, probably dialing 911. "Let's get out of here before the police come and arrest us."

"The police can't help us, Carlotta. I'm the only one who can save us."

Ed's door thumped open, and I turned to see him hurrying onto his porch.

"Mr. Lennox," I called. "I'm so sorry——" The words died in my throat when I saw he was carrying his own carton of eggs. "This is a misunderstanding," I shouted. "Don't do anything you'll regret. Let's calm down and discuss it like adults."

But Ed already had an egg in his hand. He drew back his arm with a determined frown, his enormous eyebrows forming a hairy V of concentration, and let it fly.

I watched it arc toward us in slow motion, too stunned to move.

His aim was true.

"Ouch!" Mom danced around, shaking sticky egg goo off her arm. "That hurt!"

"Would you please stop?" I yelled to Ed, over the noise of Xul's excited barks. "It's a misunderstanding, that's all. Mom thought it was you who left something nasty on our porch, and I've just explained to her that it——" I stumbled back with a gasp, then spat several words I didn't usually say. My cheek was throbbing where an egg had hit me, and goo was running down my face and shoulder.

"What the hell?" I shouted, trying to wipe the sticky goo off. Gross. It was gluing my eyelashes together and sticking my hair to my neck in an eggy clump.

Ed Lennox cackled. "Got you," he gloated. "Right in the kisser."

"You fiend!" Mom shouted. "You monster! If you think you can best the mighty goddess—" An egg hit the side of her head. "Ow!"

She grabbed an egg out of her own carton and hurled it at him. But it fell short, splattering the top rail of his porch.

I ducked as an egg sailed toward me. It clipped the side of my shoulder and more cold, sticky gunk splattered the nice shirt I'd worn to work.

Mom shrieked as another egg hit her chest, and Ed crowed with triumph. He was above us, partly shielded by his porch rails, which gave him a huge advantage. The few eggs Mom was lobbing back hadn't come close to hitting him, and on the sidewalk there was no cover to shelter behind. We may as well have targets painted on our foreheads. And Xul was capering around us, so excited that he kept getting in the way.

"Athena needs a champion," Mom shouted at me. "Artemis, goddess of the hunt, lend me your bow!"

It had been a long time since I'd allowed myself to be drawn into one of Mom's fantasies. They had a strong tendency to bite me in the ass. The reason I liked making up my own social media stories was so I could be the one in control. Far better to direct my own theater production than to be an expendable character in hers.

On the other hand, Ed Lennox was taking aim again, and I was right in his firing line.

"Screw this," I muttered, ducking across to Mom and grabbing one of only four eggs left in her carton.

She shot me an evil grin, drawing her hand back and hurling an egg that smacked against the porch sidings.

As Edward laughed louder, taunting her, I planted both

feet and sucked in a deep breath. An icy calm descended over me and I took careful aim.

"Feel the Force, Neo," I muttered to myself, mixing two different movie franchises together like a total badass, without a twinge of remorse.

Then I hurled the egg as hard as I could.

It struck Ed lower than I'd intended, hitting his chest when I'd been aiming at the sliver of slightly-less-hairy skin squashed directly between his enormous hairy eyebrows. But he yelped, staggering back, and Mom let out a loud whoop that made me laugh with sudden joy.

"Shoot again, Artemis. Your arrows fly true." Mom thrust the carton at me.

As I grabbed another egg, I realized I was grinning. Not the polite, insincere smile that appeared when my feelings were hurt, but a wide, jubilant grin that matched well with villainous cackling.

"I'll get you for that!" yelled Ed. "I'll make you regret it!"

"I'm no egg-spert," I called back, dancing from side to side to make myself harder to hit. "But you're the one who just got scrambled. And I'm not yolking!"

I flung myself violently sideways to avoid an incoming egg, and let out a scornful laugh as it smashed on the ground. "You missed!"

A car pulled up behind me, but I only dimly registered the sound, because Xul was still barking, and I was busy doing my Skywalker-slash-Neo impression again, feeling the Force and manipulating the Matrix as I aimed for the spot between Ed's brows. Cursing, he dropped the carton he was holding. With a wicked rush of glee, I realized he was out of ammo.

I gave the throw everything I had.

The egg sailed cleanly through the air, straight for Ed's

head. I was already cheering when it struck home, striking his chin and splattering goop over his mouth.

"Eat egg, Ed!" I shook imaginary pom-poms and kicked my feet in the air, doing my best impromptu cheerleader routine as Mom hooted and war-danced next to me, her long puritan's skirts hiked up and blobs of egg goop flying off her in all directions. She was grinning as widely as I was.

"We conquered evil," she crowed. "We rule the world!"

"What's going on?" asked a familiar male voice from behind me.

I spun around. "Mason!" My stomach swooped as reality crashed into me like cold water. "What are you doing here?"

Chapter Fifteen

Carlotta

Mason took in my gunk-soaked form, his expression unreadable.

"My father called," he said. "Dad yelled something about calling the police, then he hung up. So I jumped in the car."

Xul was bounding around my legs. He woofed at Mason before jumping up at Mom to lick egg off her clothes.

"Arrest those two lunatics!" yelled Ed from the porch. "I'm filing charges."

I sucked in a breath, conscious of how ridiculous I must look. Every time I blinked, my eyelashes stuck together and I had to force them apart. My hair was a sticky mess and a clump of yolk was dripping down the front of my T-shirt.

Normally I'd be overjoyed, because it was exactly the kind of look that made for social media hilarity. But Mason's gaze made me self-conscious. He'd rocked my world with that unexpected, amazing kiss, and right now he had to be wondering whether it was possible to catch crazy through oral transmission.

"No need to involve the police," Mason called to his father.

"What? Why the hell not?" Ed sounded outraged.

Mason just shook his head, lifting one hand to rub across his mouth. Was he shocked? Angry? Contemptuous? Not that I should care, but…

"You're wet again, Carlotta," Mason said, dropping his hand. "It's definitely your thing." His eyes creased, and a twitch in his cheek told me he was fighting laughter.

"If you won't do it, I'll call the police myself," Ed shouted from his porch. "The attack was unprovoked. Those two started it, and I was forced to defend myself." He stormed back into the house, slamming the door behind him.

"This is your fault." Mom rounded on Mason, jabbing her finger at him. "You and your father are in it together. Now I see what's going on here. Carlotta, Mason's the one who left that steaming mess on my porch!"

I gaped at her. "You can't be serious, Mom. There's no way you're blaming Mason."

Mason gave us the Time Out hand signal. "Wait a minute. What mess on your porch?"

"Don't pretend you don't know," huffed Mom. "You're Edward's henchman. You can't fool me."

"Somebody dumped a pile of manure outside Mom's front door," I explained.

"When?" Mason turned, and I followed as he strode toward Mom's place. "Did you see who left it? Tell me exactly what happened."

"We were out," I said. "We both arrived home at once and found it there."

He strode up Mom's rickety steps, Xul bounding behind him, and stopped at the top, peering at the turd pile. It wasn't fresh enough to steam, but it wasn't old, either. And the stink was awful.

"Judging from its size, it must be horse or cow manure." Mason shifted on the creaking boards.

"Or elephant," I suggested. "Maybe a T-Rex?"

Xul sniffed it, his tongue lolling. He looked like he was having the best day of his entire life. He hadn't bounced so energetically for years.

"That's two incidents." Mason wore a worried frown. "We need to catch your harasser before he does anything worse."

"I'll report it to the police," I said. "But I think they have bigger crimes to worry about."

Mom stomped up the steps behind us and glared at Mason. "If you didn't do this, your father must have. Dumping excrement on my doorstep is exactly the kind of vile act I'd expect from him."

Mason stepped around the poop pile and tried the front door. When it opened, he examined it. "This lock isn't secure. You need a proper deadbolt and a peephole so you can see who's knocking before you open it," he said to Mom. "Some security lights would help too, and security cameras."

"Cameras? So you can record me?" Mom snorted. "Get off my property and away from my daughter!"

"Mom, please don't be rude."

She drew up her spine, looking outraged. "I need to shower. Please escort that scoundrel from the premises, Carlotta." Striding past us, she disappeared into the house.

"May I take a look at your windows?" asked Mason. The porch was creaking and groaning under his weight, and I had to give him points for not showing fear.

"Sure. Come in, away from this stench." I walked gingerly inside, checking I wasn't leaving egg stains on the floor. Mom had disappeared into her bedroom, and her door was closed.

Mason followed me into the living room, where he inspected the windows, shaking his head. "Your locks are rusty. One shoulder blow and they'd disintegrate."

"The entire house needs some serious work," I agreed in a low voice. "I didn't realize it was so bad, and I don't think Mom's teaching salary leaves her with much to spare. Now I have a job, I'll try and contribute toward repairs."

"This is an urgent problem." He fiddled with the window latch. "Whoever's been harassing you could easily break in."

That sounded scary. "I'll get the latches fixed," I assured him.

"I'll fix them."

"Thanks, but I can't ask you to do that."

"You're not asking. I'm offering."

"It's too much."

Instead of arguing, he folded his arms and tightened his square jaw. Standing like that made his biceps bulge, and he radiated solid determination, like the living embodiment of all things right and good. All he needed was a cape.

Suddenly, I couldn't decide whether to laugh or cry.

"And in breaking news from Gotham," I muttered. "Super Muscle Man is forced to rescue his bumbling arch-nemesis, Raw Omelet Girl."

"What?"

"I lifted egg-covered hands, shaking my head. "Nothing. I just need to wash the egg gunk out of my eyelashes before I shovel the dinosaur poop off the porch. It's been an awesome day. Everything's totally fine."

Mom emerged from her bedroom with wet hair, wearing clean clothes that were bright, but otherwise startlingly normal. She went straight to the liquor cabinet and sloshed Gin into a glass.

Mason glanced at the clock, but didn't say anything about the fact she was drinking hard liquor at four thirty in the afternoon. And I was in no position to criticize, seeing as I fully intended to pour a glass for myself as soon as I'd scrubbed the porch clean.

Desperate times, and all that.

"Didn't I banish you from the premises?" Mom glowered at Mason. "Carlotta, fetch me a black candle, a Bible, and a crucifix. I need to perform an exorcism."

"I'll leave in a minute," he said. "First I want to talk about your window latches. They need to be repaired, so I'm going to fix them."

"You'll do no such thing!"

"I'm going to wash up." I tried not to look cowardly as I backed hurriedly out of the room.

When I saw how ridiculous I looked in the bathroom mirror, I took a quick picture before cleaning the gunk off my face and hands. There was no point in showering until after I'd shoveled away the poop. Besides, if I left Mason and Mom alone together for too long, I might end up having to dispose of at least one body, and I didn't want to add to the amount of shoveling I already had to do.

When I emerged, I could hear Mason talking in the living room, but incredibly, Mom wasn't shouting. Walking closer to the door, I realized he wasn't talking about window latches. His voice was pitched low and quiet, but the walls were thin enough that I could just make out his words.

"Don't you think you should tell Carlotta about what happened between you and my father?"

"It's nobody else's business," snapped Mom. "Not yours and not hers."

"You made it Carlotta's business when you dragged her into the middle of your war."

Mom said something I didn't catch, then, "Don't you dare tell her. I'll deny everything."

Mason's voice rumbled, the words indistinct. Mom said something in return, and I crept closer. Then I heard Mason say, "We forgave my father for what happened."

"The whole thing was your father's fault," Mom snarled. "He fooled me into believing he was a romantic hero. Nothing could be further from the truth."

"If Carlotta finds out about the affair, knowing you kept it from her will make it worse."

My heart was thumping hard enough to break my ribs, and my pulse was so loud in my ears, I was afraid I wouldn't be able to hear Mom's reply.

"She won't find out. Now leave. You're not welcome here."

I stepped into the room, my legs shaky. My face felt bloodless and I'd probably gone pale.

"You had an affair with Ed Lennox?" I asked Mom in a weak voice.

She glowered at Mason, her glass now empty. "This is your fault."

"Is that why Dad left us? Is it why Mason's mother took him away?"

She crossed to the liquor cabinet. "Your father was barely here. He was absent long before he officially left." She sloshed more Gin into her glass, her face flushed with anger.

"You and *Ed Lennox*?" I shook my head. "No. This is one of your fantasies. It has to be. Wait." I snapped my fingers. "You were just wearing a costume. You're

131

pretending to be Hester from *The Scarlet Letter*. This isn't real."

"It's real." Mason's voice was soft.

Mom drew herself up. "Just like Hester, I was sorely wronged. I was vilified, and abandoned, and—"

"Don't lie to me, Mom." A hot flash of rage shot through me. "For once in your life, stick with reality. Tell me the truth."

Mom sighed. "The truth." Her voice grew heavy and her shoulders sagged, her anger draining away. "The truth is that we were both unhappy." Her tone was flat, as though she had no drama left in her. "Edward fought with his wife all the time. She was an emotional rollercoaster. He couldn't predict how she'd react to anything."

I searched Mason's face, because even though Mom sounded more serious than she had for years, I couldn't trust her. He gave me a nod, his eyes full of sympathy. "My mother was unpredictable."

When my gaze went back to Mom, she met it with a flicker of defiance, as though outraged I'd turned to Mason for confirmation.

"I was doing my best," she said. "Teaching full time, while I raised you and your brother. But with your father away all the time, it was hard. Edward was going through a similar thing. We started out trying to help each other and it went further than it should have. I never meant to hurt anyone. Least of all you or Declan."

She sounded like she was being honest. This was nothing like the plot of *The Scarlet Letter*, and she didn't seem to be spinning a fantasy about being a misunderstood heroine.

Could I actually believe her?

"Dad found out about you and Ed?" I asked.

She nodded. "Your father was on one of his long

business trips when Edward's wife discovered the affair. After he found out, he left for good."

"The day Mom found out about the affair, she put me and my brothers in the car and took us to Mexico," Mason said.

Mom turned to Mason. "Edward didn't know where she'd taken you. He thought his wife would bring you back. But with each day and week that went past with no sign of you, he got more worried." Mom's expression hardened. "But that's no excuse for your father's behavior. He blamed me for the whole thing."

I clenched my hands in front of my body so nobody would notice they were trembling. As hard as it had been to be told my father would never come home again, how much worse had it been for Mason to be dragged to a whole new country?

"You knew about the affair all along?" I asked Mason.

He moved closer to put his hand on my arm, his voice gentle. "Mom told us when she took us away."

"All this time you never told me?"

That had to be why he'd ignored me when he got back from Mexico. But my fresh understanding of his actions was warring with the fact he'd known about the affair when I'd been clueless. Once again, I'd been living in somebody else's fantasy world with no idea of what was real. Believing the stories I was told, without even suspecting they were lies.

"Edward said some terrible things," Mom snapped. "He accused me of seducing him."

"Why couldn't you tell me the truth back then?" I demanded.

Mom narrowed her eyes at Mason. "Will you leave? I need to speak to my daughter alone."

Mason's jaw tightened and for a moment I thought he

was going to argue. Then he nodded. "Will you be okay?" His eyes radiated worry for me.

"I think so," I said, though I felt a long way from okay.

"I'm sorry you found out this way." He turned to Mom. "I didn't mean for the truth to come out like that, but Carlotta deserved to know."

Mom huffed, drawing herself erect. "You, sir, are Wickham in the guise of Mr. Darcy. You're a——"

"Don't start playing a role now." I cut her off, my voice sharp. "You've been more honest with me in the last five minutes than in the last twenty-nine years, and that's the only way we'll get through this."

Mom opened her mouth then closed it again, visibly deflating. She drank more Gin.

"Come on," I said to Mason, motioning him out. I walked him down the hallway, and the closer we got to the door, the worse the smell got. When I opened it, we both clapped our hands over our noses.

"I'll clean the porch for you," said Mason from behind his hand.

"No, I'll do it."

"Consider it part of my apology. When I got back from Mexico, I assumed you knew about the affair."

"If you'd spoken to me, you would have found out I didn't. And realizing you've been kept in the dark is the worst feeling in the world."

"I'm sorry." He looked stricken, but I didn't want apologies, just honesty.

"I have to talk to Mom now. Leave the poop. I'll deal with it later."

"Call me if you need anything."

I shut the door behind him and went back to the living room. Mom was on the couch in the living room, staring balefully at the glass she was holding. I sank down next to her, not caring about the egg that was still on my clothes.

"Why didn't you tell me?" I asked Mom.

"What good would it have done? Our families were already broken beyond repair, and you would have blamed me, just like Edward did." She sighed so heavily that Xul ambled over to put his head in her lap. "And though I've never cared what people think, San Dante is a small town at heart. After Edward's wife left, there was a lot of gossip, and I was worried you'd hear it. When our feud started, the neighbors talked about that instead, and stopped speculating about an affair." She stroked Xul's head.

My lips parted as her words registered and I finally realized the truth. "Your feud was a smoke screen." I shook my head. "All this time. Those nasty pranks you and Ed played on each other. The things you put in each other's mailboxes and on each other's lawns. It was all a ruse."

"It started that way. I know this is a shock, Carlotta, but my love affair with Edward finished a long time ago. Almost fifteen years."

"That's how long you've been lying to me. And not just about that. I've never been able to believe you about anything."

"But—"

"You had me convinced for *years* that I was royalty and would inherit a castle. I watched *The Princess Diaries* a million times, and spent hours practicing my royal wave."

She put her glass on the coffee table, dislodging Xul's head from her lap. Then she leaned forward, her eyes pleading. "But didn't you find it exciting?"

"Not when the mean girls at school drew a crown on my head with permanent marker."

"I couldn't stop them from being jealous."

"When my pet rabbit disappeared, you said he'd run

away to Wonderland to live with Alice. You said Snowy liked Alice better than he liked me."

Her brow creased. "Would you rather I told you Snowy was killed by a dog?"

"At least it would have been the truth. What you told me made me miserable."

"That's why I wrote you a letter from Snowy. So you'd know he was thinking of you."

"*Mom.*" I glared at her. "The letter said he'd jumped down a rabbit hole."

A hint of guilt finally stole over her expression and she frowned at Xul who'd lain down by her feet. "Well, how was I to know you'd go looking for it and get lost?"

"I was *seven*. What did you think would happen?" I shook my head. "I'm just glad I only spent one night sleeping rough before the police found me. And that it wasn't quite cold enough for my fingers and toes to turn black and fall off."

"I thought the letter would excite your imagination. It was pages long, and the rabbit hole was just one small part of it. What about the part where Snowy fought the Red Queen? You have to admit that was thrilling."

"You wrote that letter for yourself, not for me. You had fun writing it, and didn't care about what effect it might have." As awful as I felt, it was a relief to say out loud all the things I'd been thinking for years.

"Carlotta, I—"

"I never knew what was real. That's why I wanted to become an actress, so I could be sure what was make-believe. So I'd finally get to be the one in charge of reality."

I watched her expression fall even more. "You're right." She reached out and took my hand, squeezing it tightly. "I did those things, but I didn't realize..." She broke off, shaking her head. "No, I'm not going to keep making excuses. Only the truth from now on."

I stared down at her hand, desperately squeezing my limp one. I couldn't remember when she'd last held my hand. Perhaps that was my fault. When I'd started realizing the extent of her lies and questioning everything she'd ever told me, I'd pulled away. I was the one who'd put a wall between us, though she'd never tried very hard to breech it.

"Maybe some good could come from this," I said slowly. "Perhaps you could be more honest with me, so eventually I can start trusting what you tell me."

"Yes! I will, and you can." She exclaimed it so quickly, I doubted she really meant it. But her eyes looked hopeful.

"Does Declan know you had an affair with Edward?" I asked.

She shook her head.

"Are you going to tell him?"

Her lips pursed, and the heavy lines in her face deepened. She looked old and unspeakably weary. "He doesn't come home much. When he called to say his wife was leaving him, it was the first time we'd spoken in months." She hesitated. "Will you tell him about my affair?"

The question hit me as hard as if she'd swung a bat. If she refused to tell my brother, did that make it my responsibility? Declan was six years older than me, and hadn't been living at home when Dad announced he was leaving for good. Still, he'd probably feel as hurt and confused about being lied to as I did, and he was already going through a rough time with his own marital problems. It was an awful thing to have to tell him. But didn't he deserve to know?

"I need to be alone for a while," I told Mom, standing up. It was too much. I didn't know what to think anymore.

All my memories of childhood felt different now. When Mason and I used to meet up and hang out after school, had our parents secretly been meeting too?

I went into the bathroom and turned on the shower. The dinosaur poop could wait until I was ready to clean it up.

All I'd ever wanted was honesty. Was that too much to ask?

Chapter Sixteen

Mason

While Carlotta and her mother were inside talking, I borrowed Dad's shovel to clean the pile of shit off the porch. Once I was done, I washed up at Dad's, then drove back to Asher's. Resisting the temptation to check in with the surveillance team to find out if there'd been any developments, I went through the house to the back deck. I sat at the table and stared out at the sun going down over the ocean for a minute or two. Then I called Todd, my friend in the computer forensics department.

"I was just leaving the office," said Todd. "And I already told you it'd take a few days to find the information. I'll call you when I have it."

"It's urgent. Can you fast track it?"

"First I have to do the work I was employed for, then squeeze this in. Besides, cracking an anonymous account isn't something I can do in the space of a coffee break. It takes skill, and time, and—"

"You can't do it?"

He made a snorting sound through his nose. "Is it life or death? You think this FowlFetish guy is about to kill someone?"

"Probably not," I admitted.

"Then I'll track down his real identity by the end of the week."

"Okay," I said reluctantly. "Thanks." I hung up thinking I should take Todd out for a beer sometime.

The sun was almost down and the sky was darkening. I tapped my fingers on the table as I stared at the waves, picturing Carlotta's face. She'd been so pale. So shocked. And I'd had to force myself not to put my arms around her. The compulsion to make things better had been overwhelming, and I'd hated leaving Carlotta to deal with her mother on her own.

At least I could make her house secure. I'd do the work while her mother was at school.

"Hey."

The voice came from behind me, and I turned to see Asher, silent as usual and dressed in black, with Nemesis lurking in his shadow. He put two beers on the table and took the chair next to me. "Drink?"

"Thanks." I took a grateful sip of one of the beers and watched the black cat move to the edge of the deck, then jump gracefully onto the ground below, heading into the night. Probably out to steal underwear.

That made me think of Carlotta's Spock panties. It was strange to find a picture of Spock arousing, but I couldn't stop picturing his face nestled snugly over her pussy, the Vulcan's lips in the exact place I'd like to put mine.

"Where no man has gone before," I murmured, wondering if it were true.

"What was that?"

"Nothing." I cleared my throat, pushing images of Spock away. "Long day?"

"You could say that."

"More problems with your business?"

He nodded. "Always. It's complicated."

"Want to talk about it?"

"Nope."

I gave him a faint smile, wordlessly communicating the fact that I'd known he'd refuse, but I'd be there for him if he ever did need to talk. He inclined his head in return.

"I hate to ask," I said, as he took another sip of his beer. "But could you spare some builders for a couple of hours tomorrow?"

He lowered the bottle. His dark coloring made him blend in with the shadows, so he was little more than a silhouette. "To fix Trixie Watson's front porch?"

"I wouldn't ask if it wasn't urgent."

"Then they'll be at her place by lunchtime."

I let out a breath, feeling relieved even though I'd known he'd agree. "Thank you."

If there was one silver lining from our fucked-up trip to Mexico, it was that my brothers would always have my back, no questions asked. Just like they knew I'd take a bullet for them.

They also knew I'd be willing to break into houses at night and steal food and money from innocent strangers so they could eat. Been there, done that. And yeah, I recognized that my obsession with taking down every member of the Medea Cartel was probably because I was still trying to make up for not being able to better protect my brothers at the time, and so I could do a weird kind of penance for my crimes.

I didn't need a psychiatrist. I already knew how screwed up I was.

Picking up my phone, I messaged Carlotta.

You okay? Been worried.

Her answer came back a minute later.

I'm tougher than Chuck Norris. And he's the one who put 'laughter' in 'manslaughter'.

I choked out a laugh, and when Asher gave me a questioning look, I read him her joke before typing in my reply.

I'm sorry I couldn't tell you about the affair. It was your mother's secret so I wanted her to be the one to tell you.

Staring at my phone, I waited for her answer. It seemed to take a long time.

I guess it was better to hear it from Mom.

I let out a relieved breath. She understood why I'd had to keep her mother's secret, so maybe it wasn't so bad that I couldn't tell her about my undercover work. It wasn't like I wanted to lie about what I really did.

I could at least be honest about going back to work in Houston, and let her know whatever was between us would have to end very soon. But in the short time we had, I wanted as much time with her as she was willing to give. Once I went back to the nightmare of cartel life, any day could be my last. She made me feel good, and I didn't want to waste a minute of that.

Okay if I come and fix your porch tomorrow lunchtime? I messaged.

Why is fixing the porch so important to you?

Damsel. Distress. It's a thing for me, remember?

I sent the message, then realized it wasn't the whole truth. If I couldn't be honest with her about everything, she deserved as much as I could give her.

I want you to be safe… and I want to kiss you again.

I was waiting for her to reply when Asher leaned

forward. "What's happening now? You look like it's something important."

"Just talking about fixing her porch."

"If you want to send back a Chuck Norris fact, you could mention the only time he ever used a stunt double was when he had to cry on camera."

I debated with myself a moment, then typed the message in. From the delay it seemed Carlotta didn't know what to reply to my kissing confession, and sending a joke might take the pressure off.

Sure enough, a few moments after I sent it, my phone dinged again.

Chuck Norris's tears can cure cancer, so it's too bad he's never cried. P.S. My lips and I will see you tomorrow.

I grinned, reading the last part over twice.

"What's funny?"

I read Asher the first part of what she'd sent, though it wasn't the part that had made me smile.

"I like her," he said. "Good sense of humor."

"She just found out about the affair."

His bottle stopped on the way to his mouth. "How'd she take it?"

"Better than I imagined. But we should do something to end the feud between Dad and Trixie."

"I thought that's why you were fixing her porch."

"Dad's not on board. In fact, things went downhill today." I thought about telling him about their egg battle, and decided some things were too weird to dwell on.

Asher put his beer bottle down on the table slowly, and though it was too dark to know for sure, I could imagine his thoughtful expression.

"You seem entirely focused on Carlotta," he said.

"She's upset. The affair was a shock."

"What about the drug dealers next door? When are you going to arrest Santino?"

"As soon as he takes possession of a drug shipment."

"When will that be?"

"Are you getting sick of me staying here?"

"I want to know when Santino will be behind bars."

I frowned suspiciously at him. "What's going on? Is there something between you and Santino that I don't know about?"

He was silent for a while, and my heart sank. I resisted the urge to talk, letting the silence stretch, hoping he'd tell me what was going on. Asher wasn't usually one for confidences, but we'd always been close.

Finally, he let out his breath in a puff, as though he'd made a decision. "There are some things it's better for you not to know," he said. Which clearly meant he'd decided not to tell me.

"You're not involved with Santino, are you?" I asked.

"Do you trust me?"

"Of course I do."

"Then don't ask any more questions."

It was my turn to huff out a breath. "Listen Asher. I didn't think I had to say this, because I assumed you already knew. But you can always come to me for help. Doesn't matter what it is. I'd do anything for you or Kade. You know that, right?"

"We'd do anything for you too."

"I have some money saved. It's yours if you need it."

"Thank you. I don't need it, but I appreciate the offer."

"That's all I wanted to say." I drank my beer silently, hoping he'd change his mind and let me into whatever was bugging him.

Asher ran a finger down the outside of his beer bottle thoughtfully, wiping off the condensation. "Mason, I know you want to protect me, but I'm asking you not to worry. I may not be Chuck Norris, but I can handle pretty much anything."

"I know you can."

Asher was genius-level smart, and a problem solver by nature. If he'd decided to work for NASA, they'd have landed an astronaut on Mars by now. Still, I couldn't help but worry about his safety. It was just the way I was made.

"Kade's going to arrive on Friday," Asher said after a while. "Dad wants us to meet at his place when he gets here."

"Okay." But I was thinking about the fact I'd be back in Houston soon, and my family wouldn't be able to contact me. Working for the Medea cartel, I'd been able to keep my personal cellphone for my brothers to call if they needed me. But with Diamond, I couldn't risk having any link to my real identity. If Asher were in some kind of trouble, I wouldn't know, and there'd be nothing I could do to help.

Asher's teeth flashed white in the darkness. "Cheer up. Things aren't that bad."

"Not that bad?" My tone flattened. "Carlotta found out her mother's been lying to her, some asshole's obsessed with her and could escalate his attacks, you're keeping secrets, and in spite of Dad's heart problems he still refuses to eat anything that's not loaded with sugar."

"Yeah," Asher agreed, and I could hear a smile in his voice. "Hope Kade doesn't have any problems, or you'll really be screwed."

Chapter Seventeen

Mason

A faint aroma of shit still lingered on Trixie Watson's front porch as I set my toolbox down and leaned my ladder against the wall.

"Replace these rotten boards," I instructed Asher's builders. "Make sure the porch is safe to walk on." I'd promised my brother I'd let them get back to work at his construction site as soon as I could.

When I knocked, Carlotta opened the door. I was grateful to see her smile.

"Hey," I said, some of my worry about her easing because she didn't seem to still be upset. She was wearing a tailored shirt and skirt that made her look more business-like than I'd ever seen her.

That's right, she'd said something about getting a part-time office job. My mind immediately flashed to a boardroom fantasy, with Carlotta a sexy CEO demanding to be satisfied. I had to shake my head to get rid of the picture.

"Thanks for fixing the porch," she said. "And for cleaning away the dinosaur poop."

Xul came out from behind her and sniffed my legs, his tail wagging. Then he sat down to watch the workmen unpack their tools.

"I'll start with the front door lock, then come in and take a look at your windows. Okay?"

"Sure. I'll go and change, then give you a hand."

I started to bend toward the toolbox I'd borrowed from Asher, then forgot what I was doing. My entire world narrowed to the sway of her hips in her tight, sexy skirt as Carlotta walked inside. Even after she'd disappeared around the bend at the end of the hallway, it took me a moment to remember where I was and what I'd come here to do. Then I had to clear my dry throat and bend again to get the tools I needed.

Trixie's rusty old front door lock came apart in my hands, thanks to the corrosive salt air that blew from the ocean. It was an easy job to replace it, and by the time Carlotta emerged, I was already starting work on the window latches in the living room.

She'd changed into jeans and a T-shirt, and her feet were bare. She'd pulled her hair back into a short ponytail. Though I missed the skirt, she looked beautiful with her hair like that. And when she moved close to watch what I was doing, she smelled delicious, like crisp green apples.

"How are you feeling today?" I asked her.

"Still a little shocked about my mom and your dad, but coming to terms with it."

I nodded, resisting the urge to reach out and touch her. "I'm sorry you found out about it like that."

"I'm just glad I know." She leaned against the wall next to the window I was working on, then tilted her head back.

"Is that why you didn't talk to me when you came back from Mexico?"

"Yes."

"Because you blamed me?"

"What? No!" I put down my screwdriver so I could give her my full attention. "I didn't blame you." I abandoned my efforts not to touch her, and ran my hand down her arm. "When I got back from Mexico, I needed to put that hellish experience behind me. My mother had gone on and on about what your mother had done, and I couldn't…" I broke off, hating that it was so hard to put my feelings into words. "I should have spoken to you. I thought you knew about the affair, so you'd understand why I was keeping my distance."

"You didn't even want to look at me."

I put my other hand on her waist, tugging her to me. Bending my head, I touched my forehead against hers. This close, her eyes looked large and soft enough to fall into. They were usually a light brown, but they'd darkened. The upward tilt of her lips had vanished, and all I could think about was kissing the smile back onto them.

"I'm sorry," I whispered.

Her hands moved around the back of my neck, her fingers brushing the sensitive skin above the collar of my T-shirt. She let out a small sigh. "It sucks that I was the only person who didn't know. I wish Mom had been honest with me. You'd think I'd be used to her fantasies by now, but I hate them more than ever. Being lied to is the worst."

"Yeah." I swallowed, thinking about what I was keeping from her. "Listen, you know I work in Houston? I have to leave in a few days and go back to work."

"A few days?" She blinked, drawing back. "I didn't know you were going back so soon."

"And my work's so busy, it makes any kind of

relationship impossible." I shook my head, reluctantly dropping my hands. "I know that sounds like a lame excuse, but my job's important to me. I've sacrificed a lot to get where I am. When I started out, I had to make a choice. I could either be good at my job, or have a personal life. I chose my work, and there's no way to go back on that decision."

"A body guard can't have a personal life?" She didn't look convinced. "Are you like a priest who's sworn a vow of celibacy?"

"You could say I'm married to my job. I'm not celibate, but a relationship wouldn't work."

Her brow furrowed. "So what you're saying is that after you leave, I won't see you again?"

"That's right."

"So you're what? Just looking to mess around for a few days? With no possibility that it could turn into something serious?"

I grimaced, taking a step back. "You're right, it's not fair on you."

"Are you kidding? That's perfect."

I froze. "Excuse me?"

"I don't want to get hooked on you, or start trusting you, or be hurt, or disappointed. You're exactly wrong for me."

I frowned at her bright eyes and upturned lips. "Why are you saying that like it's a good thing?"

"Because now we're clear. I can use you for your excellent kissing skills and killer bod, without worrying about developing feelings." She stepped close to me, closing the gap to slide her hands back around my neck.

I opened my mouth to give voice to the second thoughts that had flared. Something about the fact that I wasn't sure how detached I could be, or how difficult it might be to walk away when I had to leave. But with one fingernail she started tracing small circles on the back of my neck, and the sensation was exquisite. Goosebumps prickled down my spine and across my scalp. Any reservations I had were lost.

Leaning into me, pushing her body against mine, Carlotta wet her lower lip with her tongue. I made a small sound, a tiny intake of breath, and her body reacted, shuddering as though she was as on edge as I was.

Her eyelids lowered. She was on tiptoe, her face tilted up to mine.

Maybe I was making a mistake and my feelings for her were already too strong for this to be a good idea. But I could barely keep that thought in my head. She was offering her lips and I needed to kiss her. The idea of carrying her into the bedroom and stripping off her clothes marched into my brain, destroying all other thoughts, like a militarized drone designed to wipe out everything it encountered.

My lungs were full of her scent and I breathed her in, my gaze on her gorgeous lips, resisting temptation for just a second longer to savor the moment before kissing her.

Then she spoke.

"Do you think it's weird that your father and my mother had sex?"

My lips hovered over hers. "What?"

"Does it make what we're doing seem strange?"

"Why would it?" I pushed my hand under the edge of her T-shirt. The warm, soft skin of her back felt like heaven. We didn't need to stop. I could shut her words from my mind and—

"Because your father ejaculated into my mother."

My hand halted. The hot lust that had marched

unopposed into my brain and conquered every other thought, suddenly fled for the hills.

I winced, drawing back. "That was an explicit mental picture I could have done without."

"If they'd gotten married, you would have been my stepbrother."

"But I'm not."

"If you were, would this be incest?"

"No." There was steel in my tone. "We're not related in any way. My feelings toward you are the opposite of brotherly, and this is definitely not incest."

She dragged in a relieved breath. "Okay. Good. That was just something I needed to get out of my head."

"Something you had to put into *my* head?"

"Whoops. Sorry." She gave me a sheepish smile. "Forget I said anything."

Though her finger started circling on my neck again, I eased free and took a step back. If only there were such a thing as mental bleach, I could use a bucket.

She bit her lip. "Was that a mood killer?"

"Little bit." I dragged a hand through my hair. "You have the number of a therapist? There's a picture in my head I'll need professional help to get rid of."

Her mouth twitched, a hint of the smile I'd been hoping to see slowly appearing. "The inside of my mind can be a twisted place sometimes. I didn't mean to dump it on you."

"It's okay. Though I'll never be able to look your mother or my father in the face again."

Leaning back against the wall, she sighed. "I know not to believe anything Mom says, but not telling me about what happened with your dad feels like a bigger lie than most of her others."

The reminder that *I* was lying to her pricked my

conscience. Though Carlotta seemed okay with the idea of a short-term fling, I felt uncomfortable not being able to tell her the truth about my work when honesty was such a touchy subject for her.

Picking up a screwdriver, I started screwing in the window latch. Probably a good idea to slam the brakes on anyway, so I could finish the job I'd come to do.

"My father was never home. I barely knew him, and even now we only talk at Christmas." Carlotta drew a circle on the floor with one bare toe, studying it as she spoke. "The last few years, I've barely spoken to Mom any more often. We've never been close." Her gaze flicked back up and she frowned. "Come to think of it, Mom doesn't seem to have any friends. I haven't been here that long, but I don't think she's had a single phone call."

"You're worried about her?"

"She must be lonely. When she gets home from school, all she does is dream up ways to annoy your father."

"I worry about Dad, too. He has heart problems and refuses to improve his diet. He's filled our old bedrooms with too much junk for anyone to stay with him, and he won't let us hire a nurse to take care of him. Every time I drop in, I worry I'm going to find him unconscious on the floor."

She sighed. "It's a shame they were both married to other people when they met. They could be keeping each other company, instead of cooking up stupid pranks to torture each other."

"Maybe they'll get back together one day."

She let out a snort of laughter. "Can you imagine? That would be hilarious."

I laughed too, mostly because she was adorable when she snorted. And watching her eyes sparkle made me ache to kiss her again.

"I need to get these latches finished," I said as much to myself as to her. "You need to stop distracting me so I can work."

She bent to grab a screwdriver out of Asher's toolbox. "How about you drill the holes and I'll take care of the screws. That'll make the job go faster."

"You know how?"

She shot me a withering look. "Bless your heart," she drawled. "Delicate womenfolk are doing all kinds of manly things these days. Using a screwdriver might be an intellectual and physical challenge for y'all, but I imagine I may be equal to the task."

I doffed an imaginary hat. "My apologies, ma'am. I meant no disrespect."

"Stand back, sir. Wouldn't want you to get hurt." She started fastening the latch, while I moved on to the next one. Her fingers were nimble and she made surprisingly quick work of it.

"You're faster at that than I am," I said admiringly.

"Are you saying I'm better at screwing than you are?"

"I'd need to do more research before I can say for sure." Unable to resist, I gave her a suggestive look.

She laughed. "Maybe I should give up my new job and become a full time screwer."

As distracting as the word 'screwer' was, she'd just reminded me about her job. I was about to ask her about it when she drew in a sharp breath.

"I've had an idea." She lowered the screwdriver, her eyes lighting up. "I could create a photo series about how I've lost my income so I take on jobs in construction. It could be an empowerment series, but with a blooper reel of mistakes to make it funny. Like I build a path and accidentally concrete my feet into it."

"You won't change your mind and close down your social media accounts?"

"Or I could nail my overalls to a wall and have to take them off to get free," she mused, like she was thinking aloud. "Underneath, I could be wearing something funny."

"Your Spock panties?" I put the drill down, as the job I was doing suddenly seemed a lot less urgent than investigating her underwear.

She blinked at my tone, which had acquired a growl. "Do you have a Vulcan fetish?"

"Apparently, I do."

"Then it's a good thing I'm wearing those panties right now."

She may as well have waved a red cape in front of a bull. I stepped closer and she turned so her back was to the wall, her eyes widening with mock innocence.

"Show me." Putting one hand on either side of her, I leaned in. "So I can take them off with my teeth."

Her lips parted and her throat bobbed as she swallowed. Her cheeks flushed.

"You're making my face go warm," she whispered. Then her voice changed, a note of alarm creeping into her tone. "Wait. Am I *blushing*?"

"A little."

"No, no, no. I can't blush. That's not possible."

I frowned, confused by her sudden distress. "You have a little color in your cheeks. What's the big deal?"

"You don't get it. To take the photos I do, I can't blush. My career depends on the fact I don't get flustered."

I drew back, dropping my hands. "I didn't mean to fluster you."

"Really? That's not what your eyes are saying."

She was right, I *had* meant to fluster her. I'd wanted to make her feel as off balance as she was making me. I needed to know if she was feeling anything close to the same level of urgent, needy desire as I was.

"What are my eyes saying?" I asked, though I already knew. If they were transmitting my thoughts, they had to be telling her I wanted to feel her thighs tighten around me as I buried myself inside her.

But she shook her head, putting her palms against her cheeks. "I can't afford to lose my only superpower."

It sounded like a joke, but her expression was so serious my heart twisted. "The last thing I want is to take anything away from you. I didn't come here to hurt you."

"But I don't get it. Why would talking about talking off my panties make me blush when being naked in front of strangers doesn't?"

"Your blush was faint. Barely noticeable."

"Really? Because my face was hot."

"It's a warm day."

Hope flared in her eyes. "Sunlight coming through the window? Landing on my face?"

"Maybe."

"I need to be sure." She stepped closer. "Say the panty thing again."

"I want to rip your panties off?"

"Like you mean it. Here, I'll get us back in the mood." She flattened her hands against my chest, then caressed down my pecs, following the lines of my muscles. Lifting her face to mine, she sucked in her breath. This time when she spoke, her voice was husky. "What do you want to do to me, Mason?"

I put my hands on her arms. "Not hurt you."

She made an impatient sound, then stepped backward, breaking free from my grip. With a flick of her wrist, she popped the button of her jeans and pushed them down, using her feet to get them right off.

Every molecule of blood in my body rushed south of my belt buckle.

"You lied." The words came out in a hoarse growl. "Those aren't your Spock panties." Somehow her waist was in my hands and I was pulling her hips against me.

"Spock's in the wash. Even Vulcans get dirty."

My hands slid to her ass of their own accord. The thin cotton felt flimsy under my fingers. Easy to tear.

"I have a confession to make." I nuzzled her ear, kissing the sensitive skin under her lobe. "I don't care what panties you wear. It's what's underneath I can't stop thinking about."

"You've been thinking about me?" Her voice was breathless, and I savored the hitch I heard, the way her words caught in her throat. Staring up at me, she was so damn beautiful, it made me want to forget caution and restraint. To forget everything except what my body was demanding.

I pressed into her so she could feel how hard I was and know how much I wanted her.

Her body softened and molded against me. Her arms went around my back and she melted into me, pushing back against my hardness.

I let out a groan of pure desire, tangling my hand into her hair to draw her face back. I'd never wanted anything so much as I wanted her.

"You're making me crazy." I told her, lowering my mouth to hers.

She bit at my lips and her tongue danced against mine, teasing me.

I lifted her off her feet and her legs locked around my waist. Her mouth was sweet and needy. Urgent and demanding. Soft and enticing.

The nearest flat surface was the dining table, and I

didn't stop kissing her while I carried her there and sat her on it. I *couldn't* stop kissing her.

When we were dating as teenagers for that too-brief time, her kisses had been my entire world. Now I knew nothing had changed. There was something earth-shattering about the way our mouths moved with each other, the way our tongues caught and our lips played. As many women as I'd kissed since then, nothing had ever come close to the pure, intense pleasure I felt when I kissed her.

Her hands were on my back, yanking up my T-shirt, running over my bare skin. I did the same to her. Her body felt precious, my touch both too rough and not rough enough. I wanted to treasure her and I needed to devour her.

Shoving her T-shirt up with one hand, I pushed her bra up with it so I could cradle one breast. Her nipple hardened under my palm. The curve was gentle but perfect, and when I ran my thumb across her nipple, it formed an erect point that made me groan with desire.

"Mason," she gasped into my mouth. "Please. I need you." Reaching to the front of my jeans, she ran her hand down my length. I was so hard, her touch was in danger of making me explode.

She hooked her legs around my hips, pulling me in closer. "You're vibrating," she gasped.

I bit her earlobe. "Sweetheart, you make me feel like I'm—"

"No." She pulled away. "You're really vibrating."

"Oh." It took a supreme effort of will to step backward and shake away the haze of lust and want. I fumbled in the pocket of my jeans and pulled out my vibrating phone.

Too late. As I tugged it out, the call cut off and the screen went black. But I knew who'd called. It was Griffin.

"Shit," I muttered.

"Everything okay?" Carlotta's T-shirt was still hitched up, her legs spread, her thin panties the only thing keeping me from heaven.

If I allowed myself to kiss her one more time, there'd be no way I could stop.

"Carlotta, sweetheart." My voice came out rough, trembling with the effort of control. "We can't do this here. Not at your mother's house."

She blinked at me, her eyes glazed. Her lips were swollen and the temptation to kiss them again was like a physical pain.

"Mom's at school." Carlotta sounded breathless, like she was at the top of a mountain.

"But she'll be home soon." I smoothed her top back down, fitting her bra carefully back into place. "We don't need to rush this. We can take it slowly. Do it properly."

"Take it slowly? Are you kidding?" Her eyes widened and her voice suddenly because a lot less breathy. "You want to take it slowly, and *now* is when you tell me?"

I swallowed hard, stepping back. "I don't want to be interrupted by your mother."

She reached up to run her hands through her tangled hair. Her face was still flushed, and she looked as frustrated as I felt.

She muttered something I didn't quite catch. From her rough tone it had to be a swear word, though it sounded like "Bumbaclot".

"Carlotta, I—"

My phone vibrated again, and I saw Griffin had sent a message asking me to call. Probably wanted to update me on whatever vicious, ugly shit Diamond was up to, or demand an update on when I'd be back in Houston.

"I'm sorry, I need to go." I stuffed my phone back into my pocket.

She folded her arms, narrowing her eyes. "Does another body need guarding?"

I put both hands on her shoulders and ran them down her arms, forcing her to unfold them. Then I took her hands. "Even if my phone hadn't gone off, I don't want our first time to be on a table in your mother's house, with the sound of hammers ringing in our ears, knowing we could be interrupted at any moment."

"I don't care about any of that."

"I do." I held her gaze until her eyes softened, then I leaned forward to kiss her. The slightest touch made my body ache for her. She was impossible to resist.

"We've waited all these years," I said. "Let's do it right."

"Is that what this is? Unfinished business from years ago?"

"This is me not being able to be around you without wanting to kiss you." I lifted one hand to twist a few strands of her hair between my fingers. "We may only have a few days, but I don't want any regrets. I want to make this a perfect memory. Something we can both think about later without wishing we'd done anything differently."

She frowned. "If we do that, we might not want it to end."

"It has to end."

She leaned back on the table, propping herself up on her hands. "Your job must be intense. Will you tell me about it?"

If only I could.

As long as I'd been undercover, the temptation to confess the truth about what I did had never been this strong. Not even close.

"I need to go. I have to return a call." I bent to start packing Asher's tools back into his toolbox, but Carlotta pushed herself off the table.

"If you leave your tools here, I'll replace the rest of the latches myself."

I hadn't thought of asking her, but it made sense. Then Carlotta and her mother wouldn't need to spend another night with insecure windows.

"Will you be careful doing the work by yourself?" I asked.

She put her hands on her hips, her brow furrowing. "I'm better at screwing than you are, remember?" Then she smiled. "Besides, leaving your tools here will give you an excuse to come back and get them tomorrow, when I might accidentally be fully naked." She tugged her T-shirt up playfully, exposing her entire lower body clad only in a pair of panties.

I closed my eyes for a moment, fighting for control, hoping she couldn't tell how close to the edge of madness she was driving me. When I opened my eyes again, I'd regained enough of a stranglehold on my self-discipline to be able to return her smile.

"I don't need an excuse to come back," I told her honestly. "While I'm gone, all I'll be thinking about is you."

Chapter Eighteen

Carlotta

Nobody in the entire history of the world had ever needed an orgasm more than I did.

My head was full of Mason. His scent was on my clothes, my lips still ached from his kisses, and the pressure of his hands was so fresh in my mind it felt as though he were still touching me.

And sure enough, when I headed into my bedroom to relieve the pressure with a little ménage à moi, my climax went off like the launch of an Apollo rocket.

Afterward, I lay drained, still dreaming about Mason.

He was an addiction. Every time his lips touched mine, I wanted to fall into him. Or more accurately, I wanted him to sink into me.

But I'd fallen hard for Mason as a teenager, and the worst thing I could do now would be to hand my heart back to him. To prevent that happening, I probably shouldn't have reached orbit while imagining he was touching me. And I definitely shouldn't be obsessing about him while lying naked in bed.

At least there was one activity guaranteed to take my mind off Mason and bring me crashing back to earth.

Yup. I checked my Instagram.

And yup, it turned out to be a terrible idea.

As funny as I'd thought the picture of me covered in sticky egg gunk was, my followers didn't agree. They thought it was a waste of perfectly good eggs, and now, as well as being a ruthless duck killer, I was a selfish consumer of the world's egg resources and an enemy to chickens.

Chikins shuld peck out her eyes, suggested one person.

Behold, Satan's hands of destruction, said someone else.

More people thought I deserved to '*dye*.' Which reminded me, I really had to add that word to my death threat filter.

Would it even be possible to win back the support of my followers? Maybe the paint-throwing duck lover wasn't an outlier. Perhaps they'd all throw paint and dump poop if they could.

A few weeks ago, I'd happened to snap a friend's dog in a cute pose, lying down with his paw over his eyes as though shielding them from something he didn't want to see. I'd captioned it, '*Maybe I should start shutting the bathroom door*'.

Not one of my followers had commented about animal rights. But now public opinion had swung against me, the same snap would probably have PETA on my doorstep within the hour.

Xul interrupted my thoughts by jumping onto my bed and settling down next to me. I patted his head and tugged on one of his floppy ears. "At least you didn't see any of the x-rated stuff, Xul. If an animal rescue team turns up, you'll tell them that, won't you?"

He just sighed and closed his eyes.

Wriggling back into my jeans while still on the bed, I found myself staring up at the posters of actresses on my wall. Sally Field had both arms in the air, beaming like she'd swallowed the sun.

"Did you ever get any death threats, Sally?" I wondered aloud.

Mason had wanted me to delete my social media accounts, but when I used to get messages from people saying I'd helped them feel better about themselves, it had been the best feeling in the world.

"Ugh," I said out loud to Xul. "Being hated sucks." But he was already snoring.

Putting both hands over my face, I couldn't help remembering an audition I went to after graduating from acting school. My eyes had been filled with stars and I was certain success, fortune, and fame were just around the corner.

The play was a comedy, the part silly, the character crazy. I'd thrown myself into the audition with everything I had. For a brief, wonderful period, I *was* that character. I owned the scene, hitting every beat perfectly, stretching the laughs, making it hilarious.

It was the best performance I'd ever delivered.

When it was over, the casting director told me I was terrible. My comedy was clownish, and he'd been inwardly cringing. He was doing me a favor by telling me that if I didn't go on a diet and get a boob job, I'd never get anywhere. Oh, and by the way, women weren't naturally funny, so I shouldn't try so hard.

Screw him, right?

If I was a clown, why not embrace it? And dammit I *was* funny!

That's when I'd started posting pictures designed to

empower women, and found the crazier I got, the more people liked it. I revealed the most personal stuff about myself, showed off my tiny boobs and big butt, and made fun of my flaws. My lack of embarrassment was my secret weapon. Thanks to Mom, I'd always been laughed at, but who knew I could earn a living that way?

"You know what, Sally Field?" I asked the poster. "I used to love acting. And maybe I'm the court jester instead of a serious thespian, but what's so bad about being a jester? Everyone likes to laugh, don't they?"

Sally beamed at me.

"Exactly!"

On a whim, I picked up my phone. I hadn't seen my old drama teacher in a decade, but when she answered my call, she said, "Hi doll," as though we spoke every day.

"Hey Judy. How are you?"

"Doing rehearsals for *Grease*." Her voice was croaky. "We open in a week, and Sandy's still messing up the songs. Danny hates Rizzo so much he keeps sabotaging her on stage. And I decided to put the Teen Angel on a wire, but every time he flies in to do his number, he wipes out the entire set." She coughed. "I've been yelling at the kids so much, I'm losing my voice."

"So it's looking bad?"

"Terrible."

"Just like you'd expect?"

"Yeah, we're pretty much on track. How are things with you?"

I sighed wistfully, remembering the exhausting and exhilarating chaos of rehearsals. "I miss the theater. Remember when we did *Cats* and on opening night Rumpleteazer's costume split all the way up the back so his bare butt was hanging out?"

Judy's laugh turned into a hoarse cough. "Still a

highlight," she croaked when she could speak again. "Sometimes I make popcorn and watch the footage again on YouTube."

"I'm in San Dante for while."

"You are, doll? Then you should come and help out with rehearsals."

"I was hoping you'd say that. But are you sure I won't get in the way?"

"Are you kidding? If you take over yelling at the kids, my voice might recover. And you can give them some pointers. Show them how it's done."

"Um. Except my short acting career wasn't exactly an unparalleled success."

"You know how to put on a good show. That's what matters."

I shot Sally Field a smile, feeling better. "Then I don't suppose tomorrow would work for you?"

"Sure. The kids will be here after school."

"Can't wait."

I hung up and looked down at Xul, who was snoring like a congested walrus. "I can't lie around all day," I told him. "I still have window latches to fix."

Xul the Destroyer farted without waking up. He didn't even wake when I made retching noises and scrambled off the bed.

In the living room, I got busy with the drill and screws. I was just finishing the latches when Mom arrived home from school. But instead of sweeping in and making a scene, she seemed subdued.

"You want pizza for dinner?" she asked. "With anchovies?"

It had to be a peace offering, seeing as she hated anchovies on pizza and couldn't understand why I loved the delicious salty taste.

"Sounds great."

"I'll order one." She touched my arm for a moment, giving me a tentative smile.

I cut her a break and smiled back. Like Mason had said, she hadn't set out to hurt me. She'd been ashamed of having an affair, and afraid I'd blame her for Dad's departure. Not that I was entirely ready to forgive her, and I wasn't sure I'd ever believe or trust her, but she was still my mother and she loved me in her own way. If I held grudges, I wouldn't have come back here at all.

My phone went off while I was waiting for the pizza to arrive. A message from Mason.

How was the rest of your day?

Knowing he was thinking about me made my thighs feel warm and tingly, though I kept warning them not to fall for him.

Still, I barely had to think about my reply.

Felt better after I masturbated.

Watching the screen, I waited for a response.

Silence.

More silence.

More silence.

Are you okay? I asked. *TMI?*

A minute later, his reply arrived.

I was drinking and almost drowned. Took a while to be able to breathe again. But tell me more. At least I'll die happy.

I grinned.

Did you know Chuck Norris actually died years ago? The Grim Reaper hasn't been brave enough to tell him.

A moment later, my phone dinged.

Don't change the subject.

I couldn't resist sending one more.

Chuck Norris doesn't cheat death. He wins fair and square.

His reply was quick.

Know any facts about Vulcans? I'm far more interested in Spock.

I laughed, and thought about it a moment before I replied.

I'm heading to the Spotlight Theater to sit in on a rehearsal tomorrow at four o'clock. Come along if you can get away. P.S. Chuck Norris proved Spock was illogical. Then he counted to infinity. Twice.

Chapter Nineteen

Mason

The next evening I went to the Spotlight Theater.

It was a small community theater with folding chairs for the audience. It smelled like paint and sweat, and the soles of my shoes stuck to the floor with each step.

Carlotta was standing in front of the stage with her back to me, next to another woman who was much older. They were watching some schoolgirls sing, *Look At Me I'm Sandra Dee*. A few pieces of furniture had turned the stage into a makeshift bedroom, and the girl's voices weren't half bad.

I chose a seat at the side of the theater so I could see some of Carlotta's face, but toward the back so as not to disturb the performers. Carlotta must have sensed I was there, because she turned. When she saw me, her expression lit up. "Come down here," she mouthed, motioning me closer. The woman she was with turned too, staring at me curiously. I recognized her as the drama teacher from school, but couldn't remember her name. She had wild gray hair and a lined face, and when she smiled a greeting I saw some of her bright red lipstick had migrated onto her teeth.

I waved a hand at Carlotta, indicating I was just fine where I was. "I'll stay out of the way," I mouthed back.

Carlotta looked like she'd protest, but one of the girls on stage suddenly started coughing instead of singing. She bent double with big hacking barks, like she was about to bring up a lung.

"Stop," yelled Carlotta, waving her hands to halt the song. "Rizzo, what are you doing? You're not supposed to actually smoke that cigarette. It's just a prop."

The girl could barely speak. "But..." Cough. "It's more..." Cough. "Authentic."

"It's also illegal. Do you *want* to spend your eighteenth birthday behind bars?"

Carlotta had her hands on her hips, and her expression was as stern as I'd ever seen it. This was a whole new side of her. Sexy teacher. Maybe I had an undiscovered fetish, because I couldn't help imagining how turned on I'd get if she were telling *me* off like that.

"Rizzo, go backstage and get a drink," Carlotta ordered. "And by a drink, I mean a glass of water. I wouldn't have guessed I'd need to be so specific, but I don't want you adopting any more of your character's bad habits."

The rest of the cast laughed, and Rizzo scuttled off, red-faced and still coughing.

"Okay," said Carlotta. "We have time for one last song. If we sing *We Go Together* again, you think you can all manage to stay on stage this time? Or shall we replace the front three rows with trampolines so you can bounce right back into the routine?"

169

Another burst of laughter from the kids. They carried the bedroom furniture offstage and replaced it with a carnival, complete with fun house. The fun house was made from bench seats and cardboard, but I had to take my hat off to whoever had painted it. And when the kids leaped all over it, singing their hearts out while they danced, cartwheeled, and twirled, my jaw loosened.

At the end of the song I stood and clapped. Loudly. And gave the kids a whistle of appreciation for good measure.

The cast looked delighted. They took long, low bows, blowing me kisses, giving speeches that involved thanking their agents, directors, and co-stars, and totally hamming it up.

Carlotta rolled her eyes. "Okay, settle down. Great job, but here are some notes for tomorrow. Kenickie, your performance was good, but your lines aren't going to learn themselves. Frenchy, excellent energy, but stick a little more to the left so you don't crowd Danny and Sandy. Doody, your tumbling is spectacular. Keep it up."

She had an individual comment for everyone, then she gave them some encouraging words as a group, telling them how well they were doing, but that they needed to keep working hard to make sure they were ready for opening night. Finally she dismissed them, and gave the drama teacher a hug before joining me.

"Impressive," I told her. "You're great with them."

"They're talented kids. And they love an audience. As soon as you walked in, their energy levels spiked."

"Glad to have helped."

"It was a fun rehearsal." She patted her stomach. "Now I'm craving something sweet. Shall we get ice-cream?"

"I want to go to your place to finish putting on the window latches."

"The latches are done. The house is secure."

"You did them all?"

She batted her eyelids. "I'll have you know, sir, there's more to me than just a pretty face," she drawled. "I can screw real good."

I grinned, offering her my arm to escort her out. "Then you deserve all the ice cream you can eat."

"You want to go to Lick It Like That?"

"Where else?"

The ice-cream parlor by the beach was only a short drive away. We used to go there when we were kids, and it turned out to have barely changed. The old jukebox was still in the corner, playing one of the songs I remembered from years ago. And the flavors were exactly the same.

"Strawberry swirl for me," I told the server. "And peanut butter?" I turned to Carlotta. "Is that still your favorite?"

Her smile was beautiful. "You remembered."

By unspoken agreement, Carlotta and I took our cones to the same corner booth we used to sit at, settling into our old seats opposite one another. Next to us was a table of four teenagers, about the same age as we were when we used to come here. Two girls and two guys, eating ice cream and laughing at something on one of their phones. Being here with Carlotta made me feel their age again. Like we'd stepped back in time and should be talking about things that happened at school.

Carlotta tasted her peanut butter cone and groaned. "This is just as delicious as I remembered." She licked ice cream off her lips, and I couldn't help but follow the movement of her tongue with my eyes. As good as my ice cream was, she looked a whole lot tastier.

"Do you feel like we're in a time warp?" she asked.

"It's exactly what I was thinking." I ran my hand over my jaw, rasping my palm against my stubble. "Tell me the truth, do I look sixteen?"

"Not a day over."

"Then do you want to make out later? I'm angling for second base."

Her eyes smiled even more than her lips did. "If you give me your homework to copy, I'll let you get to third."

Leaning across the table, I brought my mouth close to her ear. "It's a deal, sweetheart." I let my breath tickle her lobe.

She shivered, closing her eyes for a moment. When she opened them again, they were dark and her eyelids were heavy. My own relentless desire for her was mirrored back at me, and it was all I could do not to touch her.

Then her tongue flicked out and licked my ice cream. Watching her made me picture all the other things I wanted her to lick. Well, there was mainly one thing I wanted her to lick. The others were optional extras.

"Nice," she said. "But mine is better." She licked her cone again as though to confirm it.

"My turn to taste," I said.

Ignoring the ice cream she held out, I cupped her chin with my hand and tasted her mouth. Her lips were cold, sweet, and delicious. She always tasted good, but this time I couldn't get enough. I wanted to kiss her forever.

"Eww. Get a room."

I pulled away from Carlotta, flashing a grin at the teenagers at the next table.

"Old people kissing." The girl who'd spoken pulled a disgusted face. "Sick."

Carlotta laughed. "I guess we're not sixteen anymore."

"We're not old," I protested, but the teens had already gone back to their phones.

"We should give them something to complain about." Carlotta's eyes sparkled. "I said I'd let you get to third. I say we do it on their table."

I grinned at her mischievous smile. "You're not joking, are you? If you can't be trusted around impressionable young minds, we'd better take our cones outside."

We walked hand-in-hand down to the beach. The sky had turned shades of dark pink and blue, and the temperature was cooling down fast, but when I took off my shoes the sand still felt warm. The beach was quiet with only a few people walking and jogging along the tide line, and we chose a spot on the sand where we could watch the waves. There was nothing quite like sitting on San Dante's gorgeous beach. I'd miss it once I was gone.

"It's beautiful here, isn't it?" Carlotta said what I was thinking. Her ice cream was in one hand, and she juggled her phone out of her pocket with the other. "I'll take a photo of us."

"To post online? No thanks."

"You'd mind?"

"Would I mind a million people commenting on my picture?" I gave my head a firm shake. "Never going to happen." It'd be bad enough for anyone, but a potential disaster for a special agent about to go back undercover.

"Then I won't put it online. It'll just be for us."

"I don't like having my picture taken."

"Watch this." She smeared her ice cream onto her cheek.

"What the—?"

"Done." Pulling her cone off her cheek, she grinned at me with a face covered with ice cream. "Look at the picture."

She handed me her phone. The photo she'd taken filled the screen. My face was turned toward Carlotta, my expression comically puzzled. Carlotta had her cone stuck to her cheek, her eyes wide and her mouth open with mock surprise. As though something had jogged her elbow and made her accidentally face plant her ice cream.

"It's a funny picture," I admitted. "But you're mocking yourself again."

She poked her tongue out to lick ice cream off her cheek. "Normal selfies are boring. I like taking funny shots that tell a little story."

I leaned forward to kiss off the ice cream that was still under her eye. "You're so beautiful, a regular picture of you could never be boring. You don't give yourself enough credit." Catching her chin, I held her still while I kissed the stickiness away. "And as delicious as this is, I like your face even better without ice cream on it."

Carlotta pulled back, her brow furrowed. "You need to stop with the compliments. I can feel a blush coming on."

"Blushing doesn't matter, because you have more than one superpower. You proved that in the theater."

Her frown disappeared. "The kids were great, weren't they? I was proud of them."

"Are you doing theater in LA?"

"A little acting. But today was the first time I've ever been a director." Her eyes had turned luminous, reflecting the pink hues of the sunset. "I had no idea how satisfying it would be. I was trying not to overstep, but being able to make the entire cast do the songs the way I wanted? Ah-maz-ing."

"Maybe you can do some directing when you get back to LA."

She scrunched her nose. "That would be my dream job, but I seriously doubt I could get my foot in the door.

You can't walk a block in LA without tripping over at least three directors. Judy only let me take over today's session as a favor."

"Speaking of LA, when are you going back?"

She shrugged. "Being in San Dante isn't as bad as I thought. Weirdly, things with Mom have improved a little since I found out about her big lie." Her smile hitched up on one side, and my eyes dropped to trace the curve of her lips. "Also, some other good things have happened," she added.

"Like what?"

"Like this." She leaned over and kissed me until I felt something sticky and cold running down my hand and had to pull away to lick up dripping ice cream.

Not that I minded. If there was anything nicer than sitting on the beach at sunset, tasting strawberry swirl and Carlotta's lips, I couldn't imagine it. Her toenails were painted gold and her sandals lay next to my sneakers in the sand. Her bare arm was against mine, and she smelled like peanut butter ice cream, but with an extra hint of sweetness that was all her.

I'd wanted the perfect memory to carry with me to Houston, so I could call on it when things got dark. And this was it. My perfect moment. Ice cream dripping on my hand while my heart warmed as though the sun were setting into my chest instead of behind the horizon.

"How did you get that scar?" She reached up and traced the twisted line on my neck where a bullet had burned through my flesh.

My lazy, contented thoughts abruptly focused. "Car accident," I lied.

"And the ones on your arm and stomach?"

She must have seen or felt the scar on my stomach when we were fooling around at her mother's house.

"Same accident." The lies extinguished the warmth from my chest. "It was a bad one."

"Were you doing bodyguard work? Someone was shooting at you and blew the tires out, made the car roll?"

"Nothing like that."

"What do you do when you guard people? Is it like the secret service in the movies? Do you wear a little earphone in your ear? Do you order your team to patrol the perimeter?"

"Sometimes."

She grinned. "I knew it! You're guarding someone famous, and that's why you're so tight-lipped. Is it Oprah?"

"No."

"Beyoncé?"

"No."

"A Kardashian?"

"Quit trying to guess." I dragged in a breath, feeling like shit and needing to admit the truth. "All I can say is that my job's important to me. But it's not easy. I travel a lot and work difficult hours. And when I'm at work, it's like I'm someone else." It was more than I'd meant to say and I looked away, staring out to sea, trying to break the spell she was casting over me.

Even if I were falling for Carlotta all over again, my job had to come first. Maybe I was only doing it because I was still trying to make up for the past, but it didn't change the fact that I was the only one with a chance of bringing down Diamond, one of the worst scumbags to ever rise to the top of the cartel pecking order.

It wasn't fair to lie to Carlotta. And the more time I spent with her, the more I hated the thought of going back to Houston. But what choice did I have?

Chapter Twenty

Carlotta

'**D**oes masturbating too much make you go blind?'

Though I was sure I'd heard that somewhere, when I'd typed it into Google, the search came up with conflicting results.

The fact I could read the search results without squinting probably proved it was an old wives' tale. But Google did provide a helpful warning about the possibility of getting a repetitive strain injury in my wrist.

If my wrist needed surgery, I'd send Mason the bill. It was his fault I needed to spend so much solo time in the bedroom. When we kissed, I knew he wanted more, I could feel the evidence of it. But I could also feel him holding back.

Last night, he'd told me again how much more important his job was to him than any relationship could be, then barely kissed me again before dropping me at home.

Maybe that was a good thing. I liked being around him

too much. In fact, I was in serious danger of falling for him.

It shouldn't be happening, but he'd disarmed me with compliments, then charmed me with his unexpected, playful smile. I loved that he always laughed at my jokes, and how he could crack me up with his quick wit. That he was so big and tough, but a softie underneath. And how he needed to take care of people, which was incredibly sweet.

And as for how his beautiful blue-gray eyes heated up as though he were undressing me in his mind? Holy. Flaming. Fire-panties.

But falling for him would be a terrible idea.

The last thing I needed was a man I couldn't trust. And after always ranking in second place to Mom's fantasies, I wanted someone who'd value me more than his job.

None of which helped with the intense level of sexual frustration I was suffering.

At least working for Santino provided some distraction. I did some more filing, picked up more cartons, and listened to far more details about Faith's love life than I'd ever wanted to know.

But my thoughts kept inexorably drifting to Mason, and the minute I got home from work, I retired to my bedroom to double-click my own mouse. *Again.*

Opening my eyes afterward, my gaze went to my Meg Ryan poster. "Don't look at me like that," I scolded her. "You did it first, remember?"

"Are you in there, Carlotta?" Mom had to be standing just outside my bedroom door, because the volume of her voice made me jump. Had she heard my explosive orgasm?

"I didn't know you were home from school, Mom."

There was a short silence as though my mother wasn't sure what to say, even though I couldn't recall that ever happening. "We'll talk when you're up," she said finally.

When I emerged, blinking, into the late afternoon light, Mom was in the kitchen slicing cheese and a tomato for a sandwich. She was wearing navy slacks and a pale green shirt, and I did a double take when I saw how subdued she looked.

"Did you have a job interview?" I asked. "Or are you meeting with your parole officer?"

"Very funny." She looked down at her clothes. "This outfit matches my mood."

"Why? Did something happen?"

She put down the knife. "I called Declan and told him about the affair."

"You did? How did he take it?"

She sighed. "As well as could be expected."

"Poor Declan isn't having a good week." I gave Mom a sympathetic look, realizing her week hadn't been much better. "What made you decide to call him?"

"I was thinking about what you said. How I wasn't a very good mother."

"I didn't say you weren't—"

"But maybe it isn't too late to improve."

"Of course it isn't." I put my hand on her arm and squeezed. Okay, so I was a pushover. But when my mother was vulnerable and honest, my heart ached in the best possible way. For years, it was all I'd wished for.

"Things will be different, Carlotta. You'll see."

Maybe I was pushing my luck, but I had to ask. "Does this mean you'll smooth things over with Ed Lennox?"

She pulled away. "Never."

"But—"

"That man's a menace. Look. I found this stuck to the back of my car." Ripping open the kitchen junk drawer, she pulled out a strip of paper. No, not paper. It was a bumper sticker.

Warning: Driver Has Narcolepsy. Please Help By Honking.

I snorted a laugh but somehow managed to turn it into a cough.

"All those people honking behind me, and I had no idea why." She shoved the sticker back into the drawer and slammed it shut. "And Edward signed me up to the Flat Earth Society. Their magazines were being delivered to me at school, and the science teacher asked if I'd like to see his globe."

"The Flat Earth Society? That must have pushed you over the edge." I made myself keep a straight face.

"When I was away on a school trip, Edward filled my mailbox with seeds and watered them until hundreds of little plants sprouted."

I stared down as though my shoes were fascinating, but really I was taking deep breaths through my nose. When I could speak without cracking up, I asked, "Did the mailman start leaving you lettuce?"

"Carlotta, it was anything but funny."

"I know, Mom. But it's important to romaine calm and keep the peas."

"Carlotta Watson!"

My laugh burst out of me. "But Mom, you've pranked Edward too."

"I was provoked!"

"Please end your feud. It would mean a lot to me."

"The man's a monster. You can't make peace with dragons, Carlotta. You have to slay them." Picked up the knife, she stabbed it into the center of the tomato she'd been slicing.

I winced. "Just think about burying the hatchet instead of a dagger, okay? For me?"

Her brow wrinkled and her mouth pulled down into a pained expression. "I'll consider it. No promises."

My phone rang from the bedroom where I'd left it on the bed, and my heart leaped. I raced to answer it, but was disappointed when I saw Santino's name on the screen instead of Mason's.

"Hi," said Santino. "How was your first week of work?"

"Great. Hey, I don't think I thanked you enough for giving me a job. It's been a lifesaver." Faith had paid me for the week in cash, and it had been enough to cover my utility bills for my LA apartment. "You're not calling to fire me or anything?" I added, suddenly worried.

"Actually, it's the opposite. I know it's Saturday tomorrow, but do you think you could do a special job for me anyway? My cousin has an auto paint shop in Tijuana, and he's just finished spraying a metallic coating on my car. I need it picked up and I'd usually ask Faith, but she's out of action until she gets her cast off."

"You want me to go to Mexico and drive your car back here?"

"The bus will drop you a block from his shop and the whole trip should take four or five hours, tops."

I hesitated, the thought flashing back through my mind that he could be running some kind of illegal operation. But that idea had Mom's vivid imagination stamped all over it. I'd asked her to stick to reality, so I should do the same.

"I'll pay you a bonus for your trouble," he added. "And for working on a Saturday. An extra two hundred dollars on top of your normal hourly rate."

I blinked, calculating what I'd earn. "That's generous."

"I want my car back in time for a hot date on Sunday."

"Then it looks like I'm going on a road trip."

He gave me the details, and when I hung up I went out

to the living room to find Mom had disappeared. She must have eaten her sandwich and taken Xul for a walk.

My gaze went to the ladder Mason had left behind. It was still sitting in the corner of the room with his toolbox, waiting for him to come and pick it up.

Mom had no shortage of small maintenance jobs that needed doing, and it'd be a shame to waste the chance while I had the tools on hand. Strapping Mason's enormous tool belt around my hips, I tightened it as much as I could, then stuck his big drill into it before climbing the ladder. I'd start by refastening the loose curtain rail.

Being at the top of the ladder felt further from the ground than it had looked. I pulled Mason's heavy drill out of the tool belt, but as I was trying to drill a new hole to fasten the rail, the too-large tool belt slipped off my hips. Grabbing for the belt with one hand, the drill slipped out of my other hand. I lunged for it, and the ladder tipped.

For a moment the ladder teetered on the edge of going over. Then my stomach swooped and the ground rushed toward me.

Chapter Twenty-One

Mason

I was at Asher's place, looking through some information Griffin had sent, when my phone rang. Dad's name flashed onto the screen.

"We're waiting for you," he said when I answered. "How soon will you be here?"

"Be there? What for?"

"Kade's arrived from LA. We're meeting at my place, remember?"

"But it's only four thirty. I thought we were having dinner?"

"Kade got in early, and he and Asher are already here. Can you come now?"

I logged off the computer and got into the car for the five-minute drive to Dad's place. When I drove up to his house, an ambulance was just pulling away from outside. Its lights started flashing, and I stopped and stared after it with my heart in my throat. Was Dad in the ambulance? Had he suffered a heart attack? Should I follow it?

"Asher," I yelled, jumping out of the car. "Kade! Are you inside?"

I'd started toward Dad's steps when his door opened and he stepped onto his front porch.

"What are you yelling for?" Dad asked. "Come on, your brothers are waiting."

"The ambulance wasn't here for you?" I took the steps three at a time. "You're okay?"

"It must have been here for one of the neighbors." He glanced next door. "Maybe Trixie?"

I spun around and jumped back down his front steps. I was halfway to Trixie Watson's house when she hurried outside.

"Trixie, are you okay?" I called.

She barely spared me a glance, rushing toward her car. "It's Carlotta."

"Carlotta?" My chest contracted. "What happened? Is she badly hurt?"

"Stop interfering and stay away from my daughter." Trixie slid into her car and glared at me before slamming the door.

My heart was beating painfully fast. Carlotta's attacker must have come back. Fixing the window latches hadn't stopped him. He'd gotten in somehow, and now Carlotta was injured.

"What's going on?" yelled Dad from his porch. Asher came out onto the porch behind him, followed by Kade.

"Hey Mason," called Kade. "What's up?"

"Carlotta's hurt," I yelled back, sprinting to my car. Kade didn't usually spend much time in San Dante, but he'd just been here for a few days over Christmas, so another reunion could wait.

"Where are you going?" demanded Dad.

"To the hospital."

"Why?"

I tore open the car door. "What do you mean, why? Carlotta's in the *hospital*, Dad, so you can take that stupid feud of yours and stow it. Kade, I'm sorry I can't stick around now, but I'll catch up with you later, okay?"

Ignoring Dad's disapproving grunt, I slammed the door and raced off after Trixie Watson's dented orange car. After following her all the way to the hospital, I lost her in the parking lot in front of the Urgent Care Center when she swung into the only available parking space. It took me a while to find another, and by the time I got inside and went to the reception desk, there was no sign of Trixie.

I asked at the front desk for Carlotta and the receptionist told me only immediate family were being allowed in. She shot me a sympathetic look. "Sorry, love. Her mother asked me to keep you out. She's a character that one, isn't she?"

"Could you at least tell me how Carlotta is? Was she badly hurt? Is she going to be okay?"

"I'm afraid patient information is confidential."

The receptionist wouldn't budge and eventually I gave up, cursing under my breath as I strode back out.

I was almost at my car when my phone rang. Dragging it out of my pocket, I saw it was Todd. He must have read my mind.

"Tell me," I said, sliding behind the wheel.

"I tracked down the guy behind the FowlFetish account who's been sending death threats to your friend." Todd sounded smug. "Guess what? He's the same guy who hacked her account."

"You're sure?" I started the car.

"Absolutely. That duck picture she posted really got him riled. He hacked her to upload the doctored photos with the dead birds, and he's been threatening her every day since."

"Tell me who he is."

"Get this. His real name is Willie Stroker. And Willie isn't even a nickname. It was what his parents called him. The guy has a record, but with a name like Willie Stroker, do you blame him? I'd be angry too."

"You have his address?" If the guy lived close, he was probably the one who threw paint at Carlotta and left shit on her mother's porch. And today, he might have gone back to hurt her.

"Willie lives near the Lindo Lake County Park. Big lake there. Good for birdwatchers."

He gave me the full address and I punched it into my GPS. "That's only an hour away. He has to be the guy who attacked Carlotta. He's obsessed with her. Do you have his picture?"

"Sure do."

When it appeared on my phone, Willie Stroker matched Carlotta's description perfectly, complete with tattoo.

"That's him." I took off with a squeal of tires. I was gripping the wheel so hard my knuckles were white. "I'm going to make him regret everything he did to Carlotta."

"I'm going to pretend I didn't hear that." Todd sounded worried. "Listen, you're not going rogue, are you?"

"Don't worry, Todd. It won't blow back onto you."

"Mason—"

"My friend's in the hospital. She's *injured*. And I need answers."

"Willie put her in the hospital?"

"That's what I'm going to find out."

"Mason, if you don't have proof, you shouldn't go. That's not how this is done."

"Relax. I'm going to talk to him, ask what he knows. If he didn't hurt her, he has nothing to worry about." That was a bare-faced lie. The mood I was in, I'd make FowlFetish tell me everything he'd done, no matter what it took to get the truth. Guess you couldn't work for a ruthless drug cartel for six years without some of it rubbing off. And I'd do anything to keep the people I loved safe.

"You said this wasn't related to a case you were working." Todd sounded more nervous than ever, as though he could hear the rage in my voice. "If you go knocking on doors and throwing your weight around, there's going to be trouble."

"I'll leave my badge behind and pay him a polite visit as a private citizen."

"Be careful, Mason."

"He's the one who should be careful." Clenching my jaw, I pulled the car onto the Interstate and floored it.

Chapter Twenty-Two

Carlotta

I was lying under a bright florescent light with the granddaddy of all headaches. It felt like a crowd of ravers in stiletto heels were dancing inside my brain to a loud, thumping beat.

Wincing, I opened my eyes.

"Are you all right, Carlotta?" Mom sounded worried.

I blinked, trying to focus on her over the pounding in my head. There were curtains around us. It looked like I was in the hospital. Had I been knocked out?

"Sore head," I moaned.

"I'll get you something." Before I could stop her, she'd dashed out of my curtained-off cubicle, presumably in search of painkillers.

While she was gone, I did a limb check. All four were still present and accounted for, and I could wriggle my toes and fingers. I couldn't find any bandages. No visible wounds. But I *was* in pain.

Lifting one hand, I gently touched my forehead.

Ouch.

The whole area was tender, as though I'd hit something solid. Like the floor from a great height, for example. Moving my hand to the side of my head, I found a lump that throbbed when I touched it.

That's right. I'd been on top of Mason's ladder.

I must have struck my head on the metal ladder as I fell, knocking myself out. Then my face had hit the floor. That accounted for the wince-inducing dance party going on in my skull. Hopefully Mom would get me some industrial strength painkillers.

A middle-aged nurse with a kind face bustled into my curtain cubicle. "Hi Carlotta, I'm Nurse Bartlew. How are you feeling?"

I swallowed hard, because my throat was dry.

"Thirsty," I croaked.

She reached to the nightstand beside the bed, and picked up a plastic cup with a straw in it. Bringing the straw to my lips, she held the cup so I could suck up the liquid like a helpless infant. The water was lukewarm, but it went down like liquid heaven. The frenzied dancing inside my skull even slowed.

"Thank you," I said when I'd drained the cup. My voice still sounded hoarse.

"Any pain?" she asked.

"My head hurts." I swallowed again, because the water was gurgling as it dropped toward my stomach, and I wasn't sure if I'd be able to hold it down.

"Nausea?"

I clamped my teeth together and nodded.

"I'll get you a bowl." She vanished back out through the curtains.

A few moments later, Mom pushed her way into my cubicle. "I couldn't find the nurse," she said with a frown. "What happened? I came home to find you on the floor."

"Ladder," I managed. Even opening my mouth to speak a single word made me worry the water I'd consumed might come out with it.

"I saw the ladder. But what were you doing at the top of it?"

I lifted one shoulder in an apologetic shrug and swallowed, silently giving my stomach some mental encouragement. It was strong. It could hold down a little water. Easy peasy.

"It was Mason Lennox's ladder." Mom scowled. "He wanted you to climb it. And after you fell, he left you there, helpless on the floor."

Before I could defend Mason, Nurse Bartlew reappeared through my cubicle's curtains and handed me a bowl. I clutched it as my stomach did a sudden backflip. Maybe I should just let myself throw up. It might make me feel better.

"Still want to vomit, love?" Nurse Bartlew checked my chart.

I gave her a feeble nod.

"Nausea's fairly common after a blow to the head. The doctor will be in shortly, then we can give you something to settle your stomach." She turned to Mom. "We can't allow the police to take a statement from your daughter until after the doctor's cleared her I'm afraid, Mrs. Watson."

"The police?" I croaked.

The nurse put a reassuring hand on my arm. "In cases like this, it's best if they handle it. Your mother can stay with you if you'd like. You don't have to talk to them alone."

"I fell off a ladder."

Her kind eyes creased in the corners. "Uh-huh. You fell

off a ladder, or walked into a door, or tripped down the stairs. I've heard it all, love. Somehow it's never the man's fault."

"What man?" I asked, confused. Then I aimed a glare at Mom. What had she been telling them?

"More water?" asked my mother, not meeting my gaze. She slopped water from a jug into the cup and jammed the straw between my lips.

"Looks like you're in good hands," Nurse Bartlew said. "I'll pop back after the doctor's been." Before I could spit the straw from my mouth, she was gone.

I fixed Mom with an accusing look.

At least she had the grace to look guilty. "Well?" she asked defensively. "You can't tell me Mason Lennox didn't have anything to do with your fall. He rigged the ladder to topple, and I bet his father put him up to the whole thing. It's exactly the kind of thing Edward would do."

Still glaring, I motioned her closer. "Mason. Had. Nothing. To. Do. With. It." My voice was an angry hiss.

"But you don't know Edward Lennox like I do. You can't trust him, or anyone who shares his DNA."

I sank back onto the bed, too exhausted to argue. My nausea was subsiding, but the dancing inside my skull had cranked up a notch, and whoever was in there had swapped their stilettos for concrete boots. Wincing, I closed my eyes and heard Mom sigh.

"Sleep now," she whispered.

I would have answered if I could, but my exhaustion had wrapped itself tightly around me and I couldn't summon the energy to talk. I wanted to doze. And in spite of Mom's attempt to blame Mason, it was comforting to have her with me. I heard the scrape of a chair across the ground, and figured she'd dragged the guest chair closer to me.

It felt like I'd barely dropped off to sleep before I was woken by voices. When I opened my eyes, a doctor was studying me.

"How are you feeling?" she asked.

"A little better." I reached for the glass of water to soothe my dry throat, and Mom handed it to me.

"Still nauseated?" The doctor moved closer, staring intently into my eyes. Possibly checking the dilation of my pupils, or making sure they didn't drift off in different directions.

"Not really." I drained the water and handed back the empty glass.

"Follow my finger." She moved it back and forth in front of me. "That's good. Are you dizzy?"

"No."

"Can you tell me what day it is?"

"It's Friday. And I fell off a ladder. I was alone at the time and it was nobody's fault but my own."

"You remember being knocked out?" When I nodded, the doctor added, "What about further back? What did you have for breakfast this morning?"

"Toast and coffee. I remember everything. Honestly, I'm fine."

"Okay." She made some notes on her clipboard, then checked her watch. "I'm sending you for a brain scan and keeping you here overnight. You should be fine after a little rest, but it's best not to take chances."

"Oh. See, the thing is, I really need to leave now." Throwing back the blankets, I eased slowly up to sitting. My head felt weird, like it was too big for my body, but there was no way I could afford an overnight stay.

"Stay where you are." Mom leapt from her chair. "You're not going anywhere."

"Mom, I lost my insurance when—"

"I can cover the bill."

I blinked at her. "You can?"

"I have some money put aside for emergencies."

"Thanks Mom, but I don't want you to spend your emergency fund on my hospital stay."

"That's what it's for." She folded her arms and looked down her nose at me. "I was saving to buy a full-size medieval trebuchet so I can launch ostrich eggs at Edward, but this is more important."

"Your mother's right," said the doctor. "For the next twelve hours, this is where you need to be. The orderly will collect you for your scan shortly." She gave me a nod as she left.

"Thank you, Mom." I lay back gratefully. "It's really nice that you'd give up your trebuchet for me."

"I can get it on credit. Anyway, are you hungry? It's eight o'clock. I can get you something."

I swallowed bile at the thought. "I'm not hungry, but you should go and eat something. You don't need to stay with me overnight."

"Don't be silly. Of course I'm staying." She settled back into the visitor's chair she'd pulled up beside the bed, and took hold of my hand. Hers was soft and warm. "Do you need anything?"

I shook my head. In spite of telling her to go, I was grateful she wasn't leaving me alone. "I don't remember you ever holding my hand before, and this makes twice in the last few days."

She frowned. "Well, how often do I come home to find you on the floor?" Then her expression softened. "When I saw the blood under your head, I was afraid you were dead." She squeezed my hand. "Edward's worst pranks haven't scared me like that."

"I'm sorry. But it wasn't Mason's fault I fell off his

ladder."

"He booby trapped it."

"He didn't. If you told the hospital staff a man did this to me, you should make sure they know you were wrong. And please tell them the police don't need to get involved." I held her gaze until she let out a sigh.

"All right. I don't trust any member of the Lennox family, but I'll take your word for it."

"I'm sorry Ed hurt you, Mom, but it was a long time ago. I wish you could let it go."

She blinked, and for a moment I glimpsed raw emotion in her eyes. A wound that had never healed. Then it was gone.

"I'll find us something to eat." She pulled her hand from mine and stood up. "You think they serve Gin here?"

After she'd disappeared through the curtains, I looked around for my phone. I spotted it on the nightstand, but because the bed was pulled so far forward, the nightstand was behind my head where I couldn't easily reach it. And really, I still felt too exhausted to message Mason. Besides, he had no idea I was in the hospital, so why worry him?

Closing my eyes again, I drifted back to sleep.

Chapter Twenty-Three

Mason

Willie Stroker looked just like the photo Todd had sent me, and the man Carlotta had described.

When he opened his door, he was wearing a T-shirt with a picture of a duck and the words '*Release The Quacken*' printed on it. There were orange crumbs clinging to his shirt, so he must have recently consumed some kind of processed cheese snack. He was almost as tall as me and not much younger, but he probably weighed only half as much.

I was chewing on a toothpick, because I needed some kind of physical outlet for my rage and I figured chewing it to splinters might help me restrain myself from chewing on Willie's face.

Also, a lot of people took me for a big dumb thug, and being underestimated had always worked in my favor. The toothpick didn't hurt that impression.

"Are you Willie Stroker?" I asked around the toothpick, knowing full well that he was.

He looked me up and down with an alarmed expression, his gaze lingering on the scars on my arm and neck. "Who wants to know?"

I tugged my wallet out of my pocket and flipped him my badge, giving him just a glimpse. "Can I come in?"

He frowned. "What's this about?"

Instead of answering, I crossed my arms, flexing my biceps and focusing a stare on him. It was a stare I'd learned from Asher, impassive and cold. Inside, I was a pit of red-hot, seething fury. But on the outside, I was an iceberg.

He glanced from side to side. "Um. Okay, I guess you can come in for a minute, but that's all the time I can give you." He opened the door a little wider and I stepped into his gloomy hallway.

Without waiting for him to show me the way, I strode into a dank living room filled with the stink of old food. It smelled like grease and cheese, and I was willing to bet Willie Stroker had a diet as bad as my father's.

Most of the room was taken up with a large desk covered with computer equipment. A giant TV was against one wall, and a small couch was jammed in front of the desk. The TV was on, but paused. Willie had been watching porn. Two men and one woman were on the screen, frozen in a position that made me wince. But knowing Willie's history, I was grateful the movie's cast members didn't include any poultry.

"Tell me why you're here." Willie followed me into the room. He grabbed the TV remote off the couch and flicked off the screen. Also on the couch were some wadded-up tissues, a jar of Vaseline, and his cellphone.

I made a mental note not to touch anything.

"I'm here to ask you a question, Willie. Do you get off on being an online troll? Does abusing people make you horny?"

"What?"

"It's a simple question, Willie." I made my tone as reasonable as I could. "Does being an asshole get you excited?"

His eyes were wide. "Hey dude, you can't speak to me like that."

"Tell me why you send death threats to innocent women. And if you like assaulting those women in real life even more."

A flicker of realization passed over his face. "I don't want you in here anymore." He motioned to the door. "Please leave."

I moved the battered toothpick from one side of my mouth to the other. "Come on, Willie. Or should I call you FowlFetish? Either way, you can tell me about your weird sex kinks. I won't judge."

"You're a cop, right? Let me see your badge again. I want to call the station and check you're supposed to be here." He grabbed his phone off the couch.

"I wouldn't do that if I were you."

His finger hovered over the dialer, his expression nervous. "If you're a cop, you need to leave when I tell you to. Or show me your warrant."

"Did I say I was a cop? That's funny. I don't remember saying that." I moved closer. The room was so small it wasn't hard to crowd him. When I advanced, he backed up until he hit the couch.

"What do you want?" His gaze flicked to my scars, then bounced back to my face. He was starting to sweat.

"You've been harassing Carlotta Watson."

He flinched. "You can't prove that. You have nothing on me."

"I don't need to prove it. Carlotta's a friend of mine."

Swallowing hard, he dropped his phone by his side as though he'd given up on calling the police. "She shouldn't have messed with ducks."

"You hacked her account and altered her pictures." I leaned closer, making him bend backward. "You threw paint over her." I tapped him on the chest. "You left a pile of shit on her front porch." I let a little of my rage show, my voice becoming a snarl. "And you went back to her house again today and hurt her. You put her in the *hospital*."

"What?" He blinked fast. "I didn't go to her house today."

"Willie, you know it's a crime to lie to the police?" I narrowed my eyes. "It's called perverting the course of justice."

"So you *are* a cop?"

"You should get your hearing checked, Willie. I didn't say I was a cop."

He shook his head, looking confused. "It doesn't matter anyway, because I'm not lying. I didn't see Carlotta today. I wasn't anywhere near her house."

"You're sure about that?"

"I had work today, I swear. I was in the office all day and didn't even go out for lunch." He lifted his phone. "Look, I can call someone from work. My manager. He'll tell you I was there."

He was obviously scared, and I believed him. So he can't have been the reason Carlotta was in the hospital. My rage eased a little.

"I admit I did that other stuff," he said. "I threw some paint on her, but it was the stuff that washes off easily. I wasn't trying to hurt her, just scare her. And the crap on her porch, that was just because my cousin works at the zoo, and I ended up with some bags of giraffe shit. Long story. But I didn't go to her house today. I promise."

"Giraffe shit?" I mused, as though I was trying to work out what the story could be. All I could think about was Carlotta being rushed to hospital in an ambulance. If Willie hadn't hurt her, what could have happened?

"My cousin bags the shit from the zoo. People put it on their gardens."

I could have pointed out it wasn't a long story. Instead I said, "Don't forget about the death threats and all the nasty comments you left on Carlotta's social media. The effluent from your twisted brain is worse than the shit you left on her porch."

"Hey dude, I don't want any trouble, okay?"

I sighed, chewing the battered toothpick thoughtfully, as though I were considering what to do. "You know, Willie, it's too late to say you don't want trouble. Why shouldn't I arrest you, seeing as you've confessed to at least three felony charges?"

He held up both hands, straightening his back and regaining some of his bluster. "No way, man. You can't charge me with anything. You said you weren't a cop! Isn't that against the law? And you threatened me, so you can't use anything I said against me. I know my rights."

"Then we'll have to do this another way."

His hands dropped and the fear came back to his eyes. "What other way?"

I took my phone out of my pocket and showed him the picture of him I'd taken a few seconds before I knocked. "You see this?"

His face went white. "How did you…?"

"There's a window right there." I motioned to it, my

lip curled. "Next time you jack the beanstalk, try closing the drapes. What if a kid had looked in? That would be child abuse."

He gulped like a fish. "What are you going to do with the photo?"

"Nothing. Unless you keep assaulting women. Then I might decide to share it."

"Okay. You win." He sank onto the couch. "If you delete the photo, I'll play nice."

"You can start by telling Carlotta how sorry you are for everything you did to her." I nodded to his phone. "Do it now. Leave her a nice apology for everyone to see. Confess your sins. I'll wait."

He picked up his phone and typed for a couple of minutes, then looked up, his expression sullen. "Is that all? Will you go now?"

I checked Carlotta's feed on my phone, and found his apology. It was short and to the point. Good enough, I supposed.

"I'll go," I said grudgingly. "But from now on, I want you to be Mister Nice Guy. No more death threats. No nasty comments. Unless you're confessing your undying love for someone, I don't want to see it. And if I hear you've so much as thought about Carlotta again, I'll be back."

"I won't do anything else. I promise."

I went to the door and opened it. But before walking out, I shifted the toothpick to the other side of my mouth and narrowed my eyes at him. "One last thing, Willie. Who's Chuck Norris afraid of?"

"Um." His frown was puzzled. "Actually, I thought Chuck Norris wasn't afraid of anyone."

I gave him a nod. "That's because he's never met me."

Chapter Twenty-Four

Carlotta

To my relief, the doctor said my brain scan looked normal. What wasn't normal was that I was too tired to make any jokes about that result, like suggesting their machine must be broken.

When they wheeled my bed back into the cubicle after the scan, Mom insisted on staying in the uncomfortable looking chair beside me. Until I woke around midnight and found her asleep with her neck bent in such an awkward position, I convinced her to go home.

In the morning my headache was miraculously gone, and I felt fine. So good, in fact, that I dared to snag my phone off the nightstand, get online, and brave the haters.

Among all the vitriol on my feed, a weird comment popped up. A confession and apology from the man who'd hacked my account, thrown paint over me, and left poop on Mom's porch.

I read it several times, not quite able to believe it, then laughed out loud.

Maybe now some of my followers might believe I hadn't posted the gory duck photos. And it was a huge relief to know my attacker wouldn't come back.

But why the change of heart?

I was reading it again, trying to puzzle it out, when I heard footsteps. Then Mason poked his head through the curtains.

"May I come in?"

"Sure." As I eased up to a sitting position, I couldn't stop my grin. "What are you doing here? Not that I'm unhappy to see you. The opposite."

When he smiled back, his blue-gray eyes were the color of a sunny winter's day. And his disarming, lopsided smile was the perfect contrast to the square cut of his ridiculously masculine jaw.

Mason's jaw equaled a regular jaw squared. And yes, that was a math joke.

"I wanted to make sure you were okay." He winced, motioning to my face. "That must be painful."

I gently touched my sore forehead. "I probably look terrible. Not that I usually worry about how I look. Only when I see you."

He sank down on the bed, taking my hand and lifting it to kiss my fingers. "Aside from the bruises, you're as gorgeous as ever."

I wrinkled my nose, but my smile only grew. "I guess when you're around, I'll need to get used to caring."

"How'd you get hurt, sweetheart? They wouldn't tell me anything."

"I fell off the ladder and knocked myself out."

"My ladder?" His expression darkened.

"It was my own fault. I was fixing the curtain rail and slipped."

He kissed my fingers again, his lips warm on my skin

and sending tingles into my core. "But the doctor says you're going to be okay?"

"I'm fine. They wanted to monitor me overnight, but they're about to discharge me."

"You had me worried."

I wanted to ease the concern from his face, so I shuffled further over to the edge of the narrow hospital bed. "Want to lie down next to me?"

"Someone could come in at any moment."

"Where's your sense of adventure? Besides, you can stay on top of the covers. I just want a horizontal kiss. They're the best kind."

He hesitated a moment longer, then stretched out next to me. His manly bulk squeezed me in, but I wasn't complaining. His lips found mine and he gave me what I was coming to think of as a Mason kiss. Deep, thorough, and delicious. His kisses always delivered the nicest type of low-down tingles.

"You're right about the horizontal kisses," he murmured. "They are the best kind."

I was warming up, so I pushed the blanket down as much as I could with most of it trapped beneath him. I was wearing a hospital gown in an ugly shade of medical blue. Something hard was poking into my back, and it turned out to be my phone, which I'd forgotten I'd left on the bed next to me. Lifting it, I held it above us. My bruised side was closest to it and in spite of Mason's rose-tinted glasses, I was pretty sure I looked like I'd died a horrible death before a forbidden voodoo ritual had summoned me from my grave, pulling me out of the ground face first.

"A picture," I said. "For our album."

"But not for social media."

"I wouldn't do that. Not unless you agreed to it." I

lifted the phone higher, positioning the shot as best I could. "Give me a horrified look. Like you've woken up and discovered you're in bed with a zombie."

"Why?"

"Because I look like this." I pulled my mouth to the side, stuck my tongue out, and rolled my eyes back. Then I snapped the shot. "See?" I showed him the photo. "It's funny."

He studied it a moment, then took the phone from me. His lips brushed over mine, kissing me so gently it was as though he was afraid of hurting me. His kiss was so achingly tender, it shot straight to the top of my incredible sensations list. How could the softest caress from his mouth set my body on fire?

"I was worried about you," he murmured, tasting my lips with his tongue before he parted my mouth, as though he had to make sure every part of me was okay. I wanted to nip him, to show him I wanted more. But it felt so good, I just sighed into his mouth, kissing him back the same way, as though he were precious to me.

I was starting to believe he was.

He pulled away a little to smile at me, his warm eyes creasing in the corners. My own smile came from deep inside me, spreading through my entire body before blossoming on my face.

Then I heard the digital click of a camera shutter.

I blinked, confused. Where was my phone?

Turning my head, I saw Mason was holding it above us. "Did you just take a picture?"

"A better one for the album. I don't like it when you pretend you're not beautiful, just because you have a bruise, or messy hair. It couldn't be further from the truth." He looked at the shot and nodded. "This is much better." He angled it toward me.

"Holy frijoles," I breathed, staring at the photo. "We look like we're in love."

The angle of the camera meant Mason's face was mostly out of shot. Only his eyes and the top of his head were visible. But his eyes were shining. And as for me... I couldn't tear my gaze from my expression of wonder. The intensity of my emotion would have made me seem disturbingly vulnerable, except that Mason seemed to be looking at me with a similar expression. Was it a trick of the camera? An optical illusion? For some reason, it made a lump form in my throat.

"You can post that one online," he said. "Enough of my face is hidden that I can't be recognized."

"But it's not funny."

"Maybe instead of a made-up funny story, your followers need to see something real."

I blinked at him, struck by his words. Reality was exactly what I'd asked Mom for. I'd never thought about it that way before, but most of the stories I created for my followers were as removed from reality as the ones Mom used to make for me.

"Okay," I said, uploading the photo before I could change my mind. "It's worth a try."

Usually after posting, I closed the app down so I didn't obsess over the reactions. But this time, I left it open.

"People are starting to comment," I told Mason after a minute. "The first one is positive. Apparently we're sweet enough to eat. The second one just says 'Aww'. There's a third one now. And a fourth." My eyebrows lifted. "Wow. This is the first image since I was hacked that's getting positive comments." The tone of the comments had to have been helped by the confession and apology posted by the FowlFetish account, but they still blew my mind. "This is incredible. So far, my followers love this post. None of them seem to mind that it isn't funny."

A rush of relief and happiness made me want to jump out of bed, form my own one-person Conga line and dance around the room.

"Do you know what this means?" I demanded. "My followers may have finally forgiven me. What if I could convince my sponsors to come back and make a living from doing this again? You've done the impossible. I could kiss you all over."

His eyes sparkled. "Kissing me all over seems a fair and reasonable way to show your appreciation."

The blanket I had over me wasn't tucked in, so when I rolled on top of Mason, it ended up underneath me, forming a thin barrier between us. I rained enthusiastic kisses down on his forehead. He laughed, his face scrunching, as I worked my way over his eyes, down his nose and across his cheeks, attempting to cover every inch of skin. He took my face with both hands to stop me.

"On second thought, how about you focus your kisses on my mouth."

I had the full weight of my body on him, but judging by the hardness jutting into my belly it didn't seem to bother him. It was nice being on top for a change, and feeling in control. When I captured his mouth with mine, he kissed me back in that playful, sexy way I was already addicted to. His hands loosened, sliding from my face to my back. Then they froze.

His head was resting on the pillow, but he still managed to pull it back a little. "What are you wearing?"

"A hospital gown." Now I thought about it, my back did feel cold. The gown was hanging open at the back, and the blanket was scrunched between us, leaving my naked butt in the air, exposed to the full blast of the hospital's air conditioning.

He chuckled, his deliciously warm fingers caressing the bare skin of my back before drifting down to my buttocks. I shivered with arousal, feeling goose bumps springing up wherever he touched. And in the places I wanted him to touch.

"I don't think I've ever fully appreciated the hospital gown before," he murmured with his lips gently brushing my jaw. "Turns out, it's a very practical garment. It deserves a lot more respect."

I stretched my neck up to give his mouth better access. His breath was tickling my throat in the best possible way. "Mmm," I agreed. "Now I want to take this one home. What do you think? Shall I sneak it out of here?"

"Yes. One hundred percent, yes." His voice was lower. Throatier. "Carlotta, you don't know what you do to me."

"I think I might." I wriggled on his hard length and he groaned, capturing my hips.

"You're so damn sexy."

His mouth moved down my throat, and I suspected he was travelling lower so his hands could properly explore my naked body. His fingers brushed the crease where my butt checks met my thighs, making me shiver with pleasure.

I was so wet. So ready for him.

I needed his fingers to move between my thighs and caress me where I ached.

"Mason." I let out a little moan. "Will you—"

"Hello," said an amused female voice from behind me. "It's almost eight o'clock in the morning. At this hour, I wouldn't have thought there'd still be a full moon visible."

I turned my head to see Nurse Bartlew with twinkling

eyes, pressing her lips together in an obvious attempt not to laugh as she gazed pointedly at my naked buttocks.

Mason fumbled blindly for the ends of the hospital gown and tried to pull them together to hide my modesty. He clearly had a mistaken belief that I had some modesty. Maybe he hadn't seen my World Naked Day photos.

"Hello." He nodded at Nurse Bartlew over my shoulder. "I'm Mason Lennox. A friend of Carlotta's."

"I can see that. In fact, from here I can see almost everything."

I laughed, rolling off Mason. "I'm feeling much better now."

"Really?" she said dryly, giving Mason an appreciative look. "For some reason I don't find that surprising."

"Carlotta?" My mother appeared through the curtain behind the nurse, and stopped dead when she saw Mason. "What are you doing here?"

Nurse Bartlew lifted her clipboard so it hid her mouth, but her eyes still smiled. "It looked like he was about to land on the moon."

I tried not to giggle and failed miserably.

"Nice to see you, Trixie." Mason extracted himself from the narrow bed. "I presume you're here to take Carlotta home? I was just leaving."

"Are you discharging me?" I asked the nurse.

"The doctor will be here soon, so you can ask her. But I'd be surprised if she refused, considering how he's been feeling you. I mean, considering how much better you're feeling." She shot me a wink and bustled out.

Mom frowned at Mason, then at me. The hard candy in her mouth made a loud cracking sound as she bit down on it. She seemed to do that a lot when Mason was around.

"Thank you for visiting," I said to Mason. "Please come again soon."

He caught the innuendo in my tone, and his lips quirked. "I'd like to."

"Will I see you later?" I asked.

"Kade's visiting from LA, so we're having a family dinner tonight at my father's house." Then he raised his eyebrows. "Would you both like to come?" He looked from me to Mom. "I'm sure Kade won't mind cooking for a couple extra, and we can squeeze around Dad's dining table."

Candy cracked even louder. "If you think I'm setting foot in Edward Lennox's house, you're even less intelligent than you look."

"Mom." I sighed. "Please be nice."

"Carlotta can't go anywhere. She needs to rest for twenty-four hours." Mom folded her arms. "Doctor's orders."

Even though I felt fine, she was probably right. Best to be cautious.

"Rain check?" I asked.

"Okay." When he bent to kiss me, he murmured, "I'll message you."

"You'd better." I gave him a beaming smile, because I couldn't help myself. He made me feel foolishly happy.

He'd barely left when my phone beeped. When I read the message, I laughed.

Miss me yet?

I typed a message back to Mason.

Who is this? Wait. It's the pizza delivery guy, right? I miss your delicious anchovies.

A moment later my phone beeped again.

I'll bring you all the pizza you want if you steal that hospital gown.

You should know that I can eat a lot of pizza.

And I have a moon rocket ready for launch.

Mom was watching me from the foot of the bed with her arms folded. "Are you two dating?" she demanded.

I turned my smile onto her. "You know what? I think we might be."

Even the sharp, angry crack of her candy couldn't dampen my glow.

Chapter Twenty-Five

Mason

As I'd officially stepped back from the surveillance operation, I was trying to steer clear. But Asher's spare bedroom was still in use by the local team, and when I got home from the hospital I saw the DEA agent who Griffin had sent to replace me was there, so I pulled him aside for a status report.

"All we know for sure is that Santino's going to bring a shipment from Mexico, hidden in a vehicle that'll come through the Tijuana border crossing," he said. "His cousin installs secret compartments into cars."

"Nothing like keeping business in the family."

He grunted agreement. "There are a few possible couriers we're looking into. Four guys who've worked for Santino for years. Faith, the office manager, who could be faking her injury. And a couple of others, including some new girl Santino's roped in. The team watching his office says she seems green. Santino might use her because she's less likely to get searched at the border. Or she might be too much of a risk. We're not sure yet."

"Where will you intercept?'

"Santino will have the courier bring the shipment to his house. Frankie should be on hand, wanting to get paid. Once Santino's tested the product, he'll give it to his distributors and we're hoping they'll be there too. Time it right, and we should be able to bring them all down at once."

I grinned. "All tied up with a neat bow."

"We're expecting it to happen soon, and we could use your help. Could be a dozen or so armed men in the house. We're planning to have the same number, but one more on our side wouldn't be unwelcome."

"I've been ordered to stay out of sight. But I'll be armed and ready, watching from here." I motioned to the window. "If it looks like you need me, I won't hesitate." To hell with Griffin's order. If it came to a shootout, there was no way I'd stand back and watch cops die.

"We're hoping it'll be an easy bust. A blood bath wouldn't be Santino's style. He's white collar. Doesn't like getting his hands dirty."

I nodded, agreeing with his assessment. "Frankie's the wild card. He's been around a long time and isn't as stupid as he seems. But his ego's bigger than his brain, and he's been taking too much of his own product. Few months ago he shot his way out of a meeting that went sour, and he's starting to believe he's bulletproof."

"You've been doing your research."

"With him, it's personal. I knew him years ago. Been waiting a long time to see him go down."

When Mom took me and my brothers to Mexico, at first things hadn't been so bad. Mom had rented an apartment and had some casual work at a restaurant, where she hooked up with a chef who turned out to be a positive influence. Though we were barely scraping by and Mom's earnings were so low we couldn't afford much in the way of food, Mom's boyfriend would cook us a lavish meal each week on his night off. My brothers learned a trick they used to hustle a few dollars from tourists. And when we were really hungry and Mom was working late, I'd creep out to steal food and money.

If only Mom's moods weren't so unpredictable, everything might have carried on like that and been okay. But after she blew up at her boyfriend once too often, he walked out for good.

Then Mom had met Frankie. She started spending time at his place, getting high. His drugs drove our already unstable mother over the edge, and things had eventually hit rock bottom when she locked Kade, Asher, and me inside the apartment and didn't come back. After three days, Asher had managed to get us out, but he'd broken his arm doing it.

And by then they'd found Mom's body, a needle still stuck in her vein.

"Frankie has a lot to answer for," I said, my voice almost a growl.

The agent nodded as if he understood. "We'll get him."

How's your head? I messaged Carlotta before heading to Dad's place. *Are you resting?*

Going to bed. Come over and tuck me in?

Don't tempt me. Going to Dad's for dinner. I'll think of you right next door.

You could climb in my window.

If I were still sixteen, I'd jump at the idea. Even now, it was far more tempting than it should be.

What are you wearing? Maybe it was a juvenile question,

but if her answer was 'Spock panties and a hospital gown', she might find me at her window whether she was being serious or not.

Nothing but an alluring smile.

I groaned aloud. She was killing me. I had to change the subject before I really did skip dinner and risk the wrath of Trixie by barging my way in.

What are you doing tomorrow? It wasn't until after I hit Send that I thought better of arranging anything for the next couple of days. Bad idea to be in the middle of something I couldn't slip away from when the team swooped on Santino's house to make arrests.

But once Santino and Frankie were in custody, Griffin would expect me in Houston. Carlotta and I didn't have much time left.

My phone dinged. *I promised to work tomorrow. Like God, I only had one day to rest. Though I'm pretty sure He usually works longer hours than I do.*

I thought for a moment before replying.

I'd like to take you somewhere special on Monday night.

On a date? Will you pick me up? Should I dress up? Will you wear a cute bow tie and promise Mom you'll have me home by ten?

I smiled as I typed my reply. *Yes. Yes. Yes. No.*

It could well be our last night together. I'd wine and dine her, and give us both a night to remember forever.

If only I could visit her tonight. Knowing she was so close was a unique kind of torture. Still, it was great to see Kade again.

My brother met me just inside my father's front door and grabbed me in a bear hug. Though Kade was only a few minutes younger than Asher, I thought of him as the baby of the family.

Those two were about as far from identical as it was possible to get. Asher was dark, and Kade was light. Asher was serious, Kade was a prankster. Asher rarely showed what he was feeling, while Kade had the kind of infectious laugh it was impossible not to like.

I suspected the success of his TV cooking shows might owe more to Kade's easy charm than his culinary abilities. Although his culinary abilities *were* impressive.

"What's that smell?" I sniffed the air and my stomach rumbled in appreciation.

Kade dropped his voice. "I made a vegan dinner. Don't tell Dad. If nobody says anything, he'll think he's eating meat."

"Good luck with that. Dad's never met a vegetable he didn't hate on sight."

"That's because he hasn't tried them the way I cook them. I bet I can turn him into a super fan."

"I'll take that bet. If Dad doesn't clean his plate, you lose. Which means you'll have to make me a mushroom omelet for breakfast." I stuck out my hand, challenging him to shake on the deal. Kade's offer of a bet obviously hadn't been serious, but my brother never turned down a challenge and I had a serious craving for one of his world-famous mushroom omelets.

Sure enough, he shook my hand with a grin. "And if I win?"

"You won't win. I've been stocking Dad's freezer with healthy food, and he refuses to eat it. There's no way he'll finish a vegan meal."

My brother cocked his head, a mischievous smile playing on his lips. Not that Kade had any other kind of smile. He liked cooking up mischief even more than meals, and for a professional chef, that was saying a lot.

"If Dad eats his spaghetti, I want to hear about Carlotta Watson."

I blinked. "Excuse me?"

"Asher told me you've been seeing her."

"Never thought Asher was a gossip."

"You're the one who suggested the wager, and that's my price. I want every indelicate detail." He clapped me on the back. "Now come in and have a beer."

When we went into Dad's small dining room, Asher and Dad were sitting at the table. Kade took the seat next to Asher, and they both sipped their beers in unison. They may not look the same, but there were odd moments when their mannerisms matched.

"How's your surveillance going, Mason?" asked Kade. "Your team close to bagging the bad guys?"

I looked at Asher, aware that he was anxious to be rid of Santino, even if he wouldn't tell me why. "The local team expect the shipment to arrive in the next day or two, and they're getting ready to move in."

"Good to see you doing something for your mother," said Dad approvingly. I'd told him the bare minimum about why I was in San Dante, but he'd been enthusiastic when I'd mentioned I planned to arrest the dealer who'd sold drugs to Mom.

"Some kind of justice," agreed Kade. If I didn't know him so well, I might not have noticed the way his jaw tightened. But whenever our mother's name came up, Kade's normally easy-going nature grew a hard edge. He'd suffered most in Mexico, because Mom had singled him out for special treatment. He'd been her baby, but only when she was able to be a mother. Her neglect had hit him hardest.

And what had I done to help him?

I grabbed a beer and took a seat at the table, cutting off that train of thought. Going through all the things I should have done differently was pointless. While we were together, I just wanted to enjoy the company of my brothers.

"A toast to Mom." Asher lifted his beer bottle, his piercing gaze meeting mine as though he knew exactly what I was thinking. "In spite of her difficulties, I like to believe she tried to do the best she could. And I know for sure that the rest of us did."

"To Mom." We lifted our beer bottles, echoing the toast before we drank.

"Tell me about your TV show," Dad said to Kade. "Have you met anyone famous?"

"Kade's the famous one," said Asher, before Kade could reply. "He has fans who wait outside the studio door, lining up for his autograph."

"How do you know?" I asked.

"I visited him on set a few weeks ago. He was mobbed when he left the studio, and I had to stand back or risk being crushed."

Kade slung his arm over the back of his chair. "Ignore him, he's exaggerating. And to answer your question, Dad, I've met a few celebrities. Who do you want to know about?"

They talked about famous people for a while, then Kade got up to serve the meal.

"Spaghetti and meatballs," he said, putting steaming plates in front of each of us. "And there's salad for on the side."

Dad curled his lip at the salad, but dug into the spaghetti with enthusiasm. I had plenty of both. The spaghetti sauce was melt-in-the-mouth delicious, with plenty of garlic and spices.

"Do you like it, Dad?" asked Kade, giving me a pointed look.

"Delicious," Dad said with his mouth full. "What's this meat? Beef or lamb?"

"Jackfruit?" asked Asher. "Or some kind of mushroom and lentil mix?"

Kade shot him a glare, giving his head a small shake.

"What's that? This doesn't have vegetables in it, does it?" Dad peered down suspiciously.

"Vegetables can taste good," said Kade. "You might be surprised."

Dad snorted. "I know how vegetables taste." He took another big mouthful of spaghetti.

Kade flashed me his mischievous grin. "So, Mason. You promised to tell me all about your dates with Carlotta Watson."

Dad choked on his food. He coughed and spluttered, pounded his chest, then drank some water. When he could talk again he growled, "I told you to keep away from the Watsons. The whole family's unhinged."

"Be nice, Dad," I warned.

"Don't leave any details out." Kade put both elbows on the table, leaning in. "Is Carlotta still cute?"

"Cute?" I shook my head. "Gorgeous. And remember how funny she used to be? Times that by ten. Or more."

"What does she do for a job?"

"Empowering women. Helping girls feel good about themselves." I heard the pride in my voice, but couldn't manage to tone it down. "And I watched her direct a group of kids at the Spotlight Theater. She was incredible."

Kade and Asher exchanged a pointed glance.

"See," said Asher. "He's a goner."

"You were right," agreed Kade. "One of our own has fallen."

"When he talks about her, he gets puppy eyes."

"I wouldn't have believed it if I hadn't seen it for myself."

I put down my fork so I could give my full attention to glaring at them. "There's nothing the least bit puppyish about my eyes."

Kade whimpered like a dog, and Asher choked on a suppressed laugh.

"Stop," I ordered. "You think you're funny, but you're not."

"Bad dog," muttered Kade, and my brothers both pinched their lips together, their eyes dancing.

I sighed. "Okay, get it out of your systems. Let me know when you're finished."

"Don't get embarrassed. It's perfectly natural to look pathetic when you're head over heels." Kade reached over to pile more salad onto his plate.

Asher nodded. "That's right. Don't feel bad for making a fool of yourself."

"I can't be head over heels," I pointed out. "With my job, I can't even have a girlfriend."

"Good," growled Dad. "Because you're not dating the Watson girl. I won't allow it."

"You won't *allow* it?" I let out a disbelieving laugh. "You don't get a say."

"There are billions of other girls in the world. Pick one."

"You just made me want to date her." I wagged my fork at him. "If we end up getting married, it'll be thanks to you. Because you tried to forbid it."

Dad's face was turning red. "There's no way you're marrying a Watson. I won't be related to that harpy next door."

"Keep talking, Dad. You'll be seated next to Trixie at our wedding. You'll have to thank her in your speech."

"I'll do no such thing!"

"Our families will spend every holiday together. And if we have a daughter, we'll name her Trixie. Your granddaughter will be Trixie Watson-Lennox. A beautiful meld of our two happy families."

"Okay, stop it, Mason." Kade raised his hands with a laugh. "You're going to give Dad a heart attack for real. Tell him you're joking."

"That would help," Asher said. "Only Mason's not joking."

I opened my mouth to tell Asher he was wrong. I'd just been biting back against Dad's stubbornness, winding him up because there was no way I could get serious about Carlotta, even if I wanted to.

But the words wouldn't come out.

All the things I'd said to provoke Dad? Maybe I was starting to resent the fact I couldn't have them. My time with Carlotta was about to run out, and soon there'd be no more funny text messages, no more hospital gowns, or crazy photographs, or horizontal kisses. No more moon rockets, or peanut butter ice cream, or Chuck Norris jokes, or beautiful almond-colored eyes that always looked like they were smiling.

Asher was right. I was head over heels for Carlotta.

But I couldn't have her. Not if I went back to Houston. And if I didn't go to Houston, I couldn't bring down Diamond. However many people Diamond hurt and killed, I'd always know I could have stopped it. I could have saved those lives.

"You'd better be joking," growled Dad. "I won't have anything to do with the Watsons, and neither will you."

My anger rose along with my frustration, and I narrowed my eyes at Dad. "Trixie told me you put all the blame on her for your affair. Is that true?"

His mouth opened and closed a couple of times before he managed to form words. "It was all the fault of that harpy!"

"Take responsibility, Dad. You owe her an apology."

"Over my dead body."

Kade frowned. "Not very gentlemanly."

"At least end your feud with her," said Asher.

Dad glared around at the three of us. "Oh, so you're all against me now, is that it? You're going to take her side?"

"If you treated her badly, you should admit it and make amends," I told him.

"Never."

I opened my mouth to argue, but Kade the peacemaker spoke first.

"Let's change the subject. We've made our point, and now it's up to Dad to do the right thing."

"I refuse to apologize to that—"

"Dad, did you know there isn't any meat in the meatballs?" Asher interrupted.

"What?" Dad dropped his fork, his face jerking down to his plate.

Kade gave an exasperated huff. "Don't listen to Asher. What else would I have put in the meatballs? Soylent Green?"

"Soylent what?" Dad's hairy eyebrows dove together. "Is that a type of broccoli? Did you know some of the new genetically modified foods are being designed for remote brain manipulation?" He only had a small amount of spaghetti left, and he peered suspiciously at it, as though it might start giving him orders.

I took a breath, forcing my muscles to relax and pushing my anger away. Kade was right. I couldn't force Dad to do the right thing, it was up to him.

Asher dished more spaghetti onto his plate, then turned to Kade. "When are you going back to LA?"

"On Tuesday. It's just a flying visit, unfortunately."

"I'll probably be leaving around the same time," I said.

"That quickly?" Kade frowned. "I thought you were taking more time off."

"Got a call from the chief. He wants me back right away."

"How long will you be in Houston this time?"

"Maybe a year or so."

Kade exchanged a glance with Asher, their dismay obvious. They knew my work was dangerous. But if they had any idea how bad my next assignment would be, they'd probably refuse to let me go.

A year with Diamond. It would be an eternity.

Could I ask Carlotta to wait for me? Or would that make the torture worse?

"We'll miss you," said Dad, who didn't seem to have realized I was going back into a dangerous situation. Though he claimed to have unraveled some of the world's most intricate and sinister conspiracies, he had only the vaguest idea of what I'd been doing all these years in Houston.

Arranging his knife and fork together on his empty plate, Dad leaned back with a sigh, one hand on his stomach. "Nice meatballs, Kade. I'm so full I couldn't eat another bite. Unless you made something sweet?"

"Homemade chocolates." Kade got up to grab a bowl out of the fridge and after the four of us devoured the delicious treats, Asher and I moved into the kitchen to do the dishes. We tried to ban Kade from helping, but keeping him out of the kitchen was all but impossible. Apparently there were specific ways pots should be cleaned, and Asher and I always did it wrong.

There was really only room in the kitchen for one large male at a time, so the three of us jostled for space, elbowing each other and getting in each other's way. If Kade hadn't been clowning around, making Asher and I laugh, I would have thrown in the dishtowel and joined Dad who was reclining at the table with his hands folded over his stomach and his head starting to nod.

Damn, I was going to miss this.

I'd never enjoyed being back in San Dante anywhere near as much as I had this time. Mostly thanks to Carlotta, but there was nothing like spending time with my family. Listening to Kade's antics and Asher's dry humor, I wished I could freeze time. And that Carlotta could be here to join in. She'd love the way my brothers joked around. She'd fit right in, and no doubt have them in stitches.

My phone rang. A call from the agent who'd replaced me in the surveillance operation.

"We just intercepted a call from a possible courier," the agent said. "There's a good chance the shipment will arrive tomorrow morning. Thought I should warn you so you can stick close."

I swallowed a sudden hard lump of disappointment. Who'd have thought I'd ever take Frankie's imminent arrest as bad news? But the sooner it happened, the sooner I'd have to leave. And there was nothing I wanted more in that moment but to stay in San Dante.

"You okay?" asked Asher, his gaze as sharp as ever.

I took a moment before I answered. "Looks like the arrest could happen tomorrow."

"Can I be there?" Kade sounded eager. "I've never watched drug dealers get arrested before."

"Nope." I shoved my phone into my pocket.

"It's my house, so I get to watch it happen," said Asher.

"Neither of you will go anywhere near it," I told them.

Asher looked at Kade. "You want to hang out at my place tomorrow? We could remain legally inside our lawful place of residence, like the law-abiding citizens we are."

Kade made both hands into guns and thrust them into invisible holsters. "Hell yeah, I'm ready to be law-abiding."

I shook my head at them both, but I knew what they were really doing. After taking the call, I must have looked like my best friend had just died. Now I was too busy rolling my eyes at them to be depressed.

But as much as I appreciated their efforts to cheer me up, I needed a more permanent solution. Taking my phone back out of my pocket, I studied it for a moment, hesitating over whether I was doing the right thing.

Then I made up my mind.

"I need to make a call," I said, heading outside onto Dad's back porch. The night air was crisp, and from the porch I could see the Watson's house and imagine what Carlotta might be doing. She was probably in bed. Maybe she was reading, or watching a show. She could be sleeping.

I wanted to be lying beside her, to know what she looked like when she was asleep. To kiss her awake, and see her smile. To tell her I couldn't stop thinking about her.

I dialed Griffin's number and he answered on the second ring.

"It's me," I said. "I'm not coming back."

"Lennox? What are you talking about?"

"I'm not coming back to Houston. I need more time to think things through. You promised me a few weeks off, and I'm taking them."

He was silent for a moment. Then, "What do you want? More pay? A fat bonus? Name it, and I'll make sure it's done."

"It's not about the money. I'm seeing someone and I'm

not going to suddenly disappear. If I could really have something with her, I need to know."

"This is about a *woman*? Fuck that, Lennox. This is our chance to bring Diamond down, and it needs to start now. You of all people should get how goddamn important that is."

"Sorry, Griffin. I'm not going to change my mind. I've given you six years, now you can give me some time. I need six weeks. Maybe longer. I need to decide whether I'll come back at all."

"You've got a week. That's it, Lennox. That's the most I can give you, and even that's too much. Seven days, then you get your ass back here."

"Six weeks. Then we'll see."

I hung up and smiled into the night. It really was a beautiful evening. Shame Dad's house didn't back onto the ocean like Asher's, because the moonlight on the water would be stunning tonight. And I had at least six more weeks to enjoy it.

When I went back inside, my brothers were sitting at the table with my father. I opened another beer, then took my seat. "Change of plan," I said. "I've decided not to go back to Houston right away. I'm sticking around for a while."

Asher lifted his beer, tilting it toward me. "Good news."

Grinning, Kade leaned forward to clap me on the back. "That's great, bro. What made you decide to stay?"

"I decided someone else can save the world for few weeks. And I have a date with Carlotta on Monday night. Don't want to miss it." I took a sip of my beer, trying to hide my smile. But it felt like I'd opened the door on a whole new future.

I hadn't felt so good in a very long time. Suddenly, anything was possible.

Chapter Twenty-Six

Carlotta

My twenty-four hours of doctor-prescribed rest was officially behind me, and I was driving a metallic-blue Porsche SUV up the Interstate at a little over the speed limit with the window down and the music blaring.

Santino had been understanding about the delay in picking up his car, and I'd caught an early morning bus across the Mexican border. I dozed in my seat until I got to Tijuana, then followed Santino's instructions to the auto paint shop where I found Santino's newly-painted Porsche, just as he'd promised.

Before getting in, I checked the trunk and back seat, doing a careful search to make sure the car was totally empty.

Then I shook my head at myself. My brain had definitely been warped from being fed so many of Mom's fantasies. I needed to get her out of my brain and plant myself in the real world where businessmen weren't gangsters or smugglers, and there was no reason to be suspicious.

Santino's car had a delicious new car smell of leather, rubber, and money. The dashboard was silver, with cool, shiny dials and a speedo that went way beyond what my Toyota could only dream of. The black leather seats were trimmed with red, and the steering wheel had flaps for changing gears.

When I'd started the car I couldn't help the smile that crept over my face. When would I get another chance to drive a Porsche? May as well enjoy it.

I hadn't thought it would take long to get back to San Dante, but there were plenty of cars waiting to cross the border, so I played music and warbled along to sappy love songs for hours. I couldn't even pass the time by sexting Mason. Even if sending messages while driving wasn't illegal, my phone's battery was dying.

Besides, I was worried. My plan to keep Mason behind a wall of detachment had clearly failed. As much as I kept reminding myself that he was about to dump me to head back to Houston, I couldn't stop thinking about him, or wanting to message him, or wishing I were with him.

How come the man who was exactly wrong for me could feel exactly right?

When I finally made it through the border, I opened the car up on the freeway, trying to leave my troubling thoughts behind.

I couldn't stand the thought that Mason would soon be leaving, and had said he wouldn't see me again. Surely he hadn't meant *never*. If I visited him in Houston, there was no way he wouldn't be able to take a few hours off work, was there?

Or maybe I could stop myself trailing after Mason like a love-sick fool by booking myself into some sort of detox.

There might be an aversion therapy that could help. Like if I pricked myself with pins every time I thought about him.

Only I'd be a walking pincushion.

And with the amount of aversion therapy I'd need, there probably weren't even that many pins in the world.

At least the engine's throaty roar was a distraction. If I wasn't careful, Santino's Porsche would ruin me for my Toyota, and I'd never be happy driving under the speed limit again.

With San Diego behind me, it was an easy drive to San Dante. As I pulled into Santino's driveway, his garage door rolled up. A moment later, Santino appeared at the door, directing me to park the car inside. My legs were stiff from sitting for so long, so I got out slowly.

Santino was all smiles. "You made it."

"Lovely car." I handed him the keys. "I may have driven it just a little over the speed limit, but I couldn't resist."

"Car like this, it'd be a crime not to open it up."

"That's what I told the cop who pulled me over." I grinned to let him know I was joking, but he still gave me a weird sideways look, as though he didn't find it funny.

A big, blond man appeared through the door that connected the house with the garage. He was heavy set, and wearing a black polo with a thick gold necklace over it like a Russian mobster. Santino didn't introduce me, and the mobster went straight past me and opened the car's trunk. Which was weird, seeing as I'd made sure it was empty.

"Come in. I'll pour you a glass of champagne." Santino walked me into the house and down the hallway. "We're celebrating."

"What's the occasion?"

"A very lucrative business deal."

We reached the living room and my heart sank. Four men I didn't recognize were sitting around drinking. And Frankie, the bumbaclot from the party, was with them, holding a full glass of something that looked like whisky.

"Hi, baby. It's nice to see you again." Frankie's smile looked like a creepy shark.

"Oh no." I tried to back away, but I stepped into Santino and he caught my arms.

"It's okay, Carlotta," murmured Santino into my ear from behind me. "Frankie will be nice. He'll even apologize for the rude way he treated you at my party."

"I just remembered something urgent I need to do somewhere else," I twisted out of Santino's grip. "Anywhere but here."

"But baby, I still want that dinner at Pierre's." Frankie got up from the couch. "Loosen up and we can have some fun."

"Kicking you in the nuts would be fun."

Santino stepped between us, holding up both hands to get Frankie to step back. "Carlotta's good for business, Frankie. She delivered my car safely, and with Faith out of action I need her. So back off."

Frankie scowled. "Back off? You don't get to tell me that. We're partners, remember?"

"Yeah, we're partners. Which means you need Carlotta too."

I swallowed hard. They needed me? But all I'd done was pick up Santino's car.

Unless that wasn't all I'd done.

"We're good," interrupted a man's voice. I turned to see the mobster coming back in from the garage. In spite of the way he looked, he didn't have a sinister Russian accent.

Santino smiled. "See?" he said to Frankie. "We're good. That's all that matters." He turned to me and pulled an enormous wad of bills out of his pocket. "Thank you for your work today, Carlotta. Here's that bonus I promised you." He peeled off a couple of Benjamins and offered them to me.

I stared at the thick roll of notes still in his hand. Would a legitimate businessman carry that much cash? My heart was beating too fast and I was getting a terrible feeling. What if there was something illegal hidden in the car and I'd just transported it over the border?

But no, that had to be Mom's voice in my head. In real life, I didn't work for criminals. The sick feeling in my stomach was thanks to my over-stimulated imagination.

Still, I couldn't force myself to reach for the money. If I didn't take it, I definitely hadn't done anything wrong. Right?

"Keep the bonus," I said. "I don't think I want to work for you—"

A loud crash made me jump. The front door flew open and men poured into the hallway. I froze, gaping at them. Then I saw their guns.

"Police," yelled one of the men. "Nobody move."

Too late. I was already launching myself at the floor.

As I hit the ground, a loud crack rang out, like a gunshot. No, it wasn't *like* a gunshot. That *was* a gunshot.

I wriggled like a fish, pushing myself across the floor as I frantically searched for something to hide behind. But I was at the entrance to Santino's minimalist living room and there wasn't so much as a hat stand within scrambling distance.

More gunshots cracked, impossibly loud.

Raw, sharp fear flooded through me. I covered my

head with my hands, flattening myself against the floor, willing my body to melt into the floorboards.

Heavy boots thundered across the floor. Men were shouting, ordering Santino and his friends to put their hands up and their guns down.

Someone was cursing loudly, stringing together rude words and spitting them with pure venom. It sounded like Frankie.

A shout rang out over the top of the noise. "Clear at the front!"

"Clear at the back," shouted someone else, his voice muffled.

"Hands above your head, lady," growled a loud voice from just above me. "Take it slow."

I lifted my head and looked into the barrel of a gun. My limbs turned to water. I was weak and shaky. My hands trembled as I lifted them awkwardly into the air, staying put on my stomach.

The officer grabbed one of my wrists and jerked it roughly behind my back. Cold hard metal clamped around my wrist, then he yanked the other hand down too.

He pulled me up onto my feet, and I saw Frankie, Santino, and a whole lot of other men were on their knees with their hands also handcuffed behind their backs. There were far more of them than I'd realized were in the house.

It had seemed like dozens of cops had streamed in, but my terrified brain must have conjured some of them, because there were only about ten cops in the living room standing over Santino and his friends. Still, the place was full.

"What's going on?" I asked. My voice was hoarse and raspy, and I was trembling. My legs felt too weak to support me.

"You're under arrest," growled the policeman.

"I haven't done anything, I swear. I just work for him."
Talking was an effort.

"You admit working for him?"

"I don't do anything illegal. Just some office work and
picking up soap ducks."

"Picking up what?"

Before I could answer, the front door flew open and a
big man burst in, his boots thundering over the floor.
"Carlotta! What the hell are you doing here?"

My jaw dropped and I gaped at the man, sure my eyes
had to be playing tricks. Mason was here? Mason was
wearing a bulky bulletproof vest and carrying a gun?

Mason was a cop?

He turned to the officer who'd cuffed me. "What's she
doing here?"

"She's the courier."

Mason's eyes widened, then he drilled a thunderous
frown into me. "You're the *courier*? You've been trafficking
drugs?"

I tried to answer, but no words came out. This was why
Mason was in San Dante. He wasn't a bodyguard. He'd
been lying to me.

A wave of dizziness made me sag. Was this even real?
Could I be lost in one of Mom's fantasies? Was I having
some kind of hallucination?

"How the hell did you get mixed up with that
scumbag?" Mason sounded angry. Spots of red had
formed on his cheeks.

My breath hitched. The handcuffs were hurting my
wrists and the cop was gripping my arm too hard, his
rough fingers digging into my flesh. Turning my shoulder, I
tried to show Mason that my hands were cuffed behind my
back.

"Please, get me out of here," I begged.

He hesitated for a moment, and I could read his expression like one of Mom's books. He was weighing his feelings for me against his job.

The job he was married to. The job that meant everything to him.

A muscle ticked in his jaw and his eyes darkened with regret. "I wish it were that easy."

Something closed in my chest like a door slamming shut.

The cop's fingers dug harder into my arm. "I'm taking you to the station." He tugged me forward, dragging me toward the door. "You're being charged with trafficking narcotics. Do you understand?"

I couldn't answer. I was too busy trying to keep myself upright on legs that had turned to water.

Chapter Twenty-Seven

Carlotta

Being in jail was nothing like I'd expected.

Not that I'd actually expected to do time. But if I'd ever wondered what it might be like behind bars, I wouldn't have guessed how endless the hours would seem.

If I had a tin cup, I'd rattle it against the bars. If I had a ball, I'd throw it against the wall to wile the long, slow day away.

Last night I hadn't even bothered to close my eyes. All I did was count the cracks in the cold, gray ceiling. And this morning I was still counting them. In jail, it was too bright and loud to sleep. The stench of the toilet was only slightly more offensive than my thin mattress and blanket, and my cellmate snored.

I'd never imagined I could be so miserable.

Somehow I hadn't run out of tears yet. If a regular human body usually consisted of eighty percent water, my body must have been down to at least half that.

After counting every ceiling crack a million times over, I started to sing. There was only one song that suited this place: *The Folsom Prison Blues*. Only I changed the lyrics.

"*...I killed a girl in lockup. Because she set me up.*"

"Enough," groaned my cellmate, putting her hands over her ears. "Would you stop already?"

I sat up and looked over at her. All this time I'd assumed if I ever went to jail, the scariest part would be becoming someone's prison bitch and being threatened with a shanking. But I was so angry with my cellmate, she was the one who should be afraid. She should count herself lucky I had no idea how to make a shank.

"I didn't set you up," Faith said petulantly. "Blame Santino."

"Oh, I do blame Santino. He's mostly at fault, but you deserve your share." I put on a falsetto voice, mimicking the way she spoke. "Just pick up some ugly raccoon balls and soap ducks that smell like puke, Carlotta. Nothing illegal going on here, Carlotta."

"I had bills to pay." Faith sounded defensive. "And I didn't know how big the operation was. I thought they were only bringing in a small amount of drugs."

"Oh well, in that case, I'll only shank you a little bit."

Faith's sarcasm detector must have been broken, because she looked hopeful. "You get it, right? It was easy money."

"Easy?" I let out a bitter laugh. "You think this is easy?"

She let out a groan and rolled over onto her back. "How much time do you think they'll give us?" Without gel, her hair flopped over her eyes. And they'd made her take out her piercings. She looked younger and more vulnerable than when we'd worked together, and I felt a sudden pang of sympathy for her.

But unlike me, she'd known what she was doing.

"Drug traffickers get life," I snapped.

"Please, no. That can't happen." She closed her eyes. "Can you imagine doing life in jail? It's been, what? Twenty-one hours? And they won't even let me have my phone. Being locked up is driving me crazy."

"It's only been twenty-one hours?" I let out a long sigh. "It feels like twenty-one years."

For at least two of those hours, I'd been in an interview room answering questions. I'd spent at least fifteen hours in tears. And for the entire twenty-one hours, there hadn't been a single sign of Mason.

In spite of the fact he'd let the policemen drag me away from Santino's without so much as a single protest, I'd still found myself hoping Mason would sweep in and rescue me. But that hope had slowly died. Though he'd said he couldn't resist helping a damsel in distress, it turned out he was no knight.

I was on my own.

And I'd been going over and over everything that had happened, remembering how Mason had mysteriously turned up outside Santino's the evening I went to his party and fell in the pool. Then Mason had shown up at my house the next day. In fact, he'd popped up over and over again. And when he'd asked all those questions about the night of the party, how had I not realized he was pumping me for information?

Had it all been a game to him? Was he using me to get to Santino and Frankie the whole time?

Once again, I was forced to go back through my past and adjust the way I remembered everything to line up with the facts instead of the lies I'd been fed. It felt even worse than when I'd found out about Mom's affair and saw my childhood in a whole new light.

All I'd wanted from Mason was honesty. But he hadn't just tricked me. He'd made me feel important. He'd made me believe he cared about me. Then he'd jerked reality out from under my feet, and made me doubt everything.

That was what hurt most of all.

Chapter Twenty-Eight

Mason

Griffin sounded angrier than I'd ever heard him.

"What the fuck happened, Lennox?" he growled. "I heard you're screwing one of the cartel's couriers, and you charged into the middle of the bust. Tell me it's not true."

My hands were fists, the phone clenched so tightly my knuckles were white. But I kept my voice calm, channeling Asher's level of cool. "It wasn't that bad. The targets were cuffed and on the ground. I stayed out of their line of sight." At least, I hoped so, but I couldn't be a hundred percent certain. If they'd seen me, my cover could have been blown, but at the time I hadn't cared.

"First you pass up a chance to bring down Diamond, and now this? You were my best agent. The golden fucking star of the agency. What's got into you?"

"I'm calling to offer you a deal. I'll come to Houston and bring down Diamond, however long it takes. And in return, the DA will drop all charges against Carlotta

Watson. She was the courier, but she had no idea there were drugs in the car. She was a patsy who didn't know what she was getting into. If her case went to court, the prosecutor would have their work cut out to get a conviction."

"You think I can convince the DA to let off a drug trafficker?"

"I know you can."

He was silent for a moment. When he spoke again, the anger was gone from his voice. "I'll need you to get your ass to Houston tomorrow morning."

"Promise me she'll walk free, and I'll catch an early flight."

I couldn't believe I was committing myself back into the nightmare of Houston. Months or years of constant lies, of looking over my shoulder, of becoming one of the scumbags. My stomach was full of bile. But I'd already spent hours on the phone with every big shot I knew, pulling strings, making promises, trying every other way I could think of to get Carlotta out of this mess. Griffin was my last chance.

"I'll see what I can do," he said.

"I'll be at the lockup in an hour. Make sure Carlotta's out by then so I can drive her home."

"Jeezus wept, it'll take more than an hour. You realize the fast talking I'll have to do?"

"I'll be there in an hour."

He huffed out a loud breath. "For fuck's sake, Lennox. I'll tell them to call you when they're letting her out."

"Tell them to make it quick."

"You'd better be in my office tomorrow morning, ready for briefing." Griffin hung up.

I found Asher and Kade sitting out on Asher's back deck, drinking sodas and talking.

My heart was hurting, but I grabbed a soda and sat down with them as though I didn't have a care in the world. I even managed to force a smile onto my face. This would be my last drink with my brothers. No point in spoiling it by making them worry.

Asher seemed lighter and more relaxed since the drug bust. Putting Santino behind bars had eased some weight from his shoulders. But he took one look at me and put his drink down.

"What's wrong?"

"What do you mean?" My forced smile faded.

Kade frowned. "Tell us what happened."

Should have known I couldn't hide anything from them.

"I'm going back to Houston in the morning." I stared out at the ocean, pretending to be fascinated by the surfers riding waves.

"For how long?" demanded Kade.

"I don't know. A year. Probably more. Maybe less, if I get a lucky break."

"I thought you'd decided to stay in San Dante," said Asher.

"I changed my mind."

"You cut a deal."

I said nothing. They'd been watching the arrest with me from the window when we saw Carlotta being pulled to her feet in handcuffs, right in the middle of it. I'd rushed over without a second thought. Funny how she was able to do that to me.

Kade rocked back on his chair. "I guess you had to agree to go back? If only you'd known Carlotta was working for those guys, you could have stopped her."

"Yeah," I said glumly. "I would have stopped her. Only that could have tipped off Santino to the fact we were watching him. And Frankie might not be behind bars right now." I pointed my soda bottle at Kade. "Remember how it felt when we were locked in the apartment and Mom didn't come home? Frankie was responsible for that." Then I swiveled the bottle toward Asher. "You broke your arm to get us out of there. Now Frankie won't get to screw up any more lives. He's in jail where he belongs."

"At what cost?" Asher frowned. "Now you have to sacrifice yourself again."

"I couldn't be more glad Frankie's going to jail," added Kade. "But you deserve to be happy. You shouldn't have to give that up."

"Going back to Houston will be good. My work's important, and I can do a lot of good there. Save some lives."

Kade's mouth twisted. "How can you work undercover when you're such a bad actor? It's obvious you don't want to go. Stop pretending."

"If you insist on going, at least ask Carlotta to wait for you," said Asher.

I shook my head, wiping condensation from the side of my soda bottle with intense concentration.

"Why not?" asked Kade. "After all, you're sacrificing yourself for her."

"You can't tell her anything." I glared at my brothers. "Promise me. Not a word."

"We won't," said Asher. "As long as you tell her how you feel about her before you go."

"I can't. That wouldn't be fair on her."

This operation was so dangerous, I might come back in a body bag. Not that I'd admit that to my brothers. And no matter how shitty it felt, I had to keep lying to Carlotta.

"Stop being stubborn, and just be honest with her," Kade said, as though it were really that easy.

I stared at the surfers, riding the waves without a care in the world. The setting sun was spectacular, the sky almost as beautiful as when Carlotta and I had sat on the beach and eaten ice cream after her rehearsal. My chest ached at the memory of licking ice cream from her cheek. The sensation of happiness had been so strong, I could still feel its echo.

I'd made a serious mistake trying to create perfect memories with Carlotta that I could take back to Houston. It had only made things harder. I had to stop thinking about her. Stop dreaming about her. Stop being reminded of her every damn time I saw a sunset, or heard a woman laugh, or smelled peanut butter. Because everything in the damn world seemed to make me think of her.

My phone rang and Griffin said, "They're letting her out now."

I didn't waste any time getting to the jail where Carlotta was being held. But when I pulled up outside, she was already walking out with her mother. Trixie had an arm around Carlotta, and with a jolt I realized it was the first time I'd ever seen her mother hug her.

Carlotta was pale, with dark circles under her eyes. She looked exhausted and miserable. Getting out of the car, my chest tightened so it was hard to breathe.

"What are you doing here?" snapped Trixie. "My daughter doesn't want to see you."

I ignored her, meeting Carlotta's gaze. "I need to talk to you. Please."

Carlotta had no reason to trust me, no reason to agree. My name would have been left out of any deal Griffin might have made, so she'd have no idea why the DA had decided to drop the charges and release her. As far as she knew, I was the asshole who'd walked away when she needed me most.

But maybe she saw the pain in my eyes, because she nodded and stepped away from her mother.

"Give us a moment, Mom."

In spite of her mother's angry protests, Carlotta followed me to a quieter spot that wasn't in the shadow of the large, depressing jail.

When I turned to face her, all I could say was, "I'm sorry."

She rubbed her bloodshot eyes. "Okay." Her tone was flat. Like she was too exhausted to care.

"I had no idea you were working for Santino."

"You're a cop."

"Sort of."

"Sort of?"

"I really do work as a bodyguard, but I also work for the DEA. The part about me being an agent is a secret. Nobody can know."

She closed her eyes for a moment, her expression pained. "I'm sick of secrets."

"I'm sorry," I said again, hating myself for what I was about to ask. "But I need you not to tell anyone. Not Natalie, or your mother, or anyone. Can you do that for me?"

"You're asking me to lie for you?"

"I'm asking you not to say anything."

She looked up at the sky, her hands twisting in front of her. "Mason, I'm tired. I just want to go home."

I had to touch her. More than anything, I ached to put my arms around her, pull her against me, and promise never to let anything bad happen to her again. Instead, I rested one hand lightly on her arm, so she could pull away if she needed to.

"If I'd known you were working for Santino, I would never have let this happen."

She stared down at my hand with a blank, detached look, as though it was something foreign and unwelcome, but she didn't care enough about it to push it off.

I took a breath, trying to stop my throat from closing. "I lied to you about my job. But nothing else was a lie. The way I feel about you is true. It's real. More real than anything I've ever felt."

Her eyes lifted to mine. They were glistening. She was fighting tears, but her expression was tight. As though she just wanted to curl up in a ball and cry herself to sleep.

"Carlotta," snapped her mother. "It's time to go."

"I have to leave for Houston in the morning," I said.

"What are you going to do in Houston?"

"I can't tell you."

"How long will you be gone?"

"I don't know."

"You still can't be straight with me? Even now?"

I wanted to ask her to wait for me. To tell her that I loved her, and I would give anything, do anything, to keep her safe. That I wished with all my heart we could be together.

But that wouldn't be fair. I couldn't pretend I was coming back for her when I might never be able to.

Still, it was impossible to fight my urge to hold her. Putting my arms around her, I drew her to me. Her body stiffened as I pressed my lips against her forehead, even as I closed my eyes so I would always remember the feel of her skin and the scent of her hair.

"Goodbye," I whispered.

And somehow I managed to let her go.

Chapter Twenty-Nine

Carlotta

The dictionary definition of stupidity had to be falling back in love with the guy who'd already taught me how bad heartbreak could feel.

But that's exactly what I'd gone and done. And now I wasn't just chewing on a crap sandwich, I was getting chunks of existential despair stuck in my teeth.

What made it worse was that I was back in my tiny studio apartment in LA, and someone in the next-door apartment was playing Wham at full volume. *Wake Me Up Before You Go Go* was pumping out so loudly, my lamp was trembling. It was annoyingly difficult to lie around feeling like my heart had caught fire and burned out the inside of my chest when *Wham* was cranked up.

The weird thing was, in spite of the fact I'd been caught in the middle of what felt horribly like one of the fantasies from my youth, for the first time in my life, I knew without a single doubt what was real.

My feelings for Mason were one hundred percent real. The ache in my heart wasn't a fantasy, or make-believe.

Fact. I loved Mason.

Fact. Mason had made me feel special and treated me like I was precious.

Fact. I missed him with an intense longing that was hard to bear.

Also a fact, he'd made it very clear he didn't want a relationship. He hadn't been entirely honest with me, and when it came down to it, he'd chosen his job over me. But even knowing that, the feelings I had for him weren't going away. They weren't even dimming.

I needed to talk to Nat.

When she answered her phone, I could hear the café's coffee machine hissing in the background.

"Hey," she said. "Are you listening to *Wham?*"

I rolled onto my back and tucked the hand not holding the phone under my head. "My neighbor is."

"Edward Lennox is playing *Wham?* Is that one of the ways he tortures your mother?"

"I'm not in San Dante. I'm back in LA." I glanced out of the window at my magnificent LA view, consisting of a metal roof and thirteen rusty air conditioning units.

"You're in LA?" Her voice rose. "You left without telling me?"

"I'm sorry. I got here the day before yesterday. I needed some alone time to get my head straight and the guy sub-letting my apartment had moved out, so when they let me out of jail, I bolted."

"The line's crackling and I thought you said they let you out of jail." She chuckled. "Funny, right? What did you really say?"

"You know how I was working for Santino? Well, it

turns out that him and that creep Frankie were part of a drug ring."

"What?"

"I only found out when I accidentally trafficked ten pounds of cocaine across the border."

"WHAT?!"

I winced, jerking the phone away from my ear. She'd almost deafened me. "I thought I was just delivering Santino's car. Then a bunch of cops showed up."

"You trafficked drugs and got arrested? You went to *jail?*"

"I spent a day and night in lockup before they dropped the charges. Thank goodness they believed me when I told them I had no idea about the drugs, or I'd be in serious trouble."

"Oh my God, Carlotta." Nat sounded breathless. "I can't believe this has been going on without me knowing."

"Sorry I didn't call you earlier. It's been a whirlwind."

"Please come back to San Dante. Life's so boring without you. You're the perfect best friend for a writer."

"I miss San Dante more than I ever thought I would. I especially miss you." I hesitated. "And weirdly, I kind of miss Mom. You think that means I've contracted some kind of brain disease?"

"I miss you too. But what about Mason? He must have flipped out when he found out you were in jail."

"Mason's back in Houston. His vacation's over."

"He's gone? What, for good?"

"He ended our relationship, but I'm not sure he really wanted to. When he said goodbye, he looked miserable." I hated not being able to tell her the whole truth about Mason being a DEA agent, and that he'd left me in the dark about whatever he was doing in Houston. Having to lie was almost as bad as being lied to, especially when I couldn't be honest with Nat.

"So you won't see him again?" she asked.

"I don't know. I think I'm in love with him."

"Wait. Stop. Are you telling me that since the last time we spoke, you've smuggled drugs, spent time in jail, gone back to LA, *and* fallen in love?"

"It's been a busy few days."

"You're not kidding. What the heck have *I* been doing with my life?"

"I wish none of it had ever happened. I might not even get to see Mason again."

"Houston isn't that far away. You could just go there and tell him how you feel."

"Maybe I'll call him. Even if our relationship's over, I could tell him I want to be friends. There could still be chance." Hope flickered in my chest.

"Are you going to stay in LA?"

"I'm not sure yet. I'm trying to get my old waitressing job back, because I don't know what else to do. To go back to San Dante, I'd need to sub-let my apartment again, or end my lease." I let out a sigh. "It's been so great having you as my best friend again, you know? I wish we could live in the same city."

"I'll always be your best friend, but yeah, I know what you mean. It's a lot more fun when we get to hang out together." A loud grinding sound started, probably the coffee machine at the café, and she raised her voice to talk over it. "At least your Instagram followers seem to like you again."

"But so far none of my sponsors have replied to my messages, so I'm not making any money."

"You're not going to do any more drug trafficking?"

I snorted. "Not if I can help it."

Muffled voices came through the line, then Nat said, "I'm really sorry, Lottie, I have to go. More customers have come in. Call you back later?"

"Sure."

"Love you." She hung up before I could tell her I loved her too.

Weird how I hadn't wanted to go back to San Dante, and now I didn't want to be in LA. After living in different cities for years, it was only natural Nat and I would grow apart. But now we were real best friends again, and talking to her about my broken heart was the best medicine there was.

And later, I'd probably call Mom to check in on her, which is something I would never have thought to do before. I couldn't help but cheer up a little as I imagined how surprised Mom would sound when I said I was just calling to say hi.

Cyndi Lauper's *Girls Just Wanna Have Fun* started playing at lamp-shaking volume, and I sang along, doing my best attempt at head banging while horizontal. I even threw the blankets off so I could wave my feet in the air. According to scientific studies, it's impossible not to sing along to Cyndi Lauper, and even in my heartbroken state I had no defense against science.

Then my phone dinged. One of my sponsors had replied to the message I'd sent them.

Dear Carlotta. Thank you for staying in touch. Please give me a call to discuss the promotion of our skin care range.

My breath caught.

They wanted me back?

Then I read the next sentence.

We'd like to schedule another naked shoot.

I sat up on the bed and dialed her number. The brand manager's name was Carol, and in contrast to the silent black hole my emails had been falling into since the gory duck photos, she greeted me warmly. But when she started to talk about doing a naked shoot, I cut her off.

"The thing is, I want to take different kinds of shots from now on," I said. "They'll still be funny, but I want to be more authentic, and I'll probably leave most of my clothes on."

"Oh?" She sounded surprised. "But your brand is—"

"My brand is changing. It's maturing. But if you stick with me, I think you'll like what I do next. Let me come up with some concepts, and you'll see for yourself."

She hesitated for a long time. "I'm sorry," she said finally. "We like what you were doing before the unfortunate duck incident. If that's not what you want to do now, we may need to rethink working with you again."

I took a breath, wondering if I was making a mistake. Reviving my Instagram career was all I'd wanted. But the entire point of what I did was to help other people feel good about themselves, and I could only do that on my own terms. Starting with not letting other people dictate which parts of my body I chose to show.

Besides, like Mason said, I had more than one superpower. I could design my future the way I wanted it. From now on, I was firmly in the director's chair, taking control of my life.

"That's your choice," I told Carol. "You'll see how my new brand evolves over the next few weeks. If you like what you see, please call me."

I hung up and dragged a hand through my tangled hair, taking a deep breath and getting mentally prepared. I had one more phone call to make. The most important call of all. This one would help me decide what happened next, where I lived, what I did. Because there was one thing I wanted more than anything, so if Mason said he was willing to talk in person, I was ready to get in my car and start driving.

I dialed Mason's number.

There was a click, then a recorded voice came on the line. *"The number you have called is no longer allocated."*

What?

With my stomach in knots, I hung up and dialed again, just in case there was some kind of mistake. But after trying a third time, I had to accept there was no mistake. The number had been disconnected.

Mason was gone.

Chapter Thirty

Carlotta: Eight Months Later

When I knocked on Asher's door, I wasn't even sure he still lived in the same house. After all, it had been eight months since I'd last seen or spoken to him. Not since I called him from LA to find out if there was a way I could contact Mason after finding out his phone had been disconnected.

But when the door opened, Asher was standing there, and he looked exactly the same. He was wearing black jeans and a gray shirt, and he was still startlingly handsome. He was leaner than Mason and his hair and eyes were darker, but the resemblance was strong.

"Hi, Carlotta." Asher greeted me without a flicker of surprise, almost as though he'd been expecting me. "I heard you'd moved back to San Dante."

"I arrived a few weeks ago, and I have an apartment here now." I gave him a rueful smile. "This place is like a small town the way gossip spreads. I should have figured you'd hear."

"Come in." He opened the door wider, stepping back, and I glimpsed someone else inside. A woman gazing curiously at me. Did Asher have a date?

"No, that's okay." I stayed where I was. "I just want to ask you something, and it'll only take a second."

"You're still looking for Mason." It wasn't a question, but I nodded anyway.

"Do you know how I could get a message to him?"

"I'm sorry. I still have no way to contact him. That hasn't changed."

A familiar chasm opened in my heart. "So you haven't heard anything at all? Nothing in eight months?"

"Nothing. I don't know what he's doing, or when he's coming back."

"Do you even know if he's alive?" The fear Mason could be dead had wormed its way into my brain one sleepless night a few months ago. As more and more time went by, that fear had taken root and grown. Though it sounded ridiculous to voice it out loud, like one of Mom's fantasies, I needed to know Mason was okay.

Asher stepped forward, letting the door swing shut behind him, and put a reassuring hand on my shoulder. "He's alive. I'd know if he wasn't." Though I'd always found it hard to tell what Asher was thinking, his voice was gentle and his eyes were soft. But my heart still lurched with dread. Asher hadn't scoffed at the question, and he wasn't acting like my fear was irrational. That had to be a bad sign.

But whether Mason was in danger or not, there wasn't a thing I could do about it.

Wiping my hand over my face, I resigned myself to the truth.

Asking Asher had been my last chance to find Mason.

My last dead end. Eight months since he'd vanished, and there was nothing left to try.

"Come in," said Asher. "I'll get you a glass of water."

"No. Thanks. I need to go." I got back into my car and drove to Nat's café.

It was time to face reality.

I took several deep breaths and gave myself a pep talk before going into Nat's. She was behind the counter scribbling in a notebook, and the café was deserted. She looked up when I walked in and gave me a smile.

"I thought you might be my new chef turning up to work," she said. "Good thing I don't have any customers, because he's two hours late."

I leaned against the counter. "That sucks. I'm sorry." After a series of bad chefs, Nat's latest one was by far the worst.

She moved to the coffee machine and started making me one without needing to ask. Just one of the many reasons I loved her.

"How are rehearsals going?" she asked.

In spite of the heaviness of my heart, I managed a smile. "So much fun. I love being a director. I just hope my first show isn't a total disaster."

Judy had called me when she decided to retire from the Spotlight Theater, and I'd jumped at the chance to replace her. Now I really did have the best job in the world, and I loved my small apartment a few streets from Nat's café. My sponsors were back, and I was posting messages of empowerment again, and doing it exactly the way I wanted.

In fact, my life would be pretty much perfect if I weren't pining after Mason.

"I'll come and see every performance," promised Nat

over the sound of the coffee machine. "I'll sit in the front row and cheer."

"You're the best. And guess what? I'm going on a date tonight."

Her eyes widened. "You are?"

"Mason's been gone a long time, and I don't know if he's ever coming back. He has no idea I have feelings for him, and maybe he doesn't feel the same way about me."

She handed me a coffee, her expression sympathetic. "Time to move on."

"Dating is the only way I'll ever get over him."

"Who are you going out with?"

"His name's Rex." I held up my phone to show her the picture on the dating app. The guy I'd picked was as far from Mason as it was possible to get. Slender, blond, and clean cut. No visible scars. A finance executive with the most unimaginative profile I could find. "We're meeting at that new French restaurant on Ocean Drive in a few hours."

"He looks nice. And I hear that restaurant has great food."

"I bought some new underwear, just in case."

"First date and you're buying underwear? Lucky Rex."

"And I bought some beer and wine, in case I decide to invite him back to my place for a nightcap to kick things off."

She blinked. "You're serious about this."

"Deadly serious. I'll do whatever it takes to get over Mason, and Rex could be my rebound guy."

"Rebound Rex?"

"Just what I need to mend my broken heart and set me on the road to recovery." I sipped Nat's delicious coffee with a sigh. "Although good coffee makes even the pain of a broken heart easier to bear."

"Rex is only one letter away from sex. Maybe it's a good omen?"

"I hope so. It's been so long since I had sex, I've forgotten which one of us gets tied up."

She laughed. "Don't ask me. The last time I went on a date was back when people thought flip phones were cool."

I was cautiously optimistic about the whole evening, but when I walked up to Rex at the restaurant that night and he stood to greet me, my heart sank. It wasn't that he was bad looking. He was quite handsome, but in a not-Mason kind of way. And he was too small. Not smaller than me, but only half Mason's size. His jaw wasn't square enough. And when he put out his hand to shake mine, his biceps didn't have their own zip code.

"Hi," he said with a toothy smile that was nothing like Mason's playful grin.

I smiled and said hello, trying to convince my rebellious brain to stop with the comparisons. Rex seemed nice enough. A good first step back into the world of dating.

"You're really in finance?" I asked as I sat at the table he'd reserved. "I know this is a weird question, but can you prove it?"

He looked startled. "I'm actually a Financial Analyst. I work for a bank, researching companies to determine whether they'd be a good lending risk."

"Is that interesting?"

He shrugged. "It pays the bills."

His answer placed him about as far from Mason being married to his job as I could ask for. But I wanted to be sure he was right for me.

"Do you have any unusual hobbies?"

"Not really. I have a modest investment portfolio and do a little share trading."

"Do you read fantasy stories?"

"I like biographies."

"Favorite TV show?"

"I just watched a fascinating documentary about the rise and fall of virtual currencies."

There was a glass of water waiting on the table, and I took a sip, trying to wrestle my feelings into submission.

Rex's answers were perfect. He seemed honest, and too rooted in the real world to lie or make up stories. He held down a steady, easily-verifiable job, and would probably retire early with a healthy 401K.

While Mason had been exactly wrong for me, Rex should be completely right. So why did I have an overwhelming urge to fake a sudden bout of diarrhea so I could take off?

"May I take your order?" The waiter was hovering over us.

Before Rex could answer, I said, "Please give us a minute or two." Then I turned back to Rex, searching for some way to increase my enthusiasm for him. I wanted my thighs to quiver and my insides to turn gooey like they used to for Mason, but so far they were refusing to cooperate.

"What's the most exciting or unusual thing that's ever happened to you?" I asked, a little desperately.

"I had a near-death experience."

"That sounds interesting." I leaned in hopefully. "Did you go toward the light and get told by a dead relative that it wasn't your time yet?"

"Oh, no. Nothing like that." He picked up his menu and ran his gaze down the options. "It was the middle of the night. I got out of bed to go to the bathroom and fell down the stairs. Could have died."

I took another sip of my water before forcing a smile.

"Great story. Hey, did you know that Death once had a near-Chuck Norris experience?"

He frowned, lifting his gaze back to me. "No. Is that a joke? I don't get it."

The waiter moved back to our table. "Would you like to order now?"

I gave the waiter a sad smile and shook my head. Rex wasn't going to be my rebound guy after all.

"I'm sorry, Rex." I made my tone as kind as possible. "I'm afraid I can't do this. It's not you, it's me. You seem really nice, and I wish I could enjoy eating dinner with you and get to know you, and more than anything I'd like to have sex, because it's been a really long time and I want to climb back on that horse and go for a very long ride. But someone broke my heart, and the truth is that I don't want to date you because you're not him. That's messed up, I know. I'm working on it. But I guess I'm not quite there yet."

"Oh. Well, thanks for being honest." He hesitated. "What was that you said about the sex thing?"

"That I want to have sex?"

"Did you mean with me, or…?"

"No. Sorry. That wasn't clear, was it?" I shook my head ruefully. "I'm sure you're a wonderful guy, Rex, and the perfect woman is out there for you. But I have to go now."

I left him in the restaurant and drove home with an empty stomach and an unbearably heavy feeling of despair.

Once back in my apartment, I took a shower, scrubbed my face clean of makeup, and put on the clothes I'd be sleeping in: a baggy old shirt with *I Only Speak Sarcasm* printed on it in faded letters, and a loose-fitting pair of cotton shorts with a large hole in the crotch where the stitching had unraveled. Then I climbed into bed. It was only nine o'clock and my hair was damp from the shower, but who cared? I was too depressed to bother drying my hair or staying awake.

I'd only just pulled the blankets over me when there was a knock on the door. I sat up and frowned. Who the hell would come over to see me at nine o'clock at night? Could it be Nat? Was she in some kind of trouble?

I padded to the door and cracked it open, peering out.

My heart stopped.

"Mason," I gasped, pulling the door all the way open.

Wearing dark jeans and a fitted T-shirt, he filled my doorway. His eyes were creased with worry lines and stubble darkened his ridiculously square jaw. His cheeks looked more shadowed than the last time I'd seen him, and his posture was tense, as though he was on edge. A nasty purple bruise bloomed above one eye.

"Hi Carlotta." His gaze ran over my hair. "You're wet."

Chapter Thirty-One

Mason

Carlotta's hair was damp and a little shorter than last time I'd seen her, and her face was pink as though she'd just washed it in scalding hot water. She was wearing a baggy, faded T-shirt, and shorts with loose threads hanging off them. I tried not to scan every inch of her like a voracious, desperate man, but after missing her every minute of every day, I sure felt like one.

She was even more beautiful than in my dreams. So beautiful, it hurt my heart to look at her.

"May I come in?" I forced my voice out around the lump in my throat.

Her expression was still shocked as she stepped back. She seemed lost for words.

Because I was afraid I was staring at her like some kind of ravenous animal, I forced my gaze away, scanning her apartment instead.

"I like your place." I tried to act normal, attempting to break the tension. "How long have you been here?" It was a small apartment, but she'd decorated in bright colors and I liked the tall palm in one corner. Her style was quirky but comfortable, just as I would have imagined.

"Where have you been?"

With relief I let my gaze snap back to her, drinking her in again. She was an oasis after an endless desert, and I wasn't sure how I'd ever get enough.

"In Houston."

"But I looked for you in Houston. I searched the phone directory. I called every Lennox in the city."

"I used a different name. I wasn't Mason Lennox there."

"Oh." She swallowed, and I could see what she was thinking. I was bringing more lies into her life, and I had no right to do that.

"What's this?" Searching for some way to change the subject, I picked up a feather boa that was draped over the couch.

"I'm directing *Chicago* at the Spotlight Theater."

"You're the director there now? Congratulations."

"Are you really here?" she asked softly, like she was still trying to process it.

"I'm here." I rubbed my hand over my rough chin, realizing I should have shaved. I'd had such a deep need to see her, I hadn't wanted to delay even a few extra minutes. But with my battered body and unshaven face, I'd brought a little of Houston into her home, and even that small amount was too much. The thought of that ugliness ever touching her was abhorrent.

"Are you all right?" Some of what I was feeling must have shown in my face, because she suddenly sounded concerned. "Sit down."

I sank onto her couch and ran my palms over my jeans. "How are you?"

"Better than you, I think."

She was right, but I could only give a faint nod. The last eight months had been more brutal than I could ever have imagined.

"You want a drink?" she asked. "I have beer."

She didn't like beer and I'd never seen her drink it. She was a wine drinker, so why did she have beer in her fridge?

There was only one reason I could think of.

She had a boyfriend.

"Yes. Please." Though the realization was a lance through the heart, I kept my voice steady and didn't let my pain show on my face. Of course she had a boyfriend. I'd been away for an eternity. It was probably a good thing she'd moved on. Maybe it would make it a little easier when I had to walk away.

She got the beer from the kitchen and handed it to me, then sat on the chair opposite me. She hadn't bothered with a drink for herself.

"You look tired," she said. "And you're hurt. You have bruises."

"I came here straight from the airport."

"Are you going to tell me what you've been doing?"

She was too calm. This wasn't going the way I'd expected. I'd thought she might shout at me, but she was very still.

In Houston, being able to tell what someone was thinking could mean the difference between life and death, and Carlotta had always been open with her emotions. But she seemed almost as blank as when I'd said goodbye to her outside the jail, before I'd left San Dante. I had no idea what was going through her mind.

I took a swig of the cold beer while I steeled myself for what I'd come here to say.

"When I left, I couldn't answer any of your questions

about what I was doing. But now my undercover work is finished. I still can't be totally open about that part of my life, because it might endanger other agents. But my part is done and I've come to tell you whatever you still want to know."

She flattened her palms on her bare thighs and stared down at them a moment, as though trying to sort through her thoughts. "You were pretending to be a bodyguard so you could get information about drug dealers?"

"I was a bodyguard for an evil scumbag. One of the worst. I was there to help put him behind bars, and my team managed to do it." I'd come here because I needed to tell her the truth, but now I was in front of her, the words were even harder to say than I'd expected. "The things I saw have changed me. Hardened me. I'm not the same man I was. I don't know if I'll ever be the same."

She deserved the truth, but it wasn't enough. How could I describe the constant jumpiness, or the certainty a shooter was waiting around every dark corner? Worse was how terrible sights had started to slide off me, as though cruelty had become normal and hell was a place I could feel at home.

She frowned. "What happened to your face?"

I put my beer on the coffee table and lifted one hand to the bruise above my eye. "The arrest got physical. I was forced to restrain someone." Then I dropped my hand to the twisted scar on my neck. "I lied to you about being in a car accident. This is a gunshot wound." I touched the scar on my forearm. "This was a stab wound." I lifted my shirt to show her the scar on my stomach. "Another stab wound. And a bullet also nicked my calf. That scar is barely noticeable."

Her eyes were wide. When she took a breath, it didn't seem steady. "Mason…" She broke off, and I had no idea what she had wanted to say. Her hands clenched on her thighs, forming fists.

I waited for her to keep talking. When she didn't, I said, "I'm done in Houston. Finished."

"What does that mean?"

I wanted to tell her that I loved her, but I'd left her for eight long months. She had a new life, one that didn't include me.

My jaw tightened as I fought a sudden need to hurt the man she was dating. With every cell in my body, I hated that he was the one who got to be with her.

But I forced my muscles to loosen. This wasn't Houston. Violence might have stained my soul black, but it had no place here.

When I spoke again, my voice was level. "I'll never work undercover again. I haven't decided what I'll do now, or where I'll go, but I wanted you to know how sorry I am that there were so many things I couldn't tell you. My biggest regret is that I had to lie to you. I wish I could have been honest, and things could have been different between us."

"I wish that too." Her voice was thick, and I saw unshed tears in her eyes, glimmering in the overhead light.

I stood up, furious with myself for hurting her again. Though I'd come to explain, I'd dragged in with me the pain and darkness I'd never be able to escape. It had been a mistake to bring it here. I'd been chasing a dream that had already slipped though my fingers.

"I need to go," I said.

"You can't." She stood up too. "Please, don't." Her tears were threatening to spill. "I've missed you Mason. More than anything, I want to trust you. But I don't want to be lied to anymore."

My heart was pounding. Hope had lit a faint spark in my chest, and I could barely stand the pain of it.

"Lying to you is the last thing I want to do." My voice came out rough. "So here's the only secret I have left." Unable to help myself, I curled my hands around her arms, finally touching her like I'd longed to do for eight endless, unbearable months. "My heart will always be yours, Carlotta. I'm not asking anything from you. I know it's too late for us. But I want you to know I love you."

Chapter Thirty-Two

Carlotta

My breath was trapped inside my lungs, which seemed to have forgotten how to exhale. "You what?" I rasped.

This was a different Mason to the one I knew. This Mason was wounded, and not just his body. He face held a dark seriousness that hadn't been there before. His eyes were troubled and my memory of his playful smile seemed like it must have belonged to someone else.

"I need to go," he said again, letting go of my arms. Striding to the door, he pulled it open and stepped outside. "Don't worry, I didn't come here to ask anything from you. You have a life that doesn't include—"

"I love you too."

My breath caught on the words. I could hardly believe I'd said them. Was this really happening or was it a dream? Could Mason really be in love with me?

He froze, his gaze fixed on mine. His brow was

furrowed and his expression unreadable. It was as though he were finding this as hard to comprehend as I was.

"You don't have to say that," he said slowly. "You don't owe me anything. If you heard something about why the charges against you were dropped, you need to understand that I never expected anything in return."

"You had the charges against me dropped?"

His frown deepened. "You didn't know?"

I shook my head, too overwhelmed to process what that could mean.

"So why did you say you love me?" His tone was so rough, he sounded angry.

A spark of fury flared into life inside me, burning hot, and I strode toward him with my fists clenched. "I'm saying I love you because I've spent the last eight months missing the hell out of you and wishing you'd never gone away." Stopping in front of him, I had a powerful urge to pummel my fists against his chest, and settled for a hard shove that barely made him sway. "For future reference, Mason you big dummy, when a woman says she loves you, she expects a totally different reaction."

His frown slowly softened. Then some of the darkness eased from his face. His eyes seemed to lighten and his lips pulled up. His smile wasn't exactly playful. But he was Mason again, the man I loved.

My anger softened along with his expression. When he let out a chuckle it sounded hesitant, like he'd all but forgotten how to do it. But warmth filled my chest and I found myself grinning back at him. My heart started dancing.

"You don't have a boyfriend?" he asked.

"Not unless you want to apply for the job."

His face was transforming like the best magic trick I'd

ever seen. Instead of barely suppressed pain, it was filling with something like wonder.

"You're still willing to take a chance on me?" he asked. "After everything I've told you?"

"That depends. Are you still married to your job?"

"Actually, I'm unemployed. I handed back my badge."

"Then I just have one more question."

Mason nodded, his shoulders going back as though he was bracing himself. "Ask me anything."

"Do you still have a moon rocket?"

He stared at me for a moment longer before the last of the darkness slipped away, vanishing from his face.

"I'm going to kiss you now." His voice had gone hoarse. "And I guess we'll find out."

"Do you want to come inside first?"

His face was already halfway to mine, but he paused and glanced around as though recognizing his surroundings for the first time. "What am I doing out here? Yes, I suppose I should come in first." I stepped back, and he moved back inside my small one-room apartment and shut the door behind him before putting his arms around me.

"Carlotta." He breathed my name as though it were a prayer. "I missed you every moment I was gone."

I pressed myself against his wide chest, pulling him closer. He smelled so good it made me dizzy. "Me too. But I need to know if we're at the kissing part now, because I don't think I can wait any longer."

A hint of playfulness in his smile made my heart soar. "That's exactly where we are."

Then his lips were on mine, first soft, then demanding and desperate. Mason always kissed me like he owned me, but this kiss was more than that. It was far deeper. He kissed me like I was a lighthouse guiding him through treacherous rocks. Like he'd been stumbling down a dark, dangerous path, and he'd finally glimpsed light.

He kissed me like he needed me more than life itself.

And I kissed him back the same way.

Somehow we made it to the bed, stumbling together with one mind. We fell onto it with me underneath him, still kissing as though we'd die if we had to stop.

With his weight on his hands, he lay over me, his large body pressing into me in a way that felt incredible and drove me crazy with frustration at the same time.

His lips lifted from mine, leaving me gasping with need. "I didn't want to make love to you before you knew everything about me." He kissed me again. "Not while I still had to lie to you about what I did."

"That's why we've never done more than kiss?"

Instead of answering, he pressed his lips back to mine. His mouth was as hot and demanding as his gaze. I wrapped my legs around his hips, and his hard length rubbed where I needed it.

That's when I realized the true benefit of having answered the door in my sleep clothes.

No. Underwear.

My thin cotton sleep shorts with the unraveled stitching in the crotch opened like the gates of heaven, allowing Mason's rough denim jeans to rub against my bare flesh. The sensation was intense, and when his tongue flicked inside my mouth as well, I just about exploded.

"Oh God," I panted. "Stop. I can't..."

"What's wrong? You okay?" His brow furrowed and his eyes travelled down my body, but I had my legs wrapped around him, clamping his hips to mine, and I wasn't about to let go.

"Feels amazing. Changed my mind, don't stop." I nipped his lip for emphasis, then struggled with his T-shirt, trying to pull it up. But it was caught between our bodies and as much as I fought with it, his weight prevented me from getting it off.

"Mason," I gasped. "You need to be naked. Can you help me make that happen?"

He drew back, smiling down at me. It had to be a trick of the light, but I could almost see my own reflection in his eyes. He was looking at me with such warmth, it lit me up from the inside.

"You're incredible," he murmured. "I've wanted this for so long. I missed you like air or water. You have no idea how much."

"I have a pretty good idea. I feel like I've been waiting for you to make love to me for an eternity. And now I'm afraid I'm going to grow old and die before it actually happens."

He smiled, his lips hitching to one side in a way that both broke my heart and remade it again.

"We're not going to hurry." He nuzzled under my jaw, pushing my face up, before kissing his way down my throat. "I've been in a war zone, fighting my way through occupied France. After eight long months, I've finally reached Paris and I've just walked into the Louvre. I'm not going to rush straight to the Mona Lisa." Leaning onto one elbow, he ran his hand under my baggy T-shirt, pushing it up as he went. "There are other works of art to appreciate first."

"Spoiler alert, my breasts weren't painted by Rubens." I gasped as his hand reached my nipple and his fingers teased it.

"They're better than a Rubens." He bent his mouth to my breast. "Better than a Van Gogh." He flicked his tongue across my nipple. "Better than a Michelangelo." He took it into his mouth and sucked.

I fisted the sheets, curving into his mouth. What my breasts lacked in size, they made up for in sensitivity, and what he was doing to them set all my nerve endings alight.

"You like that?" he murmured.

"Yes. Yes. A hundred yeses."

"And this?" He kissed his way down my stomach while I wriggled in anticipation.

Then he froze. "There's a hole in your shorts."

"Is there?" I tried to sound innocent. "Does it look like the Mona Lisa down there?"

"She's never looked better." He lifted his face to shoot me a heart-stopping lopsided grin. "You think I can make her smile?"

I tried to reply, but all I could manage was a loud groan of pleasure as his fingers explored the gap in my shorts, finding bare, slippery skin.

Then the warmth of his breath gusted over my aching flesh. A moment later, his tongue lapped me. I moaned, spiraling into a place of pure sensation. Mason seemed to know my body better than I did. Every stroke of his tongue sent me soaring further into heaven. I cried out Mason's name again and again as the pleasure crested and became too much to contain.

The Mona Lisa didn't just smile. She exploded into a million ecstatic pieces.

Afterward, my entire body felt charged with sensitivity, and as Mason kissed his way back up to my mouth, I gasped and trembled. My throat was a little sore, like it got at concerts when I sang at the top of my lungs.

"You okay, sweetheart?" Mason's voice was low and hoarse.

"Um. I think so." I licked my dry lips. "How loudly was I crying out?"

"Well, the police could be about to kick the door down, looking for the woman I just murdered."

"I'll protect you." I promised, sliding my hands around my neck. "But I can only do that if you're naked. Otherwise…" I gave the best shrug I could manage while lying down, with every bone in my body turned to liquid goo. "It would be impossible to defend a man with clothes on, however much I might want to."

"Well, if I have no choice…" He rolled off me and with his back to me, pulled off his T-shirt, then his jeans.

I took the opportunity to fully remove my T-shirt, which was bunched under my arms, and my ripped shorts, which were covering nothing.

When Mason turned back to face me, I felt my jaw loosen and my heart leap. "Holy father of dragons. That's not a moon rocket, it's an outer planet exploration vessel."

His eyebrows rose. "Excuse me?"

"You have the nicest cock I've ever seen. The biggest, longest, most magnificent…" I stopped, because he was laughing. "What? That was a compliment. Don't laugh."

"It's funny to hear you say 'cock'. I thought you'd use a more unusual word, like something old-fashioned."

"Trouser sausage? Pizzle? Wang? Schlong?" I snapped my fingers. "What about if I call it a cork? You could fork me with your big cork."

He groaned. "That should sound ridiculous. Why is it so damn sexy?"

Lying back over me, he dropped his mouth to my neck and kissed up to my jawline. His lips felt magical. The way they ignited me was like a spell. He moved to my mouth, catching my lower lip gently between his teeth, then soothed the bite with his tongue. When he pulled his mouth away from mine, I tried to capture it again. But he moved back to my jaw, to kiss around to my ear.

His breath tickled my lobe, making my body shiver. I lifted my spine, arching up into him, needing to feel him everywhere. My hands were all over him, exploring his muscles, touching him everywhere I could reach. I wanted every inch of him against every inch of me.

I needed him inside me, and I couldn't wait.

Wrapping my legs around his hips, I pulled his hard length against me. "I'm on the pill," I murmured.

He smiled without breaking our kiss, so I felt it rather than saw it. "That's the second best thing you've ever said to me."

Then he pulled one of my legs higher with his hand, and pushed his entire length into me.

I'd thought nothing could feel as good as his mouth.

I'd been wrong.

"Mason," I gasped. Then, "Oh, God."

He didn't hesitate. He pushed in again, driving in hard. His gaze was on mine, falling into me. Was that awe in his eyes?

"Carlotta," he whispered. "My heart."

I gripped him hard, digging my fingers into his shoulders like I was hanging on for dear life. And I was. Below me the ground was shaking, another orgasm already starting to rock me. He slid one hand behind me, pulling me to meet him as he drove into me.

The ground split apart.

I tumbled into the waiting crevasse, dragging him down with me.

Maybe I heard us both crying out together, but I couldn't be sure. I was too busy having the best orgasm of my life.

Chapter Thirty-Three

Mason: Eight Weeks Later

Hand in hand, Carlotta and I wandered through the living and dining areas of the fifth-floor apartment that could be our new home. Together we stopped in front of the big windows that looked out over San Dante beach, and Carlotta let out a low whistle.

"Check out that view." She sounded impressed.

"We can see everyone on the beach, but they can't see us." I squinted down at a group of teenagers in a circle on the sand, five floors below us. "Wait. Are those kids smoking weed? Does that look like a joint to you?"

Carlotta let out a surprised laugh, and the sound was so light and full of joy, my heart felt full. I'd do just about anything to keep hearing her laugh like that, preferably every day for the rest of my life. If I achieved that goal, I'd die happy.

"You'd better run down and arrest them, Detective

Lennox," she teased, turning her bright smile on me. "Don't let any criminals get away."

"You're Detective Lennox now, Mason?" Emmy Eaves, the realtor, came up behind us. I remembered her a little from school, but Asher knew her a lot better and had highly recommended her services. This was the fourth place she'd shown us, and I thought it could be the one.

"He is." Carlotta squeezed my hand. "Mason just started on the force here in San Dante."

"Congratulations."

"Thanks." Truth was, I still couldn't believe my luck. After spending so much time with the local team that arrested Santino and Frankie, they'd asked me to join them. Compared to the hell of undercover work, it was a dream job. Luke was my new partner, and I got to come home to Carlotta every single day. What could be better?

"Do you two like the apartment?" asked Emmy. "It's stunning, right?"

Looking into Carlotta's shining eyes, I saw her answer there without needing words. We were in perfect agreement. "It's exactly what we were hoping to find," I said.

Carlotta squeezed my hand. "I want to have another look at the master bedroom."

"Take your time," said Emmy. "I'll wait right here."

Carlotta led me in to the sunny room. It had plenty of space for our oversized bed, and sunlight was slanting in through the big windows, making the space warm and inviting.

"Can't you imagine waking up here together and looking out at the view?" She sounded happy, but her brow was furrowed. "Mason, I love it. But are you sure we can afford this place?"

I put my arms around her, pulling her against me. "Don't worry. Thanks to my brother, we can afford it."

"Can you believe what Asher did? He's so sneaky."

"Sneaky doesn't even begin to cover it." I gave my head a shake, still in awe of Asher's ability to dream up schemes. "I knew he was hiding something from me, but didn't want to push it. You know what he's like with secrets."

"Well, I do now. Remind me never to play chess with him."

"If I'd had any idea what he was planning..." I let out a breath. "I'm still not sure whether to hug him or kill him."

"Hugs. No question." Pulling free to take another look at the walk-in closet, she let out a sigh. "I love this place. Can't you just imagine our clothes hanging here?"

I nodded. "Your hospital gown will go there. And your Spock panties will be in the dresser over here."

"Along with a new pair of panties I bought. You'll love them. They have bacon on the front and eggs on the back."

"Sounds delicious."

"Breakfast of champions." She grinned, stepping closer for another kiss. I put my arms back around her and happily obliged.

Emmy put her head into the room. "Did you see the —? Oh, I'm sorry." She flushed a little, beating a hasty retreat.

I let Carlotta go. "We scared her."

"Let's move, before she thinks we're getting naked in here." Laughing, she grabbed my hand to pull me into the dining room. "There's enough room for a big table in this room. We could invite all our family and friends over."

"Including your mom and my dad. They're going to

have to get used to spending holidays together. And I want us all to have regular dinners. My family and yours, with no arguments, insults, or pranks."

She grinned. "Is it bad that I'm looking forward to seeing their faces when we break it to them?"

I pulled her close. "I had no idea how evil you can be."

"Because I didn't want to scare you by revealing all my secrets at once."

I kissed her forehead, breathing in the fresh scent of her hair. "How long do you think it'll take for me to learn everything about you?"

"How long have you got?"

"If I haven't discovered everything by the time we're in our eighties, I'll just keep looking. Sound fair?"

Her answering smile was so wide, I had to kiss her again. And slide my hands down to fondle her incredible butt. Because getting to do that whenever I wanted was one of my favorite things about being with her. Although I had to admit, my list of favorite things was already long, and kept getting longer.

Emmy came back in. "My Lord. You two are cute and all, but do you ever stop doing that?"

Carlotta grinned, pulling me closer. "Not if I can help it."

I lifted my hands off her butt and looked over at Emmy, who had a hand over her eyes but a smile on her face. "Why don't you get the paperwork, Emmy? We're going to make the seller an offer."

Emmy dropped her hand and strode toward the door. "Great. If you're going to buy the place, then I guess you two can do whatever you want in here. Go wild."

"Are you sure about that?" Carlotta looked gleeful. "Wild is my wheelhouse. It's where I do my best work."

Emmy rolled her eyes. "Maybe we should head to my office to do the paperwork. What do you say?"

"Sensible," I agreed.

Before I could follow Emmy out the door, Carlotta caught my hand. "I can't believe this'll be our home," she said. "My dreams are coming true."

My heart was overflowing, but I pushed my lips to the side, pretending a caution I didn't feel. "We shouldn't celebrate yet. We still have to buy the place, end our families' bitter feud, and make sure Asher hasn't plotted any more diabolical schemes. We have our work cut out for us."

"And I'm looking forward to all of it."

"I'm looking forward to tasting your bacon panties."

"Are you two coming?" Emmy's voice came from outside. "No, wait. Don't answer that."

Carlotta started for the door. "Come on. The sooner we buy this place, the sooner we can fool around in it."

"You should write marketing pitches for a living," I followed her to the lift. "I'm sold."

We went outside into the bright sunshine. From the building's entrance, we had a good view over San Dante's white sand beach and the rolling surf. I dropped my sunglasses onto my eyes before smiling at Carlotta. She was right about our dreams coming true. I could hardly believe this was really my life. It was so far from working undercover in Houston, those memories barely seemed real.

Carlotta bumped her shoulder against my arm. "I can't wait to invite your dad and my mom to lunch at our new place and make them eat together. Let's do it soon, okay?"

"You're pure, unadulterated evil." I pretended to frown. "Is it too late to change my mind about all this?"

She grinned and caught my hand. "Way too late. You're stuck with me and my evil ways."

"For life?"

"Play your cards right."

My heart soared. "Oh, I intend to," I promised.

* * *

Dear Wonderful Reader,

Thank you for reading Mason and Carlotta's story! I hope you enjoyed it.

If you're wondering what devious schemes Asher has been plotting, all will be revealed in the next book in the series, *No Fooling Around.*

And please make sure to join my newsletter for updates on new books in the series, giveaways, competitions, and other fun stuff. Go to www.taliahunter.com and you'll get a free bonus just for signing up!

About the Author

Talia Hunter is a bestselling author who likes to pair loveable heroines with the hunks who deserve them.

She recently moved to Australia, where she's constantly amazed and not at all freaked out by the weird and wonderful critters. When she's not writing, you can usually find her with a glass of wine, a good book, and a jumbo-sized can of bug spray.

She loves to laugh, and if you feel the same way you can keep up with her new releases and special deals by following her on Amazon and on Bookbub.

Also by Talia Hunter

THE LENNOX BROTHERS SERIES
No Ordinary Christmas
No Laughing Matter
No Fooling Around

THE LANTANA ISLAND SERIES
Boss With Benefits
The Engagement Game
The Devil She Knew

THE RICH LIST SERIES
Rocking The Billionaire
Mastering The Movie Star
Bossing The Billionaire
Pleasing The Playboy

Printed in Great Britain
by Amazon